By The Same Author

AMBER ROYER

SOMETHING BORROWED, SOMETHING 90% DARK

**GOLDEN TIP
PRESS**

In memory of Yuki, the sweetest bunny and the model for Knightley in these books

Chapter One
Saturday

"Hurry back," I say as I take a seat at the baroque-looking chair behind my friend Tiff's heavy mahogany desk. Some of her coworkers are looking at me curiously, which makes me a mite self-conscious.

Tiff has a cup of pens on her desk – most of them printed with the real estate firm's logo. But one of them is an unexpected sparkly purple pen with a springy hummingbird at the top. I pull the pen out of the cup and make an experimental squiggle on the sticky note pad handy on the desk. It's glittery purple gel ink.

I can't help but smile. There's a reason Tiff and I are friends. Every once in a while, she lets her fun side show.

I start sketching Knightley, my bunny, whose silhouette is the logo for my craft chocolate shop. I draw him holding a magnifying glass. It makes sense. Sitting at this oversized desk makes me feel like the girl version of Sam Spade or something.

The front door opens, and a woman strides into the office. She's mixed race, with thick hair that cascades halfway down her back. She's wearing a red dress and leopard-print pumps. There is a colorful gauzy scarf around her neck, her only acknowledgement that it is cold outside. It looks hand-printed. At first I think this woman must be another of Tiff's coworkers, but she stops at one of the other desks and asks something. The guy sitting there points over to where I'm sitting, and the woman heads towards me, looking puzzled.

I put Tiff's hummingbird pen back in the cup, feeling like my Sam Spade daydream has conjured up a femme fatale. Which doesn't fit into my real life, at all. I'm not even an official detective. I'm a chocolate maker, here delivering some custom minis for Tiff to hand out to her clients.

"You're not Tiff," the woman says in a vaguely accusatory tone.

Ironically, I relax. I've had a killer call me out before, challenging me to solve a case, and I've had people ask for help solving murders. So it wouldn't have been impossible that someone would have tracked me here to ask for help. But all this woman wants is a real estate agent. And she's in the right place. After all, this is a real estate agency.

"Tiff will be back any minute," I say. "I'm Felicity. I own the chocolate shop down on the Strand." The woman blinks at me. I can feel her taking in my pale skin, my brown hair, the sprinkling of freckles across my nose. And the basic navy tee and jeans combo I'm wearing. And how none of it explains why a chocolate maker is sitting at a real estate agent's desk. To fill the silence, I finally say, "Tiff and I have been friends for a while."

The woman laughs. "Not nearly as long as she and I have. I'm Lydia. Tiff and I went to the same high school." She leans over the desk, offering a hand for me to shake. Why does this feel like she's being super competitive?

Still, I shake her hand and say, "It's nice to meet you." Even though so far it hasn't been.

"Lydia?" Tiff says. She's come back from the ladies' room wearing her bridesmaid's dress, with bare feet. The dress has a tutu skirt and a green and teal color scheme that makes her look a bit like a peacock.

Lydia takes one look at it and busts out laughing. "What on earth are you wearing?"

Tiff says, "A dress that makes me feel beautiful."

Tiff always looks professional, with her chemically straightened hair and meticulously made-up face showing off her black skin to advantage. She's a fan of pant suits and power skirts. So this dress is quite the departure.

I explain, "I'm matron of honor for our friend Autumn's wedding. Tiff was humoring me by trying on her bridesmaid's dress."

"It's a beautiful dress," Lydia says, taking a step closer and reaching out to touch the tulle skirt, stretching out part of the fabric.

"What do you want?" Tiff asks Lydia dryly, batting her hand away.

Lydia had described herself as one of Tiff's oldest friends. Something tells me Tiff doesn't feel the same way.

Lydia says, "I was just in the neighborhood and thought I would say hi."

"In the neighborhood?" Tiff says skeptically.

Lydia shrugs. "I'm representing a client purchasing investment property on Mustang Island." She puts a hand on Tiff's arm. "Look, I'm not proud of how we left things, at the end of real estate school. I asked to handle this one personally, when I found out it would be near the quaint little island you moved to."

Tiff frowns. "How did you even know I was here?"

Lydia looks embarrassed. "I've been following your Facebook page for years." She hesitates, then says, "Please. Can we talk? There's something going on, and I could use my one logical friend right now." Her gaze flicks down to Tiff's dress, like she's having second thoughts.

Tiff crosses her arms defensively over the low-cut bodice and says, "I have a showing in an hour. But tomorrow, I'm doing an open house. Swing by eight-ish, while we're setting up." Tiff nods towards me.

Lydia looks over at me. "Are you going to be there too?"

I say, "I'm mainly responsible for the snacks."

At least, my shop is. My pastry chef is the one making the cookies that will make the open house smell and feel like home. I'm just popping them into the oven to bake, at the property.

Lydia hesitates, but finally she says, "See you in the morning." She starts to walk away, then turns back and says, "That dress really does make you look beautiful. Like a ballerina or something."

Without waiting for a response, she leaves.

"Wow," I say.

"You said it," Tiff says. "Lydia and I have a complicated history."

"I get that," I say.

Tiff says, "The way this skirt swishes is going to be spectacular on the dance floor."

"Absolutely." I try to get myself back to matron-of-honor mode. Autumn let each of her bridesmaids choose a unique dress in her color scheme. These dresses are important to her – and therefore to me. But not as important as Tiff's happiness. I tell her, "Why don't you change and then – " I glance down at the desk and notice a book sitting catty-corner to the sticky note pad. Weird. How had I not noticed it there before. I say, "Hey, I didn't know you read Dashiell Hammett."

"I don't know who that is," Tiff says. She steps closer and peers down at her own desk. Her eyes narrow. She asks, "Was Lydia close enough to have slipped this book onto my desk?"

"I was sitting here the whole time," I protest. "I mean, she leaned over the desk to shake my hand, but surely I would have noticed her dropping a copy of *The Thin Man* a foot and a half away from me."

"Not necessarily," Tiff says absently. She's studying the desk. "Get up," she says.

"What?" I ask. But I vacate her chair.

Tiff sits down and starts opening drawers. She says, "Lydia is a kleptomaniac. Over the years, she's stolen more things from me than I can count – including at least one boyfriend.

Sometimes, she leaves something in the object's place. She refers to this as borrowing."

"What did she leave you in place of the boyfriend," I quip, then immediately regret it as pain enters Tiff's eyes.

"There may have been a scarf."

Ouch. I can see why Tiff isn't excited about talking with Lydia tomorrow. I notice one of Tiff's coworkers eavesdropping on the conversation. I gesture with my chin, so Tiff notices, too.

Tiff drops her voice, but she doesn't look embarrassed. "Nothing seems missing from the drawers. But I think she took my stapler." Then Tiff gasps. "And she took the hummingbird pen I got at the museum."

I look down, and sure enough, the only pens left in the cup are the logo ones. And I think there might be fewer of those. "Man, she's good."

Tiff pushes the book at me. "Here. You take that, for your shop. I don't want to look at it."

Now it's my turn to stare down at the desk, at the book, and all I can think is, *not again*. I try to swallow, but my throat has suddenly gone dry. "I don't think that's a good idea."

Tiff looks at me, and the indignation over her friend's misdeeds has been replaced by anxiety. "You don't really believe that just because there's an old book, you're going to get involved in solving another murder?"

I finally manage to swallow. "Not necessarily. A few weeks ago, Naomi gave me a copy of Anne of Green Gables from when she and my mom were kids, and nothing happened."

"Your aunt is more sentimental than you realize," Tiff says. Tiff has been working with Aunt Naomi on refurbing the flip hotel that I'm currently living in.

"Unlike my mom. Apparently, she tried to sell the book in a garage sale years ago." I shake my head. I'm getting sidetracked. "It could be just a coincidence, me winding up with a book every time there's a murder. I've never been a superstitious person. So I'm not comfortable with the idea, in the first place. But do you know what *The Thin Man* is about? It's a hard-boiled murder mystery."

And she doesn't even know about my Sam Spade daydream. It's just too close. Too weird.

"So why take the chance?" Tiff says. She laughs, but it sounds hollow. "Don't worry. I'll donate the book to the library."

"But you already gave it to me," I say. "I feel like now I have to take it – in case it turns out to be important."

Tiff looks like she's about to say something else, but then she bites it back and heaves a sigh. "Take it, don't take it. I'm going to go change. I really do have a showing."

I pick up the book. It's such a thin volume, hardcover, with the black-and-white image of a man in a hat and old-fashioned suit standing there on the cover, with one hand in his pocket. The only color on the front of the book is a rectangle printed in red, with *The Thin Man* printed vertically. I carefully open the book. It shows the publication date as 1934. I don't know the exact year the book was published, off the top of my head, but I'm guessing this is a first edition, or close to it.

It takes everything I've got not to toss the book back onto Tiff's desk. Which is stupid. I own a shop that has a book section. I can't keep freaking out every time I see a really cool book in the wild.

Tiff comes back, no longer an iridescent ballerina. She's back in her real-estate-agent look. She pats at her hair, even though it is already perfectly in place. She says, "I don't know why you're holding that book like it is radioactive. I think you actually enjoy solving murders."

I admit, "There is a part of me that likes helping solve cases. I like the puzzle aspect of it, and everything I've learned about psychology. But the untimely death of a human being – that is an awful, unnecessary thing. Believe me. I've lived it."

I lost my husband to a senseless accident, a year before I came home to Galveston, Texas to open my craft chocolate business. I was stuck, in my grief and in the past, and had sorely needed to do something different. My life has changed so much since I returned, with the support of an increasing circle of family and friends, a growing business that has become a gathering place in the community, and a renewed sense of wellbeing and self-worth. About the only thing that is the same as my life in Seattle, where I'd been a happily married physical therapist, is Knightley, my little white lop-eared bunny. He was my solace after my husband's death. Now he's the mascot for my shop. And since pets pick up on so much, he's happier now that I'm happy.

But every time I interact with someone who has lost someone – it opens cracks in my grief, and takes something out of me. I guess deep loss like that never goes away entirely.

Tiff says, "That's what makes you perfect for what you've been doing. You have empathy, in a way I hope Ken or I never could."

Tiff is happily married. She works hard on her relationship. And her husband is a nice guy. I don't begrudge Tiff her happiness. Still, she doesn't have to worry about the implications of strange books falling into her life. I do envy her a little, for that.

I take the book with me as I follow Tiff out the door, and we part ways in the parking lot, her for her Audi, me towards my catering van.

As I'm sliding into the driver's seat, my phone rings. It's Tracie, one of my employees. Tracie is currently at a bridal expo, showing off some of the chocolate sculptures we do at Greetings and Felicitations. The background noise level is uncomfortable, even over the phone. I can only imagine how many people are milling around our booth.

Tracie says, "We're getting close to selling out of the boxes of truffles. Can you bring more inventory?"

"I'm on it," I say and hang up – since someone at the expo is obviously trying to get Tracie's attention.

It's our first time being invited to a bridal event, and I wasn't sure how many people would be interested in buying chocolate, when most prospective brides would be collecting samples and fliers, so I hadn't given Tracie too much to carry, in addition to the two sculptures and the marketing stuff. I'm actually ambivalent as to how much sense these kinds of events make financially, given the outlay for samples and fliers. We'll have to see how much business it brings in over the next couple of months.

I head back to Greetings and Felicitations, to grab more truffles. I go in through the shop's back door which leads to the kitchen, since I usually park farther away and cut through the alley, leaving the limited parking spots in front of the shop for customers. As I open the door, I can hear voices out front. The kitchen looks like a canister of glitter exploded onto the counters, which are covered with hundreds of teal, purple, and green wafer paper butterflies, all freshly coated with luster dust. I love the look of wafer paper, because it is edible, but allows bakers to recreate the delicate look of feathers or flower petals in a way that is light, and allows for movement. The butterflies are the beginnings of Autumn's wedding cake, which Carmen quite generously offered to make for her. Wedding cakes are not a usual part of our business, but we definitely have the room for the project.

The cake is going to have six tiers, each of them a different flavor. Drake's groom's cake will be rich, dark chocolate, of course. After all, we are a chocolate shop. So far, the only evidence of the second cake is a fist-sized music note made out of modeling chocolate, which is basically chocolate mixed with corn syrup to make an edible clay.

Baking is not my favorite part of the business – that's why I have Carmen, who runs this kitchen according to her whims, baking whatever suits her fancy on a given day, whether it is pan dulce or cakes that highlight a single-origin chocolate. Our customers love her for it. Her exclusive "today only" batches of baked goods are part of the draw.

I prefer the actual chocolate making process, which is more like making wine. I do play with flavor, highlighting the best notes of my chocolates in the full line of truffles that serve as a gateway to get people new to dark chocolate interested in trying it.

While I'm here, I decide to stash the copy of *The Thin Man* in the filing cabinet in my office. My office is near the front of the building, so I have to go through the chocolate finishing room and then the bean room to the hall, which divides the space between the customer tables and our new arts annex. My office is tiny, and just being in it makes me feel claustrophobic. That may be because I'd once been trapped in this space, by a killer intent on framing me and then staging my death. The thought of it makes me shiver, and quickly drop the book I'm holding – potential harbinger of another death – into the bottom drawer.

Miles, who works for me part-time, flags me down in the hall. He's a young black guy with neatly trimmed facial hair, who is on the football team for one of the local universities. I rely on Miles for graphic arts assistance and computer help – but he's always willing to pitch in where needed. He is handling the shop by himself today, since everyone else is busy. He asks, "How am I supposed to bill the coffee for Autumn's friends?"

A ton of people are coming into town for Autumn's wedding, and she wanted to be able to use Greetings and Felicitations as a gathering spot, so we arranged for an "open bar" for them to have coffee. They can come and go as needed through Friday morning – which will be the day after Autumn's wedding. She's getting married Thursday, in her beautiful winter-princess gown, and people will probably be partying well into the night.

I tell Miles, "We just charged her a flat fee. Keep track of the number of coffees, though. If it doesn't add up to what she paid, I want to be able to give her a refund."

"Absolutely," Miles says, pulling up the notes app on his phone. He says, "There are some really cool people here." He gestures out into the main part of the shop. "Of course, some of Autumn's writer friends are here. Plus, Autumn's brother already came in from Padre. He owns a restaurant, and they do music events sometimes, so he's the one who booked the DJ and the live jazz band. They're willing to play an impromptu jazz night in the shop, if you're interested."

"Really?" I ask, excited. I'm always looking for new ways to make Greetings and Felicitations a hub in the community. "If they're only here for a few days, that wouldn't be a lot of time to advertise it. But maybe you have some ideas about that?"

Miles adds to his note. "Already on it."

I go out to the main part of the shop to meet the band. They're all sitting at a table by the window, with some of their instruments and clearly all of their luggage stacked beside them.

One of the musicians introduces himself as Boone. He's a bit older than the others, a bald black guy with a thin silver chain necklace on top of a black sweater. He says, "I'm the tenor sax. Starsky here's on drums, Flip is piano, and Randall is trumpet."

"It sounds like something's missing," I say. After all, you typically need certain instruments to balance the sound of a jazz band. "Where's your bass?"

"That's Charlie," Boone says. "His flight came in late. Our group is all coming in special for Autumn. We used to play together back in the day – but now we live all over the country."

I gesture at the luggage. "So why didn't you all just check in at your hotel."

Randall makes a face. He's a short white guy with a receding hairline and an uneven snaggletooth grimace. "We went for a short-term rental. Only, they double booked our reservation. We're waiting for Charlie to figure out what we should do."

I wince. "That sounds awful." I really need this week to go well for Autumn. Impulsively, I say, "Why don't you all stay with me and my aunt? We're flipping a hotel. It's not technically open, but we have a lot of the rooms redone."

I really should have checked with Aunt Naomi before making that offer, but I'm sure she'll understand. She's Autumn's friend too.

"Really?" Flip asks. He's Latino, with a thin mustache and a gray wool newsboy hat giving a retro feel to his look. "That would save us so much trouble."

"What kind of trouble?" a voice asks from behind me. I turn, and there's a guy standing right behind me, picking at his teeth with his pinkie nail. He's big, and a little too close, and the way he's frowning at me makes me feel like the trouble must be my fault. I just bet he's Charlie – now that it's too late to rescind the offer to stay at the flip hotel.

"Charlie," Flip says. "I've been trying to call you for an hour. We didn't know if we needed to send somebody to get you at the airport."

Charlie shrugs. "There was something I needed to take care of. A little pre-wedding surprise." He smiles, and it softens my first impression. He's not a bad looking guy. He has reddish-blonde hair and a strong chin, and he's dressed like he just stepped out of a business meeting, instead of off a plane.

Maybe this will all be okay.

I turn away from the group, ready to leave. Only someone is waving at me from one of the tables. It turns out to be Dora Richards, one of my favorite contemporary authors. Who must also be a friend of Autumn's, since she and Autumn are sitting at the same table, each with a cinnamon chocolate chunk scone in front of them. Dora writes in multiple genres, and she currently has a fun romance series about globe-trotting spies who all manage to fall in love with unexpected people while on missions.

When I reach the table, Dora says, "I absolutely adore your shop. I'd love to use it as inspiration for a setting in my next book."

"Seriously?" I can't contain the grin that takes over my face. Because, seriously – being immortalized by Dora Richards? How is that not the greatest thing ever?

She gestures with her chin over at the case where the memorabilia from the murders I've helped solve is on display and says, "That may be one of the most unique things I've ever seen."

I manage not to literally facepalm myself. Barely. And I give Autumn a desperate look. Because I'd thought she was hoping to use the shop as a backdrop for one of her romance novels. But it sounds like she's envisioning it for one of her thrillers.

Chapter Two
Saturday

I don't enjoy crowds, so I brace myself with a steadying breath before I go inside the expo. I'm carrying a big box, so I can't exactly rush my way through. Someone calls my name.

I turn, and there's Ash Diaz, taking my picture. He's got his signature rectangular glasses and skinny tie going on. Today he's wearing a black dress shirt under a gray blazer, paired with jeans. Ash is a blogger, podcaster, and general busybody. He's also my friend – now. There was a time when I thought of him as my nemesis. I smile, and he takes another shot. It's best just to roll with it. He probably won't even post the pic, since there's no story to go with it.

"Hey," I say. "What are you doing here?"

Ash gestures at the area around us, which is lined with booths. "I go where the stories are. Not all of my current happenings involve murder, you know."

I give him a pointed look. "No, just your podcast."

Ash pockets his phone and holds his hands out to take the box I'm carrying. That's a big gesture for him. Not carrying the box – I've seen him be chivalrous before. But putting the phone away in the middle of a photo op. I'm touched.

Ash says, "The ratings on the podcast are higher than on my blog. Face it, people love hearing about a real-life amateur sleuth. I'm just covering the cases you've been involved with so far, and I already have enough material for seasons on seasons."

I sigh. "You have enough material for five seasons. Because that's all the cases. There's no reason for there to be anymore." I dismiss the nagging thought of that book in my filing cabinet. I gesture vaguely at Ash. "You've already seen how dangerous podcasting about murder can be. I don't know why you're still doing it."

After all, Logan, one of the two guys in my life, had nearly been killed after the podcast had brought my supposed skills to the attention of a killer looking for a challenge. I had nearly been killed, too. And someone else had actually died.

Ash starts walking in the direction of the Greetings and Felicitations booth. He must have already made the rounds and scoped everything out. He says, says, "What are the odds of that happening again?"

"Not great," I admit. "But that's a good thing. Whatever this weird blip in my life has been, I'm ready for it to be over. I know I've said it before, but I'm determined to get my life back to normal."

"I don't think you have much control over that," Ash says. "When I called you a murder magnet in those blog posts – I wasn't just being dramatic. I can feel it. There's going to be a next case."

"I hope not," I say, though there's dread at the pit of my stomach, because I'm already terrified something bad is going to happen.

Ash says, "I think there's something about you that makes people look to you for help, and something that draws people in trouble to you."

"Thanks?" I say skeptically.

Ash laughs. Then he says, "But I do know something you can control. Give me the scoop. Which guy are you walking out with from Autumn's wedding? My fans are already dying to know, with the deadline so close approaching. It's a pretty even split between who's Team Arlo and who's Team Logan."

I give him another pointed look, but he seems oblivious. I don't know how he found out that I had told both Logan (my business partner who was once – long story – my bodyguard) and Arlo (my ex-boyfriend from way back in high school, who is now a cop) that I was giving myself until Autumn's wedding to figure out what I want my future to look like – which means choosing between the two of them.

Which is impossible. Logan gets me on a deep level. He's also suffered the loss of someone he loved – also felt both grief and remorse. He was the one that had helped pull me out of it. And we had just seemed to fit together, when he'd been in danger – and I had literally saved his life.

But Arlo doesn't have all that baggage. He's lighter and sweeter, and kissing him makes me feel like I'm home.

Ash says, "Don't tell me you still haven't made a choice."

"I think I have," I say. "Maybe."

But I'm not about to tell Ash what I've been thinking – that second chances don't come along all that often, and that even though kissing Logan was more like diving into a waterfall, life becomes so much simpler if I choose Arlo. Except for the part where Logan is still my business partner.

But I don't know – shouldn't the right decision feel clearer? I mean, it's not just my future I'm talking about, but theirs – two people I care very much about. Neither of whom I feel I can afford to lose. And neither of whom I want to hurt – though I'm afraid I've let this go on too long to avoid that. I'm not the type of person who ever wanted to have two guys fighting over her. I had started getting attached to Logan, back when Arlo had had a girlfriend. But when Arlo found himself single, he had lobbied hard for me to see that we still had a spark. It's obvious that we do. Two guys, both of whom are great in different ways.

And in less than a week, I'm going to have to crush one of them. On the day my best friend is getting married, which should be a happy day for everyone.

If I was kind, I would choose one of them, and tell the other one before the wedding. But I'm still not sure. I mean, I keep thinking I should choose Arlo, but then I remember the vulnerable way Logan had looked at me when he'd believed his days were numbered, after he'd been targeted by a killer. It had taken a lot for him to open up, and it would be a shame to throw that away.

Ash says softly, "You have no idea what you're going to do, do you?"

I don't reply.

He says, "I knew Imogen was the one the first time we met. It took her a bit longer to come to the same conclusion."

Imogen is Ash's fiancé. They'll be getting married themselves in a couple of months.

We reach the booth, and Ash goes around behind the table to set the box on the floor.

Carmen, my pastry chef, is sitting at the table, handling sales with a portable cashbox and an app on her phone, while Tracie is on her feet, handing samples to passersby and explaining options for chocolate sculptures from her catalog of designs. She's also offering rates for custom work.

Tracie is an art student and quite a talent. She's pale and petite, with curly brown hair and an expression that makes people want to help her. Not that she needs it – she's a dynamo. I love what she's been doing at the shop – but I'm a little worried about what happens when she graduates next year. She's building up clients and expectations. It's hard to find talented help – but I can't begrudge her moving on to the next thing, when she's ready. Life is transitory – even if I personally have a hard time dealing with change – or even the potential threat of change.

Carmen waves, but she's busy with the line, so I just wave back. Carmen is wearing her dark hair back in her usual ponytail. She has an athletic build and high cheekbones, which make her look striking in her long-sleeved black tee.

Ash says, "Come check out some of the other tables. If we go around together, it will give me an excuse to get a whole new set of samples. There's a cocktail van over on the other wing that is making some killer bourbon and elderflower concoctions."

I laugh. "Sometimes I think you just went into journalism in hopes of free food."

Ash says, "I blog about that food, thank you very much." He doesn't sound the slightest bit embarrassed.

Still, it's a nice distraction from my relationship problems, to walk around with a friend. Right up until we get to the first food-related table, and someone asks us, "Have you two chosen a date yet?"

There's a twenty-something white woman with thick brown hair done in pigtails. She's wearing an outfit that can only be described as elegant outdoorsy, with jeans and hiking boots paired with a beige blouse and a pink neckerchief.

I feel myself blushing, and I start to stammer something about how there isn't a thing – let alone a wedding – between me and Ash. But Ash doesn't hesitate, just says, "My fiancé couldn't make it today, so I have our wedding planner here to help me check things out."

I don't like lying, but Carmen is doing the cake for Ash and Imogen, and they've booked space in my shop's annex for the girls to do a chocolate painting class for Imogen's bachelorette party, while the guys have a chocolate and whiskey tasting. And from what I understand, they're handling the rest of the planning themselves. So it isn't actually that far from the truth.

"I'm not a professional wedding planner," I tell the girl, who is already handing me catering menus. "Just a friend of the couple, volunteering to help out."

"You never know," she says. "We've seen more than one family friend take up the wedding planning bug, after a taste of it just helping out. Right, Agnes?"

She looks over at another girl, who is standing behind several chaffing dishes, holding a set of tongs.

Agnes nods sagely. She's in her mid-twenties, white, with her dark hair done in a single thick braid. The two girls look a lot alike – same eyebrows, same noses. They're probably sisters.

Agnes says, "Some of our best clients got their start that way. My sister and I are with Daydream Hills, a winery and herb garden in the Texas Hill Country. We offer a fresh herb-based menu, which we can deliver through our mobile catering, though most couples tend to book our guest house for the weekend, with a package that includes massages and facials, and Saturday morning goat yoga for the entire bridal party."

"Imogen would love that," Ash says, though I know for a fact he's planning to have a garden reception here on the Island.

Agnes's sister starts talking to a couple who are obviously more serious about the potential of a wedding weekend in the Hill Country.

Meanwhile, Agnes hands me a plate with an herbed goat cheese stuffed mushroom, a small puddle of spinach dip with a couple of pita chips, and a crostini with a smear of pesto, more goat cheese, and some diced tomatoes. After I've taken a couple of bites and remarked on how good they are – the stuffed mushroom really is divine, with bits of wild rice and a nice undertone of wine in the stuffing, Agnes says, "If you'd like a sample of how goat yoga works, we'll be doing a mini-class every hour on the hour." Agnes points to the area behind her, which is screened with cloth partitions. "Take a peek."

I pop the rest of the crostini into my mouth and follow Ash around the side of the table, to where there's a gap in the cloth, and we peer through. I'm looking at two very small goats, standing in the middle of a wire enclosure like a very tall dog crate, looking curiously back at me. One of them makes a soft noise and trots over to the edge of the wire.

I realize that the cheese I'm eating could very well have come from one of these goats. Which is kind of cool, honestly. "Hi, sweetie," I say to the more curious goat. It perks up its ears and moves its feet through the layer of hay covering the floor inside the enclosure.

From behind us, Agnes says, "If you're not into yoga, we can also arrange for your party to hike with the goats instead."

I turn back to Agnes and say, "If it were my party, honestly that would be more my speed." Over the past year, I've undergone an experimental treatment for asthma. Before that, even hiking wouldn't have been my thing. I'm asymptomatic, at this point, but I've had a few incidents where I've been in abnormal air conditions, which have caused problems. These extreme situations were all based around catching killers. Yet another reason to try to keep another case from falling into my life. It would be more fun to take whichever guy I wind up choosing to do something normal couples do. I try to imagine either Arlo or Logan hiking with goats. I think they would both be game – more for the chance to be outdoors than for the goats themselves.

Agnes says, "All three of the goats we brought with us are very docile. Feel free to pet them through the wire."

"All three?" Ash asks, looking puzzled.

I tell Agnes, "There's only two."

"What?" Agnes drops her tongs into the chaffing dish full of mushrooms and rushes over to us. She surveys the goats and brings both hands up to the sides of her face in alarm. "Where's Princess Buttercup?"

I study the enclosure. There aren't any gaps in the wire. It doesn't seem likely that a goat the same size as the other two could have gotten out. But it must have happened – somehow. It's not like these two sisters could be mistaken about how many goats they'd brought with them.

Ash drops his plate in the trash and puts a hand on Agnes's arm. He says, "Don't worry, we'll find her."

Agnes's sister is still talking to the couple, but she keeps cutting alarmed glances over here.

I say, "I'll go talk to someone at registration. They have that PA system for announcing prize drawings. They can probably make an announcement to keep an eye out for a missing goat, and let everyone know where to return it."

Agnes says, "Please. That would be great."

Without waiting for a response, she starts moving the cloth panels, looking under her tables and then nearby tables, glancing up at narrow display cases and artwork on the walls of the expo space. Could a goat really have gotten up there?

Ash is helping her, and they're gathering a small crowd that wants to help, so I start making my way back to the front. I'm passing an area with more cloth partitions when a hand grabs my arm. I turn, startled.

It's Patsy, Arlo's other ex-girlfriend. His more recent ex, as in the girl he had been dating when I'd moved back to town. Only, Arlo had been forced to arrest Patsy's brother for murder, and her family hadn't forgiven Arlo. After the breakup, Patsy had left town. Last I'd heard, she'd taken a job in California. So what is she doing here?

She lets go of my arm. "Sorry. I called your name, but I don't think you heard me."

Had she? I'd been focused on getting to Admissions, dealing with the crowd and scanning the rafters for goats. "It's okay," I say. "I'm just surprised to see you."

Patsy brushes her dark hair back away from her face. She's got brown hair and brown eyes and pale skin – just like me. It wouldn't be unfair to say Arlo has a type. We look a little bit alike – not enough to be twins or anything, but enough that it is noticeable. That had upset me the first time I'd met her. But once I'd gotten to know Patsy, I had realized she was a genuinely nice person. So maybe the comparison between us was actually flattering. Patsy says, "I just got into town last night. I've been here all day, since your business is on the program, and I really needed to see you."

"Me?" I squeak. What could Patsy want with me? "Can it wait?" I ask. "I need to talk to someone at Admissions about a missing goat."

Patsy arches an eyebrow at me. "Go on."

"That's it. It's missing from one of the booths. I said I'd try to help."

Patsy grins. "Exactly why I knew you were the person to come to for help myself. Let's walk and talk."

We head back towards Admissions.

Patsy says, "I got a call from my mother three days ago. My father has gone missing. I want to pay you to help me find him."

"Wait a second," I protest. "That's not the kind of thing I do."

"You've helped Arlo solve a number of cases. And you figured out what happened after Mateo went missing."

Mateo had been one of my employees at the time. And I hadn't had any idea what I had been doing. I shrug. "That was part of a murder investigation."

I have a strong sense of déjà vu. Not so long ago, an art collector had asked me to help figure out who had been trying to kill him. I'd said exactly those same words, *That's not the kind of thing I do.* I hadn't tried to help – and he'd wound up dead.

Patsy says, "I understand that it's different. But I don't know who else to go to for help."

"Have you thought about asking Arlo?" I ask, regretting the words as soon as they are out of my mouth.

Patsy winces, her pain clear on her face. "I wouldn't know how to face him. We were practically engaged, and I dumped him, and now I need a favor?" She shakes her head. "Besides, my mother tried to talk to him about it. He was nice to her and all, but it's not his case."

It wouldn't be. Arlo is a homicide detective. He doesn't handle missing persons.

A chill dances up my spine. *The Thin Man* had started with a missing father. It could be coincidence – or it could be something more ominous. If somebody else dies – I don't think I could handle it being Patsy. Or Arlo. At the mere thought of that, I feel like my heart is trying to stop deep inside my chest. I force myself to breathe.

We arrive at Admissions. I pull a guy aside, and tell him about the missing goat. He asks me to describe it.

Forcing myself to sound cheerful, I say, "If it's anything like the other two, it's about two feet tall, beige and white with dark legs and big ears and a goofy-looking grin on its face."

"Sounds like you're describing Bing Crosby," the guy quips.

I laugh, though I only have a vague idea of what he's talking about. The guy is a lot older than I am.

Patsy's laugh is more genuine. She tells him, "If the goats Felicity saw look like Crosby, chances are the missing one looks like Bob Hope."

The two share an even heartier laugh, but the moment we turn away from the guy, Patsy's face falls back into a somber expression.

That better matches my mood. I know this whole thing about the books isn't logical. But at this point, I don't care.

"Come on," I tell her. "Let's get a coffee and you can tell me what happened. I probably won't have the faintest idea how to find your father, but I can at least ask around."

"How do you want me to pay you?" Patsy asks.

I manage a freaked-out sounding half laugh. If I can keep anybody from dying this time – especially Patsy or her family – that's payment enough. Hopefully, her father just needed some alone time, or had some reason for leaving town. I say, "Don't worry about money. Chances are I'm not going to do anything worth paying me for."

The only coffee available at the expo turns out to be at a booth advertising a coffee cart service. The line for the free full-sized lattes is pretty long, so Patsy and I go across the street, to a little coffee shop I've never noticed before. Patsy found it in her phone, in a search for *coffee nearby*.

There's a grand opening flier still sitting on the counter. Which explains why I've never spotted this shop, since it would have been empty until a couple of weeks ago. It's an interesting space. The chairs are upholstered with old burlap from coffee bean sacks, which have been waterproofed. There's a big red coffee roaster in an alcove to the left of the register. Everything is reclaimed dark wood and raw brick, with pictures of coffee beans lining one long wall. There's a bin near the door, offering bags of used coffee grounds for customers to take to fertilize their plants, so nothing goes to waste. It's a confident, masculine space, and I instantly love everything about it.

It's a little intimidating, since we sell coffee at Greetings and Felicitations – but we don't roast our own. It's something we could do – the processes of roasting coffee and chocolate aren't that different. For the roasting step, it's basically the same machine. It just seems like one thing too many to try to specialize in.

I quash the feeling of professional jealousy. When I'd first opened my shop, I'd been on the receiving end of that same emotion, since I'm selling candy, coffee and books in a town that already had stores specializing in all three of those things. But I've found my place among the local Strand businesses. And the more craft businesses there are on this island, the bigger the draw for customers for all of us.

Besides, my shop has its own unique draw. Whether I like it or not. Ever since I got involved with solving murders, I've gained a following with the true-crime crowd, and my shop has become a destination. People have traveled halfway across the country just to view the books associated with the various cases. There's more security on that one display case than in the rest of the shop combined.

It's not the reputation I originally wanted when I chose my lop-eared rabbit for my logo, and painted everything in shabby chic pink and gray, but I've started to lean into it.

Patsy says, "This is the total opposite of your place. And yet – there's something about it that feels the same."

"It's the sense of good taste," I say, willingly taking the compliment.

"Why, thank you," a voice says. I look up, and the barista – or I guess the owner – comes out of the back room.

The guy is handsome, in his thirties, with Asian features and messy bangs that cover his eyebrows – making his warm brown eyes even more intense. And he's directing all of that intensity at Patsy. She lets out a cute little giggle.

The guy takes our orders, and we find a table. A few minutes later, he heads over with our coffee. I'd expected to have to pick it up at the counter, so I'm a bit surprised.

The guy grins at Patsy and says, "Looks like you found the best seat in the house."

I'd *thought* they'd been bantering when he'd taken our orders. Now I'm sure I was right.

Patsy blushes as he puts her coffee down first. It has a 3D cat made of foam playfully waving from the top of the cup. Patsy says, "Cool coffee art."

"Thanks," he says again. "I could show you how to make it, some time when we're closed. Maybe get to know each other better."

Patsy looks alarmed. Maybe she's just realized he's seriously flirting with her, instead of just being nice. "No. Thanks. That's okay."

He looks hurt for a second, then regains his composure and turns to give me my coffee. "Here you go, Mrs. Koerber."

"You know me?" I ask, too startled to play it off like I might remember him.

He nods. "It would be hard not to recognize a local celebrity, what with the podcast. But I also made it a point to visit all the businesses in town that sell coffee drinks. I chatted with Logan a bit about possibly carrying my beans for your coffee bar. He said he would talk to you about it."

"He hasn't yet," I tell him. "But it would be our first collaboration with a local business . . ." I let my words trail off, looking for him to fill in a name.

He does. "It's Nathan Kim. And the roastery name is Global Seoul."

I look down at my coffee. My latte-art creature is a rabbit, peeking over the edge of the cup, holding on with his front paws. And to make it even more perfect – it's a lop. "Aww," I say. "He looks just like Knightley."

Nathan grins. "I did try." Aww, indeed. The resemblance to my lop isn't accidental. He says, a little awkwardly, "I could show you how to make 3D art, too."

Before I can reply, Patsy says, "I wasn't trying to be rude earlier. And you weren't reading me wrong. I was flirting a little. Just – I'm still getting over someone. And it's hard, you know?"

Nathan blinks, like he's not sure how to respond to this level of honesty. Finally he nods and says, "Been there." Then he turns and walks away from the table.

The person Patsy is still getting over – that has to be Arlo, right? Even though she's the one who broke up with him. They had been close to getting engaged. Obviously, she had really loved Arlo. And now she's sitting across from me – even though recently, I haven't been able to stop kissing Arlo. For the first time, this feels awkward.

Nathan walks back over to our table. He's carrying one of the bulgogi-filled pretzels I'd seen on the menu board. He slides it in front of Patsy and says, "On the house. And if your life gets less complicated, you know where to find me."

Then he walks away again.

I start to say, "I'm sorry," though I don't know how to end the sentence, since I don't know exactly what I'm sorry for. After all, Patsy left town to get away from Arlo. And both of us had dated the guy before. Arlo had been my first boyfriend, back in high school. We'd broken up over what had later turned out to be a misunderstanding. We'd each gone our separate way in life. I'd gotten married and become a physical therapist. He'd traveled a bit before getting his life together and becoming a cop. We'd only run into each other again when there had been a murder at my chocolate shop's grand opening party – and he had been the cop sent to investigate it.

Patsy says, "I don't want this to be awkward. I chose my family pride over Arlo. I have to live with that. If you make him happy, then I'm happy for you both."

Though from the way she's clutching her paper napkin, clearly it hurts her to say that.

I say, "We came here to talk about your dad. Tell me what happened." I pick up my coffee – though it is almost too adorable to drink. The foam bunny bounces as the liquid moves. I take a sip. It is a nice, well-balanced flavor.

Patsy says, "Three days ago, my dad didn't come home from work. My mom called me, frantic, convinced he'd been in a car accident or something, because if he's going to be late, he always calls. They both keep their Find-My app open on their phones, only his stopped broadcasting a location. Before it went blank, it was showing his last location as somewhere on Padre Island, but she only saw that for a minute, so she didn't get a clear idea where. The cops seem convinced he was heading for Mexico, by way of Brownsville."

"Why would he do that?" I ask.

"I don't know," Patsy says. She tears off a piece of her pretzel and pops it into her mouth. After she swallows it, she says, "My dad is an insurance investigator."

I nearly splutter out a mouthful of coffee and wind up coughing on it instead. When I can talk, I say, "But the way your family reacted after Arlo arrested your brother. How does that make sense with your father working closely with law enforcement? He had to realize Arlo was just doing his job."

Patsy's posture goes rigid. I've hit a nerve. She says, "It's different when it's family." Then she heaves a sigh. "I think on one level Dad realized that Wallace had to go to jail. He just didn't want to sit across the dinner table from the guy who put him there. And Mom – she was just embarrassed about the whole thing. The media was already camped out on their front lawn, and it was all just too much."

"I'm sorry all that happened," I say. I don't point out that I'd come very close to being killed by Wallace, and that the media hadn't left me alone about it, either. Instead, I try to re-direct the conversation back to the current case. I ask, "Was your dad investigating anything big? Something where there was a lot of money at stake, or people with dangerous reputations involved?"

"I don't think so," Patsy says. "At least, he hadn't said anything like that to Mom or me. I tried talking to the people at his office, and they were less than helpful. They just said they had already shared his case list with the cops."

"That means they're taking his disappearance seriously," I say. "That's good."

I send Logan a text, asking if he can find out what was in that case list. After all, before he was a pilot, Logan was a bodyguard, and before that, he was in law enforcement. He still has some powerful connections. He's been able to get information before.

But the text he sends back is, *Why????? You okay?????*

Usually, Logan is happy to supply information. I guess he's hesitant here, because of the history with Patsy and her family. I guess I'll have catch him up in detail after I'm done here.

I ask Patsy, "What about your dad's car? Can't the police trace it?"

Patsy says, "It never left the lot. One of his coworkers did tell me he left around 10 a.m. that day. So theoretically, he could have taken an Uber to the airport, and then flown to Houston. But that does nothing to explain why he would be anywhere near here."

"Unless it was for an investigation," I point out.

"Then he would have told Mom. He always let her know when he was going to travel." Patsy sighs again. "I'm most worried about my parents' marriage at this point. Things have been stressful for all of us, in the aftermath of everything to do with Wallace. I've overheard them fighting a couple of times, when I visited them last month. What if my dad just snapped, and he decided to start over somewhere where he doesn't know anybody?"

"Then that would be great news," I say. The alternatives – that he was abducted, or that he might even be dead – are hard to even think about, let alone put into words. And no one has called with ransom demands. I'm not about to tell Patsy that the critical window when most kidnappers negotiate has already passed.

But if Patsy's dad left in the middle of a workday, that makes the skipping-town-due-to-anger scenario less plausible. Waiting until the next day doesn't match up with a spur-of-the-moment decision made in the heat of an argument.

Unless . . . maybe Patsy's dad is a truly meticulous type. And he knows insurance. Maybe he's trying to fake his own death, so his wife can collect the insurance and join him in Mexico later.

I know that sounds like the plot of a bad thriller. But stranger things have happened in real life.

My phone lights up with a text. I glance down. It's from Logan. He's sent me a list of the case files, even though I haven't yet answered his *You okay?* message. I should have known that he would come through.

I text back, *Thanks! I will explain later.*

Then I turn my phone around and show Patsy the list. I ask, "Does any of this look familiar?"

Patsy studies the information. "Not really. The only case on here that I can remember my dad talking about was the one with Mr. Tunaface." She points to where this name is written in parenthesis after the more realistic name Bryce Turner. "Apparently, that cat was a YouTube star, bringing in a significant amount of ad revenue. There was a big insurance policy on him – only he got lost, and the lady who took him in had him fixed and trained him to behave, so when the original owners got him back, his followers refused to believe it was the same cat."

"I'd love to see how that investigation turned out," I say, half-laughing. Though I don't see a circumstance under which Mr. Tunaface's woes could have caused Patsy's dad to disappear.

Patsy says, "I think they were going to have to pay out, since the cat's brand was basically ruined."

I nod. "Makes sense." I look down at the list. The answer could be on the screen in front of me, without me realizing it. I say, "Can I get your mom's number? Maybe she knows something about some of these people. Or maybe she remembers something from the morning before your dad disappeared."

Patsy texts me a contact, saying, "I'll let her know to expect your call."

I say, "It will probably be later today, or tomorrow. With the expo and keeping regular hours at Felicitations, we're pretty busy today." I don't mention that the main reason I'm busy all this week is because I'm trying to finish up everything I've promised for Autumn's wedding, both as her matron of honor, and as the chocolate maker in charge of her wedding favors. It seems a bit mean to bring up weddings in general to someone with a broken heart.

Only – my phone rings, and it's Autumn. My best friend is always more likely to text than call. Whatever she needs must be urgent. Which means wedding talk is bound to happen in front of Patsy.

"Excuse me," I tell Patsy. Then I answer the phone.

As soon as I've said hello, Autumn says, all in a rush, "I need somebody to calm me down right now. I just got a call from the jewelry store, where we sent Drake's ring to be sized – and they've lost it. I don't want to have to tell Drake, because he's already nervous about being in front of that many people, and he already freaked out about a scuff on his shoe."

"Okay," I say. "Take a deep breath. It will be okay."

"How can it be okay?" Autumn wails. "The band was a one-of-a-kind seventeenth century posey ring, rumored to have later been worn by one of his favorite poets. We were having it sized by a specialty jeweler who could do it without ruining the engravings."

I tend to forget that Autumn is independently wealthy, due to an unexpected inheritance, because she mostly lives like an average person. But it's a big reminder now, when she says that she's splashed out for a museum piece for her husband-to-be.

I say, "It will be okay, because the jeweler will find it. They can't afford not to, since they're responsible for the ring. It has to be somewhere. I'll go down there and talk to them in person."

Autumn doesn't sound happy, but she agrees to let me handle it. I'm glad she doesn't insist on going with me, because as emotional as she is right now, her going into the store is bound to be like using a bulldozer to pick out a fossil. I'll get a box of truffles from the stash I left with Carmen and Tracie at the expo to take with me. After all, leading with chocolate does usually make for a more pleasant experience when I'm going into a confrontational situation.

"Everything okay?" Patsy asks.

"Nothing I can't handle," I say. Though I'm not entirely sure about that. I mean, what am I supposed to do if the jeweler really can't find the ring? It's not like they can just whip up a new one. I take a steadying sip of my coffee.

Autumn texts me a picture of the receipt, with the ring's appraised value. The number is so big I take in a startled breath and accidentally snort 3D foam up my nose.

Once I can breathe again normally, I tell Patsy, "This is turning into quite the day."

"Sorry," she says. "I hate having to add to your stress. But thank you for helping me."

"I told you I can't promise anything."

Nathan is coming this way again, carrying a wad of napkins. He must have witnessed my foam-snorting, which is embarrassing. Especially if Logan does want for us to work with him.

I start to say that I am fine, but Nathan holds out the napkins – which turns out to be not napkins at all, but a rough white pouch, filled with glass marbles. He asks, "Does this belong to either of you?"

Patsy and I exchange a look. She seems just as puzzled as I am.

"No," I say. "Why?"

He says, "I found it in the back room. I know it wasn't there twenty minutes ago."

"How can you be sure?" Patsy asks. "Maybe someone who works for you left it there."

Nathan looks troubled. "I can be sure because we only have two Chemex pour over pots, and this was sitting where one of them was supposed to be. And I know nobody else would have moved that pot since I last washed it, because I'm the only one here."

I gasp at the similarities to what had happened at Tiff's office. There it had been a pen taken and a book left. Which means that so far today, a pen, a stapler, a coffee pot, a priceless ring and a goat have all gone missing. It seems unlikely that Lydia could be responsible for *all* of those thefts. But I do think I'm going to have to have a talk with Tiff's kleptomaniac friend when we see her tomorrow morning at the open house.

Chapter Four
Saturday

Patsy walks back into the expo with me. I get the feeling that she doesn't want to be alone. But she begs off before we get to the Greetings and Felicitations booth, turning and walking quickly in the other direction before I can say anything. I don't think she wants anyone from the shop to know she's back in town. The whole thing with her brother, and how things ended with Arlo must be too embarrassing.

But then I realize – maybe she just saw Arlo. After all, he's standing at the booth, talking to Ash. He's dressed in a suit, probably still on duty as a homicide detective. It's not likely he would have been called in for a missing goat, and as far as I know nobody has died, so maybe he just stopped by. Arlo's Cuban, with warm brown skin and brooding dark eyes and thick black hair, and he fills out the suit well. He also has extremely kissable lips, and I feel a little bubbly thinking about the last time we had kissed. I think about what he'd said – to stop debating what I want my future to look like, and just live it – with him. It would make him so happy if I do choose him. I imagine what the grin on his face would look like if I told him I was putting an end to the suspense.

But I'm still not sure about my decision. Especially not after spending time with Patsy. She may look a little bit like me – but we're completely different people. What if Arlo is having trouble separating us in his mind? If he loves an ideal, rather than me as a person?

I know it's a bit presumptuous to think that. Arlo knows me, from the years we spent dating in high school, and from spending time with me again over the past year. Arlo still has to be the safe choice, no matter what happened between him and Patsy. Despite me having seen the sympathetic side of Logan – and being so deeply drawn to it.

"Hey," Arlo says. "I was hoping you were coming back."

"Only for a minute," I say. "Drake's ring has gone missing from the jeweler's. I just wanted to grab a box of truffles to bribe them into looking harder for it."

"Well, this will only take a minute," Arlo says. "For once, I don't have a case. So, I'm organizing a group to go bowling tomorrow. I'm hoping you can come, so I can finally show off how good I am at something."

Which sounds fun. Only – that would give him a chance to see how absolutely awful I am at something. Still, he's bound to find out all of the things I'm bad at, sooner or later. We can't have a real relationship if I can't get over that. "Sure," I say. "It would be nice to do something normal together."

Arlo's phone rings, and when he looks at it, his expression falls into a frown.

"You caught a case, didn't you," I say, keeping my tone light and teasing.

"Maybe," he says. "I need to get this call. But if bowling doesn't happen tomorrow, then definitely next weekend, okay?"

Which is after I'm supposed to make my decision. But I did tell him that no matter what, I want us to still be friends. This could be his very calculated way of making sure I don't chicken out. I agree to go, because no matter what, Arlo will always be important to me.

As Arlo turns away, Ash gives me a significant look. I assume he's judging Arlo's merits and trying to communicate something about the future of my potential relationship, but what Ash says is, "I'll give you a ride over to the jewelry store. It will be a lot more low-key than showing up in that catering van of yours."

"I'll have you know – the shop has been doing a lot more catering. We've partnered with Enrique to do desserts for his pop-ups." Enrique is a Galveston-area chef who does pop-ups and catering, while still in college. Greetings and Felicitations has started working with him, providing desserts on some of his gigs. Especially his current gig. He's catering the reception for Autumn's wedding.

Ash does not look impressed. "I don't care what your shop does. You really need a private investigator's car. You know, not immediately obvious."

I start to protest that I'm not a private investigator, that I only seem to wind up in the wrong place at the wrong time, and get the information needed to solve a crime. Only – I did just take a case. I still haven't decided whether I should tell Arlo that I'm helping Patsy, and Arlo is bound to pick up on something if I hesitate, so I grab Ash's arm and say, "Fine, we'll take your car."

I march Ash towards the front of the expo before Arlo has the chance to get off the phone.

As we clamber into his Honda hatchback, Ash asks, "What happened with you and Patsy?"

Of course, he noticed me leave with her. Ash is far more observant than he seems. It's like his car – unassuming on the outside, but meticulous on the inside, with all the latest electronic features.

"Her father's missing," I say.

Ash's eyebrows go up, leaving the confines of his square glasses. "And you're on the case?"

I feel myself blush. "I didn't mean to – it's just, I got a copy of *The Thin Man*."

He puts the car back into park. "That can't be good. That's kind of a gritty book."

"I know," I say. "I always preferred the film version, with Myrna Loy. They traded a lot of the grit for charm. Plus, she gets a lot better dialogue in the movie."

Ash nods slowly, "But as far as you know, nobody's dead."

I gesture back inside the convention center. "Arlo just got a call. So you never know."

Ash shakes his head, "But that would be his case, not yours."

"And then you wouldn't have anything to podcast about," I tell him. "There have been some weird goings-on, if you need to fill air time. Since your blog is all about current happenings."

As we drive to the jewelry store, I fill Ash in on all the thefts, and the possible connection to Tiff's frenemy. Ash has learned the hard way to be a more responsible journalist, so I don't think he'll make any accusations without proof. But when he parks outside the jewelry store, he does make notes. It looks like he might launch a little investigation of his own.

Ash says, "I have a number of articles in the works, even if this doesn't pan out. Did I tell you I'm doing a feature on the goat yoga sisters? They're going to let me interview them in their RV. Cute animals are the second biggest draw for my blog – after true crime."

I tell him, "I guess I'll have to check out your blog more often. I don't remember a lot of animal features."

He says, "It's a more recent thing. I covered a dog surfing contest this summer, and people started telling me about animal related events. Obviously, if I cover their events, they're more likely to drive traffic to the blog."

We go into the store, and a Latina woman in her mid-forties comes out of the back and makes her way up to the jewelry case that faces the front door. We study each other across the glass. Her gaze keeps darting back to the back room. But finally, she forces a smile and says, "What a lovely couple! I guess you're here to look at rings?"

I look at Ash, about to burst out laughing, but Ash puts an arm around me, pulling me into a side hug. "Why, yes we are."

I force a smile, too, trying to avoid giving Ash an *are you crazy?* look. But then I realize what he's doing – something is obviously wrong – the woman is glancing toward the back room again. Ash is trying to get us a moment to figure out what's up. I hand the woman the box of truffles and tell her that they're from my shop. Then, I tell the woman, "Maybe we could just have a moment to look on our own."

Though it's going to be an awkward transition when we tell her why we're really here, there's nothing to do but play along.

The woman looks relieved. She says, "Let me know if you need anything," and scurries towards the back room.

I have to stop myself from following her. It's so odd. I mean, who closes the door to the back room of a jewelry store, when there's customers needing to be watched, to prevent theft? I whisper to Ash, "You don't think there's a robbery going on?"

He shrugs and walks over to the men's wedding bands. He points at one of the rings in the case and says, "That's similar to the one Imogen picked out for me. Simple, but not too simple, you know?"

The ring in question is made of platinum, with a row of five small diamond chips. It suits Ash. Obviously, Imogen knows him well.

But that's beside the point. I whisper, "We need to call the police."

"I already sent a text," Ash says. "The dispatcher is in my LARP group."

That was good thinking on his part. Making a call could have alerted whoever's back there. I say, "Then let's go outside and wait for them."

Ash says, "I think we should find a way to get a peek into that back room. When she comes back out, we're at the perfect angle to see inside." He gestures at the rings. "Which one would you pick for Arlo?"

"If she comes back out," I say. Part of me wants to rush back there and try to help. But that would probably make whatever is going on worse. I take a deep breath and try to slow my mind, enough to deal with all of this rationally. I gesture at the rings and tell Ash, "I think you're getting a bit ahead of yourself. You remember how I freaked out when Autumn got engaged so fast."

"I remember," Ash says. "But I know you. Once you make a decision – you go for it, whether it's a chocolate flavor or a suspicion about a murder suspect."

He's not wrong. But those aren't decisions that would affect the rest of my life. I look down at the bands. There's certainly more variety available in men's rings than when Kevin and I had gotten married. There's one in matte black tungsten, with a shiny channel down the center, that immediately makes me think of Logan. But Arlo? It takes a minute, but I spot a rose-gold band with a thick line of warm-toned wood down the center.

"Maybe that one?" I say. "But seriously, I haven't made a decision yet."

The store's front door is opening. I turn, and there's Logan, asking, "Haven't made a decision about what?"

Can this day possibly get any more awkward? Logan is tall, and well built, with a strong jaw and piercing green eyes. He's from Minnesota, and has a bit of Midwest ruggedness to his face. Is it any wonder I'm attracted to him? He's wearing a dark tee under his pilot's jacket, paired with his usual jeans.

"I haven't decided what I'm getting Autumn for her wedding gift," I lie.

Logan looks confused. "I thought you got her that big piece of wall art?"

Darn Logan, and his excellent memory. I wave a dismissive hand. "What are you doing here, anyway? I thought you had a flight today."

Logan says, "I just got back. Drake called me. He said his ring has gone missing, and he asked me to find it. He doesn't want Autumn to know that he knows about it, because she seems nervous about everything going right."

I can't help but laugh. To think at first I had been worried that Autumn and Drake might not know each other well enough to decide they were ready for marriage. But there's the noise of something heavy falling over in the back. The smile slides from my face. There really is something going on back there. There's no time to wait for the cops.

And it's a good thing Logan showed up. As much as I'm still ambivalent about violence – one of the main reasons Logan's private-security-and-who-knows-what-else past has given me pause throughout our entire relationship – it's nice to have a big guy who carries a gun on hand when there's a potential crime in progress.

I tell him, "The saleslady seemed nervous."

Before I can elaborate, Logan says, "You two stay here."

He vaults the gate into the employee area behind the cases and heads with purpose to the closed door. My heart squeezes with worry as he prepares to open it.

There's another noise. Logan tries the handle, and when it doesn't work, he kicks the door open.

The woman screams, as she gets shoved towards Logan, and someone runs out the building's back door, slamming it behind them. Logan takes off after this person.

Ash attempts to vault the gate the same way Logan had, and he makes it across, though he does an awkward dance into his landing on the other side. I take the time to open the gate and follow him to where the woman is standing, looking in dismay out the open door. I feel guilty that we had hesitated to step in to help. Despite the fact that waiting had been the more logical choice. Anything could have been happening while things were falling over back there.

"Are you okay?" Ash asks, and for a second I think he's talking to me.

"I guess," the woman says. "He threatened to kill us all if I did anything suspicious. But then he didn't hurt me, when he could have." She looks like she's in shock. The truffles I had brought her are scattered on the floor. When she sees me looking down at them, she says, "He thought you'd given me a weapon. He made me open the box. And then, when he saw it was just chocolate, he knocked it out of my hand. I'm sorry."

I lead her to a nearby chair, next to a table with gem setting equipment. I ask, "What happened?"

She gestures helplessly at the open back door. "He came in, asking about a piece he had commissioned. But I couldn't find it. He was convinced it was in the store somewhere, so he started opening drawers and rummaging through things – then he pulled a gun on me and demanded I open the safe. When I told him I couldn't, he forced the safe open and . . ." Trailing off, she flaps her hands towards the mangled safe door.

"And he stole whatever was in there," I finish the sentence for her.

"No," she protests. "The safe was empty. I told him there wouldn't be anything in there. We outsource a lot of our work."

I tell her, "We're actually here looking for an item y'all also said was lost. It's my friend's wedding band."

The woman narrows her eyes. "I thought you said you were looking at engagement rings."

"Nah," Ash says. "She's just an undercover bridesmaid."

"Matron of honor," I correct him. "And there's something more going on here than a simple lost item." I lean towards the woman and ask, "What happened to all the special jewelry?"

The woman's eyes go wide with recognition. "I thought you looked familiar. You're the amateur sleuth, from the podcast."

I smile. "I would have thought the chocolates would have given it away." Sometimes it is good to be recognized. Maybe she will feel more comfortable giving us information.

"I'm the podcaster," Ash says. "And Logan's – loosely connected to law enforcement."

The woman sighs. "I'd love to help you out. But I just work here. I don't own the place."

"But that doesn't mean you don't know anything. What's going on?" Ash prompts.

The woman says, "The jeweler we use for a lot of our more delicate pieces didn't show up on Wednesday, when he was supposed to drop off the finished jewelry. We've tried to contact him, and it looks like he skipped town. We've reported it to the insurance company, and they've assigned us an investigator, but there's nothing we can do at this point except damage control. So when people have been calling asking about their jewelry, we've had to say it's been lost. Which isn't exactly a lie."

Logan comes back in the door. He's alone. It's disappointing he didn't catch the would-be thief. Logan looks at me. "Do you think that posey ring would be worth enough to tempt a jeweler to bolt?"

I shake my head. "Drake's ring cost about the same as a nice car. So enough to drive out of town on. But not enough to start a new life in Aruba."

"What about the piece that guy commissioned?" Ash asks the woman. "Was it that valuable?"

She gets up, goes over to a filing cabinet, and pulls out a manila folder with a sketch inside. "Hardly. It was a flower-shaped pendant, inlaid with peridot and rose quartz. It was a reproduction of a lost family heirloom." Behind the sketch, there's a photograph of the piece in question. In the photo, a woman wearing Victorian-style clothing is standing at the base of a staircase. The pendant is eye catching. But it's not worth leaving town over.

I gesture at my phone, then when I have the woman's permission, I snap a picture of the photo.

Logan says, "Give me the jeweler's contact information. I can make a few calls and see if I can find out anything."

The woman pulls up the information in her phone and sends the contact to Logan. She says, "Like I said, I'm not the owner of this place. And after this – " She gestures at the open door. "I'm not coming in tomorrow. I need a personal day. You need to talk to Vic." She sends Logan another contact.

"Right," Logan says. He turns to me. "I guess you just couldn't resist one more case before the wedding, Fee."

The way he says it, it's like he realizes I'm going to choose Arlo over him, and he sees this as some kind of going-away thing for us to do together.

Despite the fact that we're still business partners, so we're going to be doing things together all the time.

I laugh, and it sounds nervous even to me. "It's not really a case." I hesitate, "And it sounds like you're the one who's going to get the information to solve it."

"Maybe," Logan says. "If it's that simple."

I keep thinking about that, all the way home. Nothing is that simple these days.

When I open the door to the hotel lobby, I hear piano music, floating out from the dining room, which is down a long hall. I'd half-forgotten we even had the old piano, leftover from the old hotel's glory days. This place must have been amazing, then. Tiff and my aunt have put so much work into the restoration, and the updates. Whoever winds up running this place after it gets flipped is going to have one special space.

But this hotel has become my home, as I've watched the transformation step by step. I don't even want to think about finally flipping it.

I make my way down the hallway to find the musicians all gathered around the piano, listening to Boone play. He's really good. After a bit, Boone stops and turns to Randall and says, "Here's where I want you to come in."

I accidentally jostle one of the tables, and at the slight noise, all the musicians turn to look. "Don't mind me," I say. "That sounded great."

Boone says. "Thanks. We do try." He plays a few notes of a jaunty melody, then he adds, "I just wanted to thank you again for giving us a place to stay. Your aunt is one sweet lady.

She made us some jambalaya just as good as any I've ever had in New Orleans."

I smile. "I know Galveston is a bit out of the way, but there's a lot of good food."

Boone nods. "I've played here before, when I was doing my music full time. But that was back before I got married. Galveston has always had such a vibrant music scene. It's good to see that things haven't changed."

"Really?" Charlie asks. "It's such a small island."

I shrug. "We have this big historic opera house. They have concerts there all the time, though some of it is tailored to kids these days. It's been around since the late 1800s. I did a report one time for school, with a couple of paragraphs about how they had a benefit concert for flood sufferers after the 1900 storm."

"That opera house has killer acoustics," Boone says. "But there are also so many smaller venues, clubs and bars, and even the resorts."

I scrunch up my nose. "A lot of those aren't really my scene."

The musicians all kind of shrug, but it's not mean, more like they get it. We're all different.

Starsky says, "You should have seen the Balinese Room, back before Hurricane Ike leveled it. Everybody played there. Sinatra, Bob Hope and Duke Ellington. Everybody." He tells Charlie, "You should have been playing with us back then. They let us open one night for the Commadores."

I know a little bit about the Balinese Room. I'm pretty sure it wouldn't have been my scene either, despite the big-name draw. Galveston had a reputation for being Vegas before Vegas was actually Vegas, and the cops had spent a lot of time trying to shut that place down.

Charlie turns to me and says, "My late wife was a huge Sinatra fan. We only met-" His voice breaks with grief that still sounds raw. He clears his throat. "Boone introduced us. My wife and I, I mean. Although, he introduced us to Sinatra that night too."

I do the math. Sinatra died in the late 80s. So Charlie and his wife must have been married for roughly thirty years. He doesn't look old enough for that.

"I'm sorry for your loss," I say softly. I mean it. I can empathize with what he's going through right now, and I'm glad he has good friends to help get him through it.

"Thank you," he says. We make eye contact, and I can tell he realizes I've been where he is.

There's a bit of awkward silence, as nobody seems to know how to get back the easy vibe.

I say, "So you all have day jobs?"

Flip says, "We have to. Music is more of a hobby. I'm an investment banker. Charlie's the CEO of a startup firm, and Boone's a teacher."

Starsky says, "I'm between gigs. I was waiting tables at Denzel's restaurant until a few days ago. But there was a misunderstanding with a customer, and it didn't end well."

"But Autumn's brother is here for the wedding," I protest. "Aren't you worried about seeing your former boss?"

Starsky makes a face. "What's he going to do? Fire me more? I'm hoping, now that he's had time to think about it, he'll offer me my job back. Especially after he hears me on drums."

I sincerely hope so. I really don't need a source of potential conflict at Autumn's reception. As matron of honor, I'm determined that this event goes perfectly for her – and I already don't know what to do about the ring.

The guys get back to practicing. I leave them to it.

I run into Aunt Naomi as I head for the elevator, and tell her I'll be back down in a bit. I want a moment to think about what might have happened to Patsy's father, and to look more closely at the case list Logan forwarded me. So I go up to my suite and I sit down on the floor, where Knightley can get close, since he's more comfortable closer to floor-level. Knightley hops out of his cage and makes his way over to me. I feed him his treats and pet him while I scroll through the list. He seems particularly insistent for attention tonight, pressing his head against my hand. I gently touch the soft fur on his ears. It doesn't take much to make both of us happy.

It's not a huge list – just the cases that Pete has open, or has recently closed. Most of them seem reasonably routine. A burglary where art and jewelry had gone missing. A restaurant with a significant kitchen fire. A high-end home that had burned to the ground. A boat theft. A flooded wine cellar, where the entire collection had been destroyed. None of it looks like a reason to harm the insurance investigator. Which is good, of course. I'm still hoping that Patsy's dad went on sabbatical, and he'll make contact when he is ready.

I do have questions about some of the cases, though. Particularly where the insured item is one guy's hands, and the incident apparently involved a touch football game. And another that involved the theft of someone's guitar. I mean, how did that even make the list for the caliber of cases Pete was investigating?

I tell Knightley, "You feel like it's social time, don't you?"

Though I'm really just giving him my own thoughts.

My suite in the flip hotel is up on the fourth floor, but Aunt Naomi and I share the lobby as our impromptu living room. I scoop Knightley up and plop him in his carrier. I bring the lop down with me, so he can hang out on the area rug while Naomi and I catch up. Knightley doesn't like the feel of bare wood under his feet, so once we're settled, I don't have to worry about him going anywhere.

Naomi makes us cups of hot tea, and asks, "Are you okay? You look incredibly sad."

I move from the sofa down to the rug, so I can pet Knightley some more, which is always comforting. Knightley nibbles at my pants cuff, rubbing his head against my leg in solidarity.

I try to explain exactly why I'm sad. Finally, I say, "I've felt grief throughout the whole process of planning Autumn's wedding. Everything reminded me of what me and Kevin did, how happy we were, how unfair it was that he died. But I didn't feel any of that at the bridal expo – even when someone implied I might be the one getting married."

Naomi gives me a sad smile. My aunt looks like a slightly older version of me. Tonight, maybe a slightly wiser version, too. She says, "Sweetie, you're finally moving on. That isn't something to feel guilty about."

"I know," I say. "It just feels like I'm letting go of something. Which is sad."

"Which *is* sad," she repeats. "But the fact that you're still alive, and now you're at the point where you're going to be okay – that's pretty happy too."

Chapter Five
Sunday

The next morning, there are already two cars in the driveway on the property for Tiff's open house. I recognize Tiff's Range Rover. Which means the Elantra must be Lydia's. Unless she stole it, too. Although that comment feels a bit snarky, so I mentally take it back.

At least Lydia couldn't have stolen Drake's ring, since it had never made it back into town. Although, if she had been the one who had taken the posey ring, being able to just ask her to give it back might be easier than trying to track down the jeweler who actually took off with it.

I am going to have to ask her, no matter how awkward it is, about some of the things she did take. I pull a big box out of my catering truck. It has baking sheets, cooling racks, and the cookie dough Carmen whipped up for me. I peek inside the Elantra as I walk up the long driveway, but there's nothing in the car, except a paper cup in one of the cup holders. Maybe the car is a rental. Or Lydia is extremely fastidious. I balance the box up against my hip as I turn the knob to go into the house.

Immediately, something feels wrong.

"Tiff?" I call.

"In here." I think she's crying.

I step on something crunchy. Here, in the hallway, there are pieces of curved glass, plus shattered fragments – and the tell-tale wooden collar of a Chemex coffee maker. Those things are super heavy duty. The amount of force needed to smash a

Chemex would be spectacular. And there's a rounded hole in the wall plaster, just above my head. What happened in here?

"Tiff? You okay?" I call again.

The only response is loud sobbing coming from the kitchen. It's a big house, with an open floorplan. I can see through the living room into the kitchen, and there's no one standing there. The weeping must be coming from behind the island.

I put down the box and pull out the pepper spray I always carry in my purse. I make my way cautiously across the room. It sounds like Tiff might be hurt. But if whoever hurt her is still here, I don't want to put her in more danger.

But I don't hesitate, the way I did at the jewelry store. Maybe it's because Tiff is one of my closest friends. Maybe it's because her crying hurts something deep inside of me. I try to ignore the way my heart is thudding, how being in this lovely, oversized home while the hairs at the nape of my neck stand on end is surreal. I duck down – stupid, I know, since I've already announced my presence, and carefully peek around the edge of the island. There's Tiff, on her knees, a wide run in her tights. But she's not the one who has been hurt.

Lydia is lying there, unmoving, while Tiff clutches her hand. One of the heart-shaped metal bookmarks Autumn had bought for her guests' gift bags is on the floor by Tiff's side, flecked with blood. The bookmark is made of a single, solid piece of gold-toned metal, with a thin gap running down the middle of it. It's an elongated, slightly curved heart with a pointed end, maybe five inches long, and now it's a bit bent. It takes me a second for my adrenaline-fuzzed brain to realize that Lydia has been stabbed.

And the first thing I can process is, *Huh. That's odd that the victim gave us her own murder book – and got stabbed with the bookmark.*

Which isn't actually logical, I know. Likely Lydia wouldn't have had the bookmark, since we had put together the gift bags over at Autumn's house a week ago.

Tiff looks up at me, terror and sorrow in her eyes.

I nod down at the bookmark. "You didn't, did you?"

It takes Tiff a beat to catch my meaning, then her eyes go even wider. "Of course not!"

My legs feel like Jell-O, as adrenaline in my body switches from fear to anxiety. "Is she dead?"

Tiff nods. "But I think she pulled the bookmark out, and used it to scratch a message on the cabinets."

Obviously, Tiff is right, but I still can't help but lean down and check Lydia for a pulse. Nothing.

I look at the cabinet near her shoulder, and there, crudely carved, is the name Vic. Which is what the woman at the jewelry store had said her boss's name was.

I pull out my phone to call Arlo, to report the death, but then I realize I should talk to Tiff first, so it gets reported right. I ask, "What exactly happened?"

Tiff brings the back of her free hand to her face, wiping at her eyes. Her voice trembles as she says, "I got here a few minutes before you did. There was somebody still in the house. I didn't really get a good look at them, because whoever it was tried to brain me with that Chemex pot. I ducked, and the killer ran out the back."

I stand up and look, and at the far side of the living room, the back door is still wide open. "That makes sense."

Tiff says, "I started to call the cops, and my office – since whoever was here might have gotten in using the lockbox on the front door. Any real estate agent could have gotten the code. But then I heard a soft metal sound. It had to have been Lydia dropping the bookmark. And when I saw-" She starts crying again. I give her time to get ahold of herself, without interrupting. Eventually, she says, "I forgot all about calling anybody."

"That's understandable," I say. I gesture down at the bookmark. "You didn't touch that, did you?"

"No." Tiff says the word with horror.

"That's good," I say. "At least your fingerprints won't be on it."

Tiff looks relieved – but then her face goes ashen. "They might be. If that bookmark is one of the ones from Autumn's gift bags – I was the one who took all those dangly price tags off of them. And I did have one of the extra ones at my office. Felicity, I think I'm being framed."

"Oh no." Anxiety spikes through me. Could my friend really go to jail? I take a steadying breath, try to think more logically. Surely, there's not enough here to make Tiff a real suspect. I tell her, "We still need to call the cops. I'll tell Arlo that all of the bridesmaids' prints could be on the bookmark." I put a hand on Tiff's shoulder. "In the meantime, I think you should come sit on the couch."

"But I don't want Lydia to be alone," Tiff protests. "Some uncomfortable stuff might have gone down between us, but we were friends."

"Then she wouldn't mind you doing what you need to pull yourself together before the police get here."

Tiff nods, and rests Lydia's hand gently on the tile. She lets me help her up. Tiff looks back sadly as I lead her over to the couch. She sits down in the middle of it, her hands clasped neatly together.

I move over to the open door, looking out into the back yard as I make my call to Arlo. This is a luxury property, so it's no surprise that there's a pool. Some water has been splashed up onto the cement – probably by the robotic pool cleaner. There are footprints on either side of the water – some heading away from the house, made by a person wearing shoes with distinct treads, probably sneakers. And there are several less distinct ones heading towards the house. Which could be from the same person, if the prints had been given more time to dry. They also could have been made by Lydia herself. I think about what I'd seen in the kitchen. I'm pretty sure Lydia had been wearing ballet flats. I snap a few pictures, since the prints will likely be gone by the time anybody else gets here.

Arlo finally picks up the phone, with a friendly, "Hey, Lis."

"Hey, yourself," I say back, trying to keep my tone light.

But Arlo says, "What's wrong?"

I tell him, "I'm here at Tiff's open house. And Tiff's friend has been murdered."

"Are you alone? Is Tiff there?" Arlo asks. He sounds anxious.

"She got here before I did." I slip outside – hopefully out of Tiff's earshot – before softly saying, "I found her kneeling by the body. But she was in shock. I know what it is going to look like, but she didn't do it."

Arlo asks, "Is there any chance the attacker is still in the house? You and Tiff need to leave-"

"No," I say, and I explain about how the murderer had tried to hit Tiff and then run out of the house. "I don't think we're in danger."

Arlo says, "I wish I could help, but this one isn't going to be my case. I've already got a case, and I'm up north of Houston, trying to figure out what the victim was doing in Galveston. I need to interview people who might have known him."

"Couldn't you have just called around for that?" I ask, not even bothering to try to hide my disappointment. "Talked to his coworkers or whatever."

"I could have," Arlo says, "except that he worked from home, doesn't seem to have had a social life, and we can't find next of kin. He was a fairly secretive guy, Lis."

Arlo must really feel bad about not being able to help Tiff, who is, after all, his friend too. Normally, he at least tries to avoid sharing information about his cases with me.

"That sounds sketchy," I tell Arlo. "Please be careful."

"Why?" he asks. "Would you miss me too much if I was gone?"

Is he seriously flirting at a time like this? "Arlo, I'm serious."

"I know," Arlo says. "Look, I'll phone in the report, try to spin it in a way that sounds sympathetic to Tiff. But I probably won't be able to be involved with the case anyway, since Tiff is my friend, too, and it might look like conflict of interest."

"What should I do?" I ask.

Arlo says, "If you're absolutely sure no one else is in the house, go back inside, lock the doors, and don't open them until somebody shows you a badge."

I take his advice, and tell Tiff, "Wait here. I'm going to check everything out." With my pepper spray at the ready, I check the house. It doesn't take long, since there's only a few pieces of furniture in each room – just enough to give a potential buyer the impression of what the space could look like. And in all four bathrooms, the showers are stone, open to the rest of the flooring. Two have garden tubs. The closets are open and empty. There's clearly nobody else here. I start to make my way downstairs when I notice a candy wrapper on the floor of the landing. Could Lydia's killer have dropped it? Or was it from one of the other real estate agents showing the house?

I lean over to examine it, but I don't touch it, in case it is evidence. The writing is in Korean, so I have no idea what it says, but there is a picture of a peach on the label. I take a pic of the wrapper, too. There's a couple of H-Marts in Houston, not too far from here, so it's not that unusual that someone would have Korean candy. I try not to jump to any conclusions regarding the new Korean coffee roaster – who doesn't seem to have any connection to Lydia, other than the possible theft of a coffee pot.

I sit down next to Tiff. I'd love to get her a glass of water, or maybe something stronger to settle her nerves, but I'm not going back into the kitchen. I know, I've had medical training, since I used to be a physical therapist, before I'd reinvented myself as a chocolate maker. And at this point in my life, I've seen a number of dead bodies, but it never gets less disconcerting. And it somehow seems rude to disturb the space where Lydia is lying with a mundane task like filling a water glass from the fridge. Still, in times of crisis, I do two things: I organize assistance, and I feed people – make coffee at the very least.

I have cookie dough, right here, but again, it would feel super disrespectful baking cookies right next to a dead body. I fidget with my phone, just to have something to do with my hands.

I realize I forgot to tell Arlo about the message Lydia had left, but since it's not going to be his case, I might as well wait and show that to the cops when they do arrive.

Tiff puts a hand over mine to still my anxious movements. I realize I'm making her more anxious, when I need to be helping her.

I ask, "What do you think Lydia wanted to talk about?"

"I'm not sure," Tiff says. "What if she knew she was in trouble and wanted my help? If only I'd made time for her yesterday, she might still be alive."

I feel the sting of that emotion, having been in a similar position myself.

"What was she trying to apologize for yesterday?" I ask.

"Back in Ohio, Lydia and I graduated high school together, and one night, we cooked up the idea of opening a real estate firm together after we graduated. You have to be sponsored by another agent for a while first, but we had the logistics of that figured out. I even took out a lease on office space. But maybe a month before we finished our real estate coursework, Lydia just skipped town. I didn't see her for several years. When she came back, turns out she'd finished school and been working for a firm in Florida."

Tiff had only recently moved to Galveston, after she and Ken had gotten serious. I'd been a last-minute replacement bridesmaid at her wedding, because we'd become such good friends, but I haven't known her that long. She's shared a lot of fun stories about her childhood making buckeyes with her grandmother, going to her older brother's football games, and riding roller coasters with her dad at Cedar Point. I know nobody's life is perfect – but I'd never imagined Tiff might have experienced anything so bizarre.

I say carefully, "I hate to speak ill of the dead, but with that story, plus the random stealing, Lydia sounds like she was a total flake."

Tiff grimaces. "I suppose she was. But she never meant to be. Kleptomania is just like any other addictive disorder. Lydia's parents sent her to therapy, and she would do okay for a while, but when things got really stressful, she would relapse. Her mom died when she was a teenager, and she had some serious problems with her stepbrother after her dad remarried, and I think she started taking things at first to get attention. By the time it was a habit – she had hurt and alienated a lot of people."

I nod sympathetically. "It sounds like you really cared about her."

Tiff says, "People tell me that I often give others too many chances, too much benefit of the doubt. But I don't think I'd like to live any other way." She manages a half-smile. "Besides, if I cut people off if they didn't make a stellar first impression, I'd have never wound up with Ken."

"Really?" I ask. "I thought you two hit it off, after you met at that baseball game."

Tiff says, "I don't even like baseball. I only went because a couple of my friends were total sports nuts. So when Ken had the jersey and the foam finger, I thought he looked like the biggest dork. Plus, the part of the story we don't usually tell is that the only reason we wound up exchanging numbers is that he spilled his nachos on me from the row above mine – and he promised to pay for my dry cleaning bill."

"Oh, wow," I say. I've never seen Ken at a ballgame, but he looks fashionable at all other times, and seems reasonably coordinated. Then again – who would be coordinated trying to balance nachos and a foam finger?

Tiff has the ability to look below the surface at who people really are. I guess that should be flattering, since she chose me as a friend at a time when I hadn't exactly been at my most personable.

The doorbell rings. Tiff and I both jump.

I get up to answer the door to Detective Beckman and a couple of other folks – including the CSI guy, Fisk. I know both of them from other times I've had to call the police and report a body. They are friendly enough. I think they know me well enough to realize I'm not a threat, or a probable murder suspect, even though I would have been in the position to help Tiff stage this crime scene.

Detective Beckman even sounds sympathetic while talking to Tiff about what happened.

But I can see the sharp way she looks at Tiff when certain details come up. She has thick, curly hair pulled back into a low ponytail as businesslike as her gray suit. Yet, I've never seen her as intimidating before. Then again, she was always there to help when I'd been in trouble, before.

She seems to already have a theory working – and it isn't in Tiff's favor. As much as I don't want to get involved in another murder case, I need to help prove my friend is innocent. Which means I'm now juggling two cases at once – the disappearance of Patsy's father and the murder of Tiff's friend. I can't deal with all of this on my own.

So after I point out the name *Vic* carved on the cabinet, and tell Detective Beckman about what the girl at the jewelry store had said about asking for Vic when we go back, I text Logan to meet me at the diner we both like, so we can get a late breakfast and start looking into all of this.

Chapter Six
Sunday

By the time everything is done with the police, all-day breakfast is still on the menu – but it's more time for lunch. So at the diner, I get my usual burger and fries. Logan has a club sandwich and potato salad. He's wearing his usual tee and jeans combo, but the pilot's jacket he usually wears with it is slung over something on the seat next to him.

"Who has Cindy?" I ask. Cindy is Logan's Bichon Frisé. He's technically fostering her until my mother gets back from Europe in a few days – but the tiny dog has Logan wrapped around her paw, and we both know it.

"I left her at my apartment. She has the run of the living room, but she didn't want to go out before I left, so I should probably get back soon so I can walk her."

"Oh." I hadn't even thought about Cindy when I had texted. "We could have gone somewhere with a dog-friendly patio. There are tons of them on the island. Next time, there's a place on the beach-"

"So there's going to be a next time?" He's grinning again, his easy confidence back.

"Just eat your sandwich," I say. I pick up my hamburger. Instead of biting into it, I say, "Tiff insisted on going home, once we were allowed to leave the crime scene. She said Ken was worried sick, and she needed to get back to him. She was still shaky when she took her keys."

Logan says, "Tiff is a careful person. I'm sure she wouldn't drive if she wasn't able."

"Probably," I say. "But what if she was targeted? After all, it was her open house, not Lydia's. What if Lydia surprised the killer?"

"I doubt that was the case," Logan says. "If the killer wanted Tiff dead, he would have killed her then. After all, if he had already stabbed Lydia, he would have no reason to hesitate."

I wince. "True. And I guess it is unlikely that the killer would follow up with another attack, since that person had been intent on fleeing when Tiff showed up. Since Tiff wasn't able to give a good description to the police, she won't be seen as a threat."

"That's true." Logan still looks worried, though.

"Do you not think Tiff is safe?" I ask. "Please be honest."

"She is probably fine," Logan says. "But there're too many variables – and even though the probability is low, I don't like to take risks with my friends' lives. I'd be more comfortable if Tiff were staying with friends out of town, or if she had been okay with installing a security system for her house. What if the killer doesn't know Tiff can't identify him?"

"What makes you think it's a him?" I ask.

"The amount of force with which that coffee pot hit the wall, and the angle used to stab Lydia with the bookmark. They both imply somebody relatively tall and particularly strong."

"How do you already know all that?" I ask. "Did you see the forensic report?"

Logan taps his phone, which is sitting on the table. "I may have gotten the preliminary information. It was rushed through, since Lydia Dunning is such a high-profile victim. The police are going to want to close this one fast, before the media gets out of hand."

"Really?" I ask skeptically. Tiff hadn't mentioned anything about Lydia being famous. And I'd certainly never heard of her. What could be so important about a real estate agent? I take out my phone and do a quick search.

The hits start rolling in. *Lydia Dunning, author of the tell-all memoir Silently Counting to Ten, claimed her stepbrother was a murderer, and her stepmother covered it up. Now we've learned that she herself was murdered.*

I look up from the article and give Logan a wry grin. "News sure does move fast in the age of the Internet." I turn the phone around and show Logan the image of Lydia's book cover, which has part of an old photo of a skinny white guy peeking out from behind a wall – glaring at the title text. Presumably her stepbrother. I tell Logan, "He did it. He had to have been livid over this book, so odds are he killed her."

"Can't have," Logan says. "Cal Dunning is dead."

"That would make it difficult," I say. I read through the rest of the article. I can't help but wonder how much of this Tiff knows. It did not sound like Tiff even knew her friend wrote a book. I tell Logan, "At least since the killer is a guy, it's unlikely that Detective Beckman will decide that Tiff did it."

"Not necessarily," Logan says slowly. "Just because the angle implies somebody tall killed Lydia doesn't prove it. Tiff is still a viable suspect, especially since Lydia stole her car and her boyfriend and moved out to the Keys. She even took money that was supposed to be in escrow for a commercial property they were buying jointly."

I feel my mouth sliding open as I process how the different parts of Tiff's story fit together. Tiff had said she had taken out a lease so that she and Lydia could have office space for their real estate agency – but there could have been escrow for a property that was rent-to-own. Maybe the office space had been in a converted house, or something. Which looks a heck of a lot like motive. I force my mouth closed. Then I say, "So the best way to help Tiff is to figure out why Lydia was really killed."

Logan says, "I knew you were going to say that. And since it came in so handy last time, I've been putting together a gift for you."

"What do you mean?" How could a gift I haven't gotten yet already have come in handy?

Logan moves his jacket and pulls something that had been hidden under it up onto the table. He slides it across the table to me. It's a pink and gray backpack. The colors match the color scheme I'd chosen for Greetings and Felicitations, and the silhouette of Knightley is embroidered over one of the pockets. He says, "If you're going to keep acting as an investigator, you ought to be prepared. So I got you a start on your own go bag."

I hesitantly take the backpack. This is different than the clothes-food-and-emergency-supplies bag that I keep for weather-related evacuations off this hurricane-prone island. I tell him, "If there's a gun in here, I'm giving the whole thing back to you."

"Nothing like that." He reaches out and puts a hand on top of mine. "That's not a path I'd want for you." He hesitates. "I know I've got no right to even say that. I just hope . . ." His words trail off, like a strong emotion has closed his throat.

I turn my hand around and squeeze his. I know what he hopes – that our paths can run parallel. And I have no idea how to respond to that, when I'm pretty sure they can't. I let his hand go and unzip the pack. "There's a flare gun in here. And a Taser."

Logan's cheeks redden. "Those don't count."

I laugh, and he smiles, and suddenly we're laughing together. And it's so easy and so perfect. I don't know how I can possibly give this up. But I'm going to have to. "Logan," I say, "we should talk."

His body language stiffens. "Nope. You said you weren't going to make a decision until Autumn's wedding. I've got almost a week to change your mind."

Ouch. How does Logan know exactly what I've been thinking? That I was going to tell him we need to figure out what we are to each other, without a romance. With me together with Arlo. Logan and I click on so many levels. And my attraction to him is off the charts. It doesn't hurt to give myself this last week,

to make sure of what I want – at least, if it isn't going to hurt
Logan more in the long run, with me drawing things out. But he
looks more determined than hurt.

"Okay," I say. I eat a couple of fries, trying to recapture
the easy feel of the previous moment, but it won't come. I ask
Logan, "Why do you even want to be with me? You've traveled
the world, done exciting, adventurous things. You could have
anybody. So why me, specifically."

He reaches across the table and brings his hand to my
chin, gently making me look up at him. "Because you are the
sunlight."

He doesn't elaborate, but I get it. Logan has been through
a lot. And I've been there for him, helped him to find a way back
from his self-imposed exile. Truly, Logan needs me, in a way that
no one else does. And he knows the worst of me – my lack of
self-confidence, my need to micromanage, my inability to have
kids – and none of it has deterred him in the slightest.

I look away, and find myself studying the backpack. With
it, he's offering adventure. It's like a flip of *The Thin Man* – with
me as Nick, the reluctant ex-detective who's trying to stay away
from getting involved with cases, and with him as Nora,
encouraging me to see justice through, just one last time. And
then one more. So if I want to do something normal – like having
a regular bowling night – and stop solving mysteries – Arlo is
honestly the way to go.

But I do need to solve this case, for Tiff – another person
who was there for me at the lowest point of my grief. And I need
Logan, with all his access to information, to help me do it.

As if to prove that point, Logan says, "As far as I can find
out, nobody has seen that missing jeweler since last Saturday,
when he paid his rent – with a cashier's check. But then again,
nobody expected to see him, except the jewelry store here, on
Wednesday."

"It feels like everybody's gone missing," I say miserably.
"The jeweler. Drake's ring. Patsy's dad." I put the remains of my
hamburger down on the plate and put my hands palm-down on

the table. I need Logan to answer me seriously. "This is the first time I've been involved with more than one case at the same time. And there's nothing logical that says any of this is connected. But I can't help trying to fit together Lydia's death with missing jeweler or Patsy's missing father. Is that just because I've gotten so used to trying to make the pieces fit while solving a murder that I'm trying to make totally unrelated things connect?"

Logan considers this for a long time before he answers. He says, "Human beings are programmed to look for patterns. That's just basic psychology. But the hard part about detective work is keeping an unprejudiced mind about the evidence. You have to consider the possibility that two – or even all three – of the cases are connected, without being disappointed if they aren't."

"That sounds incredibly difficult," I say. "And I don't know how to prioritize any of this. I don't want to let down Patsy. Or Autumn. Or Tiff."

Logan says, "Just follow the evidence. Once you've figured out one case, then move on to the next."

"You make that sound so easy."

My phone rings. It's Ash. Reluctantly, I answer it. I know the gist of what he's going to say before he even opens his mouth. Or at least I think I do. Typically, he'd be calling to get a scoop for his blog, now that I have come across yet another dead body. Which from his point of view probably makes me a mega mega murder magnet. But what he actually says is, "Felicity, I think I might have been the last person to see Lydia Dunning before she got attacked."

"Congratulations?" I say. "You're finally getting your own scoop for your blog."

"Not funny," Ash says. "It's a little creepy, actually. But it's not going on the blog. When I saw her, I was doing something that may be illegal."

"I'm not sure I want to hear this," I say.

"But I need to tell someone. And I know you're going to be investigating, so it is easiest if I just tell you. Then you can relay it to the cops and keep my name out of it."

"Hi, Ash," Logan says loudly enough for his voice to be picked up by the phone.

"Don't mind him," I say into the phone. "Logan's not really a cop anymore."

"He acts like one," Ash says.

"So what illegal thing did you do?" I ask.

Ash hesitates. He says, "My LARP group borrowed one of the turtles from the Turtles Around Town exhibit. We needed it for a battle mascot."

Logan leans over the table. He says, "That's defacing public property – if not outright theft."

"I'm putting you on speaker," I tell Ash.

Ash says, "We put the sculpture back. You couldn't even tell. That's why we did the whole thing overnight."

"Which turtle?" Logan asks.

"The one out front of the library. We saw Lydia coming out of a window, and she saw us returning the sculpture. We both nodded at each other in silent agreement to pretend we never saw each other. But now she's dead, and she was carrying some kind of documents out of the library, and I think maybe that got her killed."

"I'll look into it," I say, "Right after I swing by the jewelry store. I seriously need to talk to Vic."

"Sounds like a plan." Logan pops the last bite of his sandwich into his mouth and wipes his mouth with a napkin. He balls the napkin up and stands up from the table. "Let's go."

"What about Cindy?" I ask.

"We'll stop by my place and walk her before we head to the jewelry store."

Ash says, "Logan, I promise, you really can't tell we ever moved the sculpture."

I tell Ash, "I don't think Logan cares about that. Relax. We're not going to get you into trouble."

While we're driving over to Logan's place, I call the number Patsy gave me for her mother. I'm not extremely hopeful of getting an answer. I'd called a couple of times last night, but it had gone straight to voicemail. This time, though, Patsy's mom answers after a couple of rings. She sounds exhausted. I can't imagine what she's been going through the past few days.

After I explain who I am, she tells me that Patsy told her I might call.

She says, "I don't know what I can tell you that the police haven't already followed up on. I'm sorry my daughter bothered you about this."

I say, "I told her I couldn't make any promises. But I want to at least try to help. I need to ask some uncomfortable questions, but remember, it's because I want to help."

"Patsy said you were overly polite. Just ask what you need. And call me Mary Anne."

I say, "Okay. Were there any problems between you and Pete? Any reason he might have wanted a little time apart? Patsy said she is afraid that her brother's arrest has stressed your relationship."

"From tactful to blunt at the speed of light," Mary Anne quips. "But you know every relationship has problems. Lately, Pete was really stressed about work. And I suppose I could have been more supportive about it. We had a couple of fights about him working overtime when we were having a dinner party, and one time when he forgot to call. I'd made pork chops for dinner, and by the time he actually got home they were dry as dust. But that's hardly anything to leave home over."

She's right. But something obviously happened. "Do you think there might have been a problem at work? Maybe the overtime got to be too much?"

Mary Anne laughs. "Pete would have just quit if that was the problem. He could have taken any of half a dozen other jobs. He loves being an insurance investigator. He says it's half the fun of being a cop – with none of the danger. He keeps track of every case of fraud he uncovers, and how much money he's saved the firm. The total is into the billions."

I say, "But they weren't going to give him that sum, were they?"

I mean it ironically, but Mary Anne takes it as a serious question. "Of course not. We aren't rich. So nobody would have taken Pete for ransom, if that's what you're thinking."

I hadn't been thinking that, since it has been three days, and there haven't been any ransom demands. I'm actually worried that we aren't going to find Pete at all. If he's not using his credit cards, and hasn't been spotted anywhere – that's not a great sign.

I say, "But you weren't having money troubles. Nothing that would have caused Pete to be desperate."

"Of course not! Didn't I tell you he's been working all that overtime?" She makes a noise, like she's exhaling a heavy breath while moving the phone against her face. "But you know what? He did say something about going to the pawn shop a couple of times. I assumed he was still looking for a new amp for his guitar, but it is possible he pawned something."

"Okay," I say. Wallace had told me that he and Patsy grew up in north Florida, before he had moved to New York for his business. "It would be hard for me to get to Tallahassee just now. Do you think you could check with the pawn shops he liked to visit? See if they have receipts for anything?"

"Oh, we're not in Tallahassee anymore. Pete took a transfer, a couple of years ago, after the kids left home. But sure, I can do that." Mary Ann seems to be writing something down. Finally, she says, "It's really nice of you to be helping Patsy, after everything that happened. You probably don't know, but she was a late bloomer. She had some lonely, awkward days in high school. Even wound up taking a family friend to prom her senior year. She still won't go to family parties where he might be present. So this thing with Arlo was one of the only times when our Patsy was truly happy. I just wish Pete could have gotten over it. It wasn't fair to make her choose between her family and her boyfriend. So – just try not to rub her face in it, okay?"

"I wouldn't do that," I reassure her.

I hang up, still re-evaluating everything I'd thought about Patsy. She seems so much more self-confident than I am. Is she faking it? Or did something happen in her life to make her finally stand up for herself?

Logan parks the Mustang outside his apartment complex. He acts like he hasn't heard anything of the conversation that just transpired – though I'm sure he did. I go inside with him to check on Cindy.

The dog is beyond excited to see me. Logan goes into the kitchen and grabs us each a bottle of water from the fridge. He says, "I would offer snacks, but I put all of your favorites in your go bag. In that back zipper pocket you didn't even bother to open."

"Really?" I say. "Even those Siracha coated peas I like?"

"Especially those." Logan hands me the bottle of water.

"What about those plantain chips?" I ask.

"With the lime? Absolutely." He steps even closer. He leans in and kisses me, and I kiss him back, despite my resolve. After all, he knows me so well. And he's a really good kisser.

It's a perfect moment, until Cindy, from a combination of too much excitement and no recent potty break, starts peeing loudly on the rug.

Chapter Seven
Sunday

When we make it to the jewelry store, there are several people behind the counter – all trying to help one person. Arlo.

He's got his phone out, showing them a photograph of a young guy wearing a blue blazer over a pale green tee. The pic looks like it might have been taken in the 1980s. When he sees us walk in, he pockets the phone. Right. He doesn't want us getting caught up in his investigation.

Although – what is he investigating that has brought him to the same jewelry store Autumn's ring disappeared from?

Arlo arches an eyebrow at me. He leaves the counter and pulls us over to the door for a more private conversation. "One murder case not enough for you? You here to get involved in mine?"

"I think we've got enough investigations of our own," I say, though I can't help but be curious how this shop dovetails into his case.

Logan says, "But when we solve our case first, we'd be happy to help you out."

Arlo smirks at Logan. "Very funny. Sorry I can't offer to return the favor, since the case you're digging into would be conflict of interest for me."

Logan shrugs. "Then let's say dinner. Whoever is still working pays for the other two."

"Sounds reasonable," Arlo says.

Are the guys seriously trying to turn this into a competition? By default, that lines me up with Logan. And I don't like the idea of taking sides in this.

I say, "If we cooperate, we'd be likely to solve both cases faster. These are people's lives we're talking about here. We need to stay dignified."

Logan says, "I always respected the dead when I was a cop. It's no different now. But the puzzle of the who and the how – there was always something exciting about the challenge of it. I think it's a balance of the two that keeps us going."

"Agreed," Arlo says. "You put that very well. Care to share anything else? Like what brought you here?"

"We're here about Drake's missing ring," Logan says.

"That was from *this* jewelry store?" Arlo asks.

Oh, boy. Who *doesn't* know about the ring? Autumn was trying to keep it quiet. But there's no use denying it. I nod, and add, "And Tiff's friend left a dying message – the name Vic scratched into wood. It's possibly Lydia was trying to identify her killer."

Arlo looks back at the counter, where there's a tall guy – presumably Vic – trying to pull something up on a laptop. There's a much younger guy, who's on his cell phone. But Arlo isn't looking at either of them. He's studying the petite woman with the short dark hair, who is using a rag and a bottle of Windex to remove some fingerprints for the glass while leaning on a single crutch. She's looking right back at him, curiosity shining in her eyes.

"Vic," Arlo says. "As in Vikki Spinelli, the five-foot woman with her leg in a cast over there?"

I do a double-take, and Vikki starts looking at me instead of Arlo. Okay. So this isn't going to be as straightforward as I thought. If the police believe that Lydia's killer was tall and strong – it's even less probable that Vikki could have done it. I mumble, "She could still be involved somehow."

Maybe she even got injured in the altercation with Lydia, leading up to Lydia's death. I make my way back to the counter and ask Vikki, "So what happened to the leg?"

"Snowboarding accident," she says, scrunching up her nose at the ridiculousness of the memory. "Last week in Colorado. I get a bit competitive sometimes, and it doesn't always work in my favor."

"I get that," I say, though I am far from athletic. But I do get competitive about other things. Me playing board games is not a pretty sight. "I hope it's better soon."

"Thanks," she says. "But it's fractured in twelve places. It's going to be a while."

So yeah, there's no way she could have attacked Lydia. But that doesn't mean she doesn't know her. I show her the picture of Lydia from the back cover of *Silently Counting to Ten*. I ask, "You didn't happen to see this woman near your store over the past couple of days."

Vikki gives me an odd look. "No."

"But you do know her," I prompt.

"I know who she is." Vikki gestures at the photo. "I went to her book signing, in Boulder. Look, I thought it was the pain medication, mixed with a couple of beers from lunch, but I would swear that I saw her yesterday afternoon, leading a goat down Avenue K."

It takes me a beat to absorb what that means. If Lydia had taken Princess Buttercup from the expo – that means that the little goat is probably alone, wherever Lydia stashed her. That's not good. If she wasn't expecting on being gone long, Buttercup might not have food or water. Or whatever else goats need. We're going to have to find her, quickly.

But I don't even know where to start. Avenue K is a mostly residential street, with a park and a cemetery. That's really not much to go on. I text Tiff, asking her if she knows where Lydia would have been likely to stay while she was in town.

Really, all I know is that Lydia visited a number of public places and took some things. I consider the fact that Lydia and

Vikki's paths had intersected in Colorado. Could that be the reason for the dying message? Not saying Vic was the killer, but to get something *from* Vic? Something more important than naming her killer? I ask, "Is there any way Lydia might have taken something from you at the book signing? Or maybe given you something?"

"You mean because of the kleptomania," Vikki says.

I guess Lydia must have talked about it in her book. I'm really going to have to read that thing.

"Yes." I decide to be blunt. "She wrote the name Vic as she was dying. That has to be you, right?"

"Not necessarily," Vikki says. "There's also Vic that works at port parking for the cruise terminal, and that kid who works at McDonald's."

"Okay," I say slowly. Though neither of those sound likely to be connected to Lydia or her murder.

Vikki says, "There wasn't anything extra tucked into my book when I got it back from her. I don't know what else to tell you."

I glance back at the guys, who are talking softly to each other. They're so focused on their own conversation, I doubt they've heard a word Vikki has said. Something about their dynamic has changed, though it is hard to identify exactly what. Logan, whose body posture usually reads as open, has his arms crossed. And Arlo is looking at the floor.

I really hope that whatever decision I make at Autumn's wedding doesn't ruin their friendship. For a panicked moment, I wonder if the only kind thing to do would be to give up both of them. But – then none of us would be happy.

"Are you okay?" Vikki asks.

"Yeah, fine," I say quickly. I turn back to face her, and try to focus on the case. "I'm trying to remember the name of the woman who was working last night. I'm not actually sure she told me."

"That was Mirabel."

"Mirabel. Is she okay? She seemed really shaken up about everything that had happened."

"She's fine," Vikki says.

"That's a relief. Tell her to come by my shop if she wants some more truffles to replace the ones that got smashed." Thinking about the scene last night, I have an idea. "Did you happen to catch any security video of the break-in?"

Vikki gestures towards Arlo. "Like I just told your friend, the feed to the cameras had been cut." She hesitates. Then she nods, like she's deciding to trust me. "But you know what? Mirabel took a pic of the sketch she helped them do last night at the police station. She said she wasn't sure if she was supposed to keep a copy – but she wanted me to have a heads-up if he came back." Vikki awkwardly takes a phone from her pocket and shows me the text thread.

I study the photo. It's a guy – but he's super short. So he's probably not Lydia's killer. And he doesn't look familiar.

But that's not the only case that I'm working on. The jeweler with connections to Galveston was first noted as MIA the same day Patsy's dad disappeared. I say, "Mirabel told me that there was an insurance investigator looking into the missing jewelry. It seems like they followed up really fast."

"Considering how much that posey ring cost – believe you me, the insurance company was very concerned. They're waiting on the police to close the case, but since the jewelry hasn't been recovered, it seems likely that they will cover our reimbursement to the customers promptly."

I wince. It sounds like Autumn isn't getting Drake's ring back in time for the wedding. I ask, "Do you know the name of the insurance investigator attached to the case?"

"Hailey something or other." Vikki gestures towards the back room. "I can get you her card."

"That's not necessary," I tell her. Some of the tension goes out of my shoulders. And yet, I'm a little disappointed. It would have connected things so neatly if Patsy's dad had been the investigator involved in the case. But nothing right now seems like it is going to be that straightforward.

Vikki says, "It's such a shame about Roland. He really was the most talented jeweler I've ever known. And a decent guy, you know? I can't believe he's dead."

Wait. I feel like I missed a step here. Roland – presumably the guy who took off with Drake's posey ring – is dead? Of course he is. Otherwise, why would Arlo be here, in such an official-looking capacity? If I hadn't been so caught up trying to get my own investigations to intersect, I would have realized that Arlo's murder case resolved one of our missing persons. Trying to hide the fact that I feel really dumb, I tell Vikki, "I'm sorry for your loss."

She nods, and for a second it looks like she might cry. I'm guessing Roland meant something to her, something more than just a work colleague. I wish I had more to offer her than empty condolences. Hopefully, Arlo can figure out what happened to Roland, and she can at least have closure.

Vikki doesn't seem to know anything else that would help me sort out what is going on, so Logan, Arlo, and I leave.

Once we're outside, I text Autumn, asking her to swing by Felicitations later. I want to tell her in person about what happened to the ring. She will still have time to replace it before the wedding. Maybe not with something quite as special, but I can convince her to move forward, instead of holding out hope the posey ring gets found.

Arlo asks me, "Why were you so curious about which insurance adjustor will be handling the jewelry?"

Okay. So he had been listening to at least part of my conversation with Vikki after all. I say, "Patsy asked me to help find her dad. I was just wondering if it might have been him. It would have given him a reason to be in Texas, after all."

There's a brief moment of pain in Arlo's eyes. I've touched a sensitive subject. He says, "Patsy's dad isn't really a bad guy. If things had been different, I think we would have gotten along well."

"I get that," I say.

Arlo says, "You should be careful, looking for him. People who disappear like that – usually there's a reason they don't want to be found."

"You think maybe he was running from something," I say. "Or someone."

"It seems likely," Arlo says. "Best case scenario, he made it to the border and is happily off the grid."

I nod – but I don't really believe that. From what Patsy said, he doesn't seem the type. "Patsy would probably be okay, just knowing he's alive out there somewhere. It's just the suddenness and the questions that have her so freaked out."

Arlo starts to say something, thinks better of it, then tries again. "How is Patsy?"

From the look on his face, Arlo still has complicated feelings about Patsy and their breakup. Clearly, he doesn't like the idea of her being in emotional pain.

"She's worried," I tell him. "But other than that, she seems okay."

"Good," he says. "I'm glad that she's moved on."

Logan looks solidly at Arlo. "Are you sure that you have?"

Arlo says, "Just because you have good memories of someone doesn't mean you're still hung up on them. I want Patsy to be happy. But I want to be with Felicity. I think I've made that clear to everyone involved." Arlo turns to me, and his expression softens. "I love you, Lis. Always have, always will."

He reaches out and takes my hand in his. An array of complicated emotions pinball through me. Pain. Joy. Love. Fear. All the more reason to get this whole relationship thing settled by the end of the week.

I see Logan's jaw flex, but he doesn't say anything.

Arlo asks, "Do you want to have lunch?"

Arlo is clearly talking to me, but Logan responds, "We just ate."

Arlo gives me a questioning look.

I say, "Sorry. Bad timing."

Which has been the story every time, between Arlo and me. But something has brought us back together. We're finally getting the timing right this time – except for this little blip.

Arlo squeezes my hand. "Next weekend, then. Don't forget you already said yes to bowling on Sunday."

"I love bowling," Logan says. Though this is the first I've heard of it. "What time should we be there? I'll even bring my own ball."

I guess he really does love bowling. Who knew?

At first, I think Arlo is going to tell Logan to mind his own business, and that he is definitely not invited. But I guess he isn't ready to throw their friendship away after all, because he lets go of my hand to throw both of his hands up in the air, saying, "Why not? There's going to be a whole group from the station. Be there at 6." Arlo's phone rings. He says, "I have to take this." He points a finger at Logan. "Be very careful. I know I can't dissuade either of you from looking into any of this, even though it is stupidly dangerous. Just don't let Felicity get hurt."

"I'll protect her with my life," Logan says. It looks like he means it.

"Hello," I say. "I'm right here."

Arlo and Logan both laugh.

"Sorry, Lis," Arlo says. Then he walks away to take his phone call.

Logan asks, "Library, then?"

"Yes, library," I agree.

We head for Logan's Mustang. As we're getting into the car, he asks, "Do you know where I can get a bowling ball on short notice?"

I stare at him. "So you just lied about loving bowling?"

"I can neither confirm or deny that information," Logan says. "But I'm a competent bowler, thanks to my dad. And I couldn't pass up the opportunity to show off in front of you. After all, I have a limited time. And I need you to know I'm all in."

"I can respect that," I say. "I'll try not to take advantage."

Logan grins at me. "You're not that kind of girl."

"I'm really not, am I?" I laugh. "It's going to be an interesting few days."

We drive to the big public library, and Logan goes to have a chat with the security guy. Meanwhile, I examine the first-floor space, trying to figure out which window Lydia would have come in through. Before I make much progress, Logan comes back, looking puzzled.

He says, "The guard says there wasn't a break-in."

What? I tilt my head, giving him a confused look. "There had to have been. Ash wouldn't lie. There's no advantage to him to make up a story where he looks bad."

"True," Logan says.

I point out, "Surely there were security tapes from last night."

"Let's see if we can get access," Logan says.

So I follow him to where a different security guy is standing near the entrance. Logan explains that he is a consultant for the police, wanting to view the security tapes.

The guard says, "I need the request from the actual police, not just a consultant."

"Fair," Logan says levelly. He gives the guard Arlo's name and badge number, and the guard calls the station.

After a few minutes, the guard hangs up and tells Logan. "I can let you view the recordings, but there was no break-in last night, so I'm not sure what you're hoping to see."

"We just want to verify a few things," Logan says.

The guard trades out with somebody else who takes the position near the door, and we follow him to the security office. It must have been painful for Arlo to have to vouch for Logan, given their little competition, when the murder we're looking into isn't even his case. But he'd done it because he really does care about justice, and for that I'm grateful.

The guard helps us get settled in big rolling office chairs in front of the digital recording setup, which looks extensive, considering this is just a library. We have a rough estimate from Ash of the time when Lydia was leaving the building, and if a camera caught her, it would be going through a first-floor window facing the front of the building. So it doesn't take long to find the recording that catches her walking across the room and doing something to the window. After a moment, she slid it open and went through, out into the night.

"Well, I'll be," the guard says. "There was a break-in. Only – nothing was stolen or disturbed. We would never have even known that she was here."

"But why was she here?" I ask. "We need to reconstruct her movements to find out what she was actually doing here."

Together, the three of us work our way backwards, until we get to the point where Lydia entered the building in the first place, through that same window. The guard pieces everything together, so that we can watch the clips moving chronologically forward, using clips from different camera feeds.

And still, none of it makes sense. Lydia had broken into the library carrying the same set of files Ash had seen her holding when she left. She had walked purposefully to an exhibit in the middle of the first floor, not even trying to avoid any potential cameras. And then she had just stood there, for like an hour – the guard fast-forwards through a lot of that, when it becomes obvious she's not about to spring into action.

"What is she doing?" Logan asks.

"It looks like she was comparing something in the exhibit to something in her files," I tell him. "We need to look at that exhibit to try and figure out what."

We thank the security guard, and go find the exhibit. It's about the history of theme and amusement parks in Texas. This raises so many more questions than it answers. Why didn't Lydia just come look at this during the day, when the library was open? Why *didn't* Lydia take something from here?

My phone rings. It's Patsy's mom. "Excuse me," I say, as I step outside the office and find a quiet alcove where I can take the call.

Mary Anne says, "I'm at a pawn shop. It's farther away than the ones Pete usually goes to, but I can't just sit around doing nothing, all sick with worry, so I've been driving around all day, checking out all the shops I've been able to find."

"Oh, I'm so sorry. I wish I had some information for you."

Mary Anne makes a dismissive noise. "I'm the one with information. Apparently, my husband visited a large number of pawn shops over the past couple of weeks. I finally found someone willing to tell me what he was doing."

"And what was that?" I ask.

"He was trying to find out if anyone had brought in a specific necklace. He seemed certain that someone was going to pawn it. Pete doesn't usually handle cases involving jewelry. And I certainly wouldn't have pawned any of the pieces he gave me. Neither would Patsy. So I have no idea what he would have been obsessing over."

I don't either – but as we have been to a jewelry store twice in as many days, it seems important to find out.

Chapter Eight
Sunday

Later, back at the shop, Logan is helping me get started on the favors for the wedding party. Carmen is handling the front of the shop.

I go out front to get Logan and myself each a coffee, and to make sure there's not too much of a line. Carmen is adeptly pulling an espresso shot. I go past her, around the counter to where we have the drip coffee station, where customers can fill their own cups.

The guy waiting for the espresso has a paper bag in front of him – filled with one of Carmen's baked treats – alongside a copy of Carmen's cookbook. He taps the book and tells me, "This is the fifth one of these I've bought as a gift. *The Greetings and Felicitations Cookbook* has become my go-to for recipes I serve at my bed and breakfast."

"Nice!" I say. I gesture to Carmen, who has a pleased expression on her face. "You know Carmen has a second book in the works."

"Really?" the guy asks.

Carmen turns to give him his coffee. She says, "It's going to be full of recipes for special dietary needs, from gluten free to lower calorie. I've been including some of them in my daily baking rotation."

"Not this I hope." The guy opens the paper bag and peers inside.

Carmen says, "Don't worry. Your double fudge brownie is just as decadent as ever. I'm trying my best to have something for everyone – and for different occasions. Sometimes, I want to go all out. You should see the groom's cake I've got going for an upcoming wedding. Four different types of chocolate filling and frosting."

"Nice." The guy pays for his book, and takes his coffee and brownie. He calls back over his shoulder, "See you next week!"

She turns to the next customer. It's nice we're building up so many regulars.

I leave her to it and get back to making chocolate. I go into the bean room, where Logan is pulling a bucket of beans away from the optical sorter. That had been a splurge piece of equipment, from before I had sunk most of my free cash into the flip hotel. I've got my eye on a depositor machine for making single-origin chocolate chips, but it comes with a steep price tag. The only upside of finally flipping the hotel will be suddenly able to afford that kind of upgrade.

It smells amazing here, surrounded by all the aromas of roasting chocolate, which basically permeate the walls. That means it requires more focus to judge a particular bean's roast, because I have to separate that scent out from everything else.

I take the bucket from Logan and put a couple of handfuls worth into the tabletop machine.

We had used some of our existing bonbons and mini bars for the goodie bags for Autumn's guests. But I want to do something special for the people closest to Autumn.

Drake's great-grandmother is flying in from Jamacia, along with some of his cousins, so I wanted to celebrate his Caribbean roots. I had ordered a single bag of Jamaican-grown cacao beans, which arrived yesterday. Unfortunately I had other chocolate in the machines and couldn't process them until today. Chocolate takes days to process, so we're cutting this one close. Which is why I'm taking time out, despite everything else that's going on, to get it started.

Jamaican cacao is considered some of the finest in the world, but the trees are lower yield, and the land available for growing is small, so it is on the expensive side. Since there isn't a lot of room for error with so few beans on hand, I'm doing a roasting test using a table-top coffee roaster and maybe a cup worth of beans.

The chocolate is starting to smell just the way I want it. I pull the cacao from the roaster and dump it onto a sheet tray. As soon as it is cool enough, I hand-winnow one of the beans, removing the papery husk and cracking the bean with my fingers, tasting a couple of the resulting nibs.

The flavor notes are earthy, and I've roasted to play to the beans' strengths. There's a lemony element, and something malty that plays pleasingly with the rich chocolate brownie notes. Logan is a beer guy. I think he's going to like this chocolate.

"Here," I say. "Taste this."

I drop the nibs into his hand.

He tastes them, then after a moment he says, "This is really nice. It feels like it would go well with a stout."

Logan has been trying to learn as much as possible about the chocolate business. He keeps saying he wants to make a limited-edition bar of his own, but he hasn't quite done it yet. He has a good palate, and he's studied everything I can teach him about flavor pairings and roasting technique. So I'm not sure what he's waiting for.

I say, "I was thinking of doing small bars with crystalized rum hard candy."

Logan tastes another nib. "That could work." Then he puts a hand on my arm and says, "I know you usually make the design decisions, since you founded this business. But what if we did solid hearts instead of bars? And paired them in a two-piece box with a bonbon? Have you ever heard of Red Stripe Beer?" When I shake my head, he doesn't look surprised. Logan knows I'm not a beer person. He says, "It's a Jamaican beer. It's more of a lager than a stout, but it has a crisp edge to it that I think would work beautifully in a jelly filling."

I arch an eyebrow at him. "Are you saying you've finally decided to make your first chocolate?"

"Nah. That needs to be a bar, something where I choose the beans and roast them myself. But I'm more than happy to have a go at making beer jelly and sweet potato ganache."

"Deal," I say. I make my notes on time, temperature, and flavor. Then I move over to the big roaster and get the rest of the beans started roasting.

Logan puts his jacket back on. "I'm going to need to run to the store for ingredients. Need anything else while I'm gone?"

It's such a simple moment, him offering to pick stuff up at the store. It's the kind of thing that means more than the big grand gestures.

"No," I say. "I have everything I need. And you don't have to go right now. The chocolate won't be ready for days."

He turns to me, his keys in his hand, and I can't read the expression on his face. He says, "No errand is too small, you know. I'd bring you coffee from Kona."

He could, too, what with his airplanes. Logan's other business is as a puddle jump pilot. I ask, "Speaking of coffee – why didn't you ask me about carrying coffee from Nathan's new roastery."

Logan bounces his keys in his hand. Then he says, "I didn't want to push. What we have romantically is already fragile enough. I don't want you to feel like I'm trying to make big decisions for Felicitations, or trying to take anything over."

I understand why he feels that way. I have had a hard time delegating and sharing responsibilities for Greetings and Felicitations, since I first started the shop in memory of my late husband. I felt like everything had to be perfect, that I had to decide it all myself. I'd once asked Logan if he would feel equally comfortable if I started making decisions about his puddle jump business. But now – I need Logan to feel like he has earned his part of Felicitations, since he's worked so hard at helping it grow. He'd even financed and led the remodel of the annex.

I say, "Logan, I want you to feel comfortable here. I might not like all your ideas, but I want you to feel free to express them."

Logan puts his keys down on the counter and really looks at me. He says, "Since I've known you, you've needed something that was just yours. Something that you could control, and a space where you could be creative. I have always tried to respect that."

"I know." I start pulling out the heart molds from their place under the counter. "And I expect this shop to still be my place to be creative. But I've learned recently that if I want to find connection to the people I care about, I'm going to have to give up a measure of control. I want this to be a place where other people can be creative too. That's why we're doing the chocolate art classes and the chocolate making demos and the experiences. If I'm opening the shop to everyone else – then why not you."

"Honestly, Fee? Because you've kept me at arm's length, especially here. And I feel like maybe I should have pushed back against that. That if I'd showed you more how much I want you – that you wouldn't be about to get back together with Arlo. And if I don't change your mind, next week are you still going to want me to feel comfortable here, where you create and think and dream? And if not – are you going to want to be stuck running a business with decisions I made?"

I've never seen his green eyes look so intense. I suck in a breath.

I take my time to really think before I answer. "I know it would be awkward at first, but there is so much of you in this place. I would hate to see you leave it."

Logan starts to say something else, but Carmen comes into the room. Her gaze flicks from me to Logan and back to me again. "Felicity, the police are here to see you."

"Send them back here," I say. I look at Logan. "Please stay, if they let you."

Detective Beckman and a uniformed officer I haven't met before come into the bean room.

Beckman says, "It smells amazing in here. Imagine coming to work every day to this. I'd be sampling things all day long."

"Tell me about it, Meryl," the officer says.

Officer Beckman tells me, "Felicity, this is Officer Sabrina Price."

Officer Price and I exchange nods. She's petite, with her light brown hair cut into a bob. But she's wearing tiny earrings shaped like cupcakes. Something tells me that under other circumstances, we'd be friends. Circumstances where I felt comfortable calling her and Meryl by their first names. Like I had, before the distance I'd been feeling because of this case.

I ask Officer Beckman, "Is there something I can help you with?"

She replies, equally formally, "I need you to go back step by step about what happened at the crime scene."

I resist the urge to retort, *Didn't we do this yesterday?* After all, we'd been friendly acquaintances, and now all I feel is suspicion. But I hope this near-friendship can return after I clear Tiff. So instead of being defensive, I calmly recount exactly what happened.

When I'm done, Beckman asks, "So you never saw this alleged intruder?"

I tell her, "No. By the time I got there, Tiff had run him off."

Officer Price asks, "Why did you feel the need to visit every room in the house?"

I say, "I told you. I wanted to make sure we were alone."

I'm beginning to feel anxious. Why are they picking on these details?

Beckman asks, "But if you believed Tiff about the intruder running out the back door, why would you have needed to do so?"

And there it is. I feel my neck and face going red. "Are you accusing me of something?"

Officer Beckman holds out a piece of paper inside a plastic bag. As I take it, she says, "Real estate agents are masters of setting the scene. Take that box with the cookie dough. Baking cookies to create the illusion that an empty house really feels like a home. Staging furniture so that rooms look bigger and more open than they ever will when in use. So if Tiff had wanted to stage a murder scene, she wouldn't have forgotten the details – like the height needed for a believable dent in the wall."

"But why would she have done that?" I protest.

Beckman gestures towards the paper. I read it through the plastic. It is a hand-written letter from Tiff to Lydia. It's definitely Tiff's handwriting. The letter sounds like it was written when Lydia tried to approach Tiff after returning from Florida. It contains a significant threat to Lydia's wellbeing should Lydia come anywhere near her again. I say, "Oh, come on. This is melodramatic, sure. But you don't think Tiff would actually hurt anyone. She's one of the nicest people I know."

"That's true," Logan says. "I can vouch for Tiff as a character witness."

Detective Beckman gives him a skeptical look. "You're hardly impartial."

Officer Price says, "Several people at the real estate office reported Mrs. Henry having a tense conversation with Ms. Dunning the day before her death. And they report both Mrs. Henry and yourself inviting Ms. Dunning to the crime scene. If Mrs. Henry knew you were going to be there, it would have been taking a huge chance for her to commit a murder you might walk in on. But if she needed a convenient witness and someone to help her stage the scene – you were right there, all along."

Logan says, "Meryl, is this really necessary? You know Felicity."

Officer Beckman gives him a sympathetic look, "I'm afraid it is." She turns back to me. "Right now, we don't have all the evidence. But we will find it. I believe that you didn't kill Lydia. But if you cooperate and tell us what Tiff did, then you can avoid making yourself an accessory."

"She didn't do anything." I take out my phone and scroll back to the pictures from yesterday. "I gave you this image already. There was somebody at that house wearing sneakers. I had on these same half boots. Tiff was wearing pumps, and Lydia had on ballet flats. I never left the scene, and there wasn't anywhere to hide anything. So there had to be another person running past the pool."

Officer Beckman says, "We are still looking into the possibility that Tiff was telling the truth."

"Then why badger Felicity?" Logan asks.

"Because I wouldn't be doing my job if I didn't," Beckman says. "Because I have to follow the evidence – even if it leads to people I know."

I show them the picture of the Korean candy wrapper – even though I know they bagged the real thing. And then I point out, "What about the message scratched into the cabinets? If we had done it, why would it say Vic? If Tiff was going to go through all the trouble to make sure the height in the wall implied a guy, why implicate a 5-foot-tall jewelry store owner?"

Officer Price shrugs, like it's the most logical thing in the world. "Tiff didn't realize Vic was actually Vikki when you tried to frame her. After all, you just happened to be the one present at the jewelry store break in. You heard the name."

I feel heat behind my eyes and at the base of my nose. Being accused like this is totally unfair. I say, "I didn't do anything."

Detective Beckman, at least, seems to believe me. Mercifully, they leave.

Logan gives me a sympathetic hug. He says, "We'll figure this out. There is no way we're letting anyone frame you."

"Thanks?" I say. I go out into the main part of the shop to make sure the police and their exit haven't disrupted the customers too much. We're still busy, with Autumn's guests, and with a board-game group that have pushed together six tables.

Autumn is standing at the self-serve coffee station, stirring cream into a cup of dark roast.

I ask her, "Why didn't anyone tell me you were here?"

She says, "Apparently, you were busy. What did you want to tell me?"

The front door opens and Mrs. Guidry comes in. She's in her sixties, with curly gray hair and distinctly Cajun features, with a prominent nose. She's carrying a large flowered purse, which I've never seen before. Mrs. Guidry owns the Cajun restaurant across the street. She's an excellent cook. Unfortunately, she is also one nosy lady. She probably wants to know why the police were here.

I groan inside.

But instead of questioning me, she makes a beeline towards Autumn. Mrs. Guidry says, "I saw you pop in here. I wanted to say congratulations on your upcoming nuptials."

"Thank you." Autumn grins at her and shows off her impressive engagement ring.

Mrs. Guidry says, "I just found out you're getting married. If you like Cajun food, I'd love to offer my place to cater your rehearsal dinner. It would be an honor to host one of my favorite authors."

Autumn gives Mrs. Guidry a half hug, then says, "That is such a kind offer. I'd love to accept, but we've already booked a restaurant."

"Well, it is last minute. But you let me know if you need anything. My beignets are to die for." Mrs. Guidry hands Autumn a business card. While she has her purse open, she pulls out a copy of *Melody in Blue*. "While I'm here, I don't suppose you have a moment to sign my book?"

"Of course!" Autumn produces a Sharpie and heads over to a table to find a flat surface.

Mrs. Guidry jokes, "I suppose you're all set with your something blue."

Autumn purses her lips. "I don't believe in superstitions. I don't need anything borrowed or blue for me to know Drake is going to do his best to make me happy. And really, that's all I can ask for."

I feel bad that I'd assumed Mrs. Guidry had only come by to ask about the police. She's often nosy – but she's also generous.

I feel less bad after Mrs. Guidry turns to me and says, "I hope everything's okay. I saw the police on their way out."

"It was nothing," I say as softly as I can. After all, the room is full of customers. "They just had a few questions about Tiff's friend's death."

"That poor woman," Mrs. Guidry says. "If you ask me, I think one of those goat farm ladies had something to do with it."

I find myself squinting at her. Mrs. Guidry hadn't been at the bridal expo. How did she even know there *were* goat farm ladies in town? I ask, "What makes you think that?"

Mrs. Guidry says, "They, these two sisters from the Hill Country, Agnes and Esme, came in for lunch today. I had the news on really quiet on the TV. They were going on and on about some missing goat. Then, right when I was dropping off the appetizers, Agnes tells the Esme that she caught the dead lady from the news – they were showing a clip of Lydia Dunning – she caught her going through everything in the sisters' RV. I hate to eavesdrop, but apparently Lydia claimed that she was leaving something instead of taking anything. Agnes didn't believe her, and she threatened to call the police if Lydia didn't leave. Now, Agnes didn't say she'd hurt Lydia. But what if she found out Lydia did take something from the RV after all, and she was mad enough to confront her about it the next morning?"

Or if she found out Lydia had been the one to take the goat. Hmmm . . . Agnes had been wearing hiking boots at the expo. They weren't sneakers, but could have made tread patterns by the pool. And she's exceptionally tall. I'm going to have to find her, and ask a few questions. Of course, if I find anything concrete, I'll turn the information over to Detective Beckman. But until then, I'm not telling Meryl that I'm investigating the death.

After Mrs. Guidry leaves, Autumn asks me again, "What was it you were wanting to tell me?"

"That Mrs. Guidry makes the best Po Boy sandwiches on the island. You should really try one."

Autumn rolls her eyes. "You and your sandwiches."

"What? I'm busy a lot of times, and they're easy to eat on the go."

Autumn says, "Now you're just stalling. Tell me what you really wanted to talk about."

"Fine." I pull her into the hall, so we can talk more discreetly. I'm direct. I say, "The jeweler who had your ring is Arlo's latest murder victim. The ring didn't show up at his apartment, or in his workspace. If he had the jewelry with him, he may well have been killed for it. I'm sorry, but you're probably not going to get the ring back."

Predictably, she's upset. But she seems to have made her peace with it. Honestly, it's a good thing she doesn't believe in superstitions, because a missing ring would be enough to make some people call off a wedding.

She says, "I've already commissioned a reproduction. It won't be as special as the real thing, but at least I know he will like it."

I say, "Drake seems like an easy-going guy. I don't think marrying you is about the ring, no matter how cool of a museum piece it may be."

Logan walks out from the kitchen and finds us in the hall. He says, "I'm going to go ahead and run by the store. If now is a good time, maybe we can stop by Nathan's and talk to him about the coffee. I've checked out his pricing, and it is reasonable, considering what we're paying now."

"Sounds good," I say. "I was trying to think of an excuse to talk to him anyway. Maybe ask about the candy wrapper and the Chemex pot. Though I'm going to be completely embarrassed for jumping to conclusions again if this was a coincidence."

Chapter Nine
Sunday

When we get to Global Seoul, Nathan has his coffee roaster going. I know how delicate that process can be, so I tell Logan, "Let's grab a chair and wait."

The teenager working behind a counter gives us a questioning look.

Logan gestures towards Nathan, and the kid nods back. Then he goes back to looking at his phone. A decent number of the tables in the coffee shop are taken, but there's no line. Global Seoul hasn't been open that long, but it's such a cool space – it deserves to be busier. Maybe we can do some cross-marketing – assuming Nathan doesn't turn out to be a murderer.

Across the room, Nathan says something to the guy, who puts down his phone and moves over to the espresso machine. He pulls us a couple of espresso shots and brings them over to our table. He says, "Nate roasted this two weeks ago. You need any sweetener or anything?"

"That would defeat the purpose," Logan says. After all, Nathan wants us to taste the skill that went into roasting the coffee, without covering it up with additions.

I take a sip of the espresso. It's nice, smooth, low acidity, with rich body and beautiful crema.

Logan says, "This is good. I really hope he's innocent."

"I agree," I say as I take another sip.

After a few minutes, the noise of the roaster stops. There's the whoosh of beans being released into the cooling tray.

Nathan brings a cup of the just roasted beans over to our table and sits down. He looks confident, but excited that we're here. He says, "I knew you'd be back."

Logan says, "We want to talk bulk discounts and cross marketing."

"Absolutely," Nathan says. "You know I've got the hustle."

"Well, you obviously have the skill," Logan says. "But it seems the hustle would have taken you to more of a metropolitan area. So why set up shop in Galveston?"

Nathan spins the cup of coffee beans in front of him on the table. "A friend of mine recommended the space. She works in real estate, and said a friend of hers had moved down here and loved the laid-back vibe. I wanted to be near the beach, but not in the middle of nowhere. Galveston's a tourist town, with quirky history and a great art scene. I was working at a fun shop in New York, but I wanted to open up my own place. It seemed like Galveston was a place where Global Seoul would fit right in."

He's thought a lot about this. Which is not surprising for someone so meticulous with foam art. I think about the details of what he's just said. More than one out-of-town real estate agent showing up at the same time seems like a coincidence. So maybe they were the same person. I say, "Wait. Was your real estate agent friend Lydia Dunning?"

Nathan grins. "You know her. Nice. She used to come into It's a Grind every day when she was working on that book. We're planning on having a book signing for her here next week. We just decided to do it spur of the moment, so I haven't had time to do the fliers yet."

I exchange glances with Logan. Nathan has no idea Lydia's dead. Which makes sense. It only happened this morning, and if he's been busy at the shop all day, he may not have seen the news.

Logan seems to be waiting for me to say something. So I guess *I'm* going to have to tell him.

I say, "Nathan, I'm sorry. Lydia Dunning died this morning."

He stops spinning the cup of coffee beans. "What?"

Logan says, "She was murdered. We've been trying to re-trace her steps."

He looks both distraught and confused. "So you're not here about carrying my coffee?"

"We are," Logan assures him. "We had no idea you had a connection to Lydia."

"Are you sure she's dead?" Nathan asks. He sniffs, like he might be trying not to cry.

"Very sure," I say. "Were you two close?"

"We never dated or anything, but yeah, we were good friends. Ironically, it started when she stole my jacket. Lydia had a problem with kleptomania. But when she realized my wallet was in the jacket, she brought it back. The wallet – not the jacket. She kept that. It looked better on her than on me."

I ask, "Were there every any problems between you two? A fight? Any kind of jealousy?" I gesture towards the back room. "Some reason she might have taken your Chemex, to make sure she had your attention."

Nathan's lips narrow. "I told her about flunking out of business school, and she used that in the book. She did a meta opening where it's like the reader has been sitting in the coffee bar the whole time. We did have a fight over that, because she used my name and everything. But I got over it. I don't think she had a problem with me."

I ask, "What about that random bag of marbles that Nathan found in place of the Chemex? When it showed up, why didn't you immediately think she left it.?"

He looks over at the bar. "She hadn't been in that day. And she told me her therapy had been going well. I guess I should have put two and two together, but I always like to think the best of my friends."

"Can we have a look at these marbles? Logan asks.

"Sure." We follow Nathan over to the bar. He goes around behind it and pulls the marbles pouch out of a box marked Lost and Found.

Next to the box, there are a couple of open bags of individually wrapped candies. One of them is the same kind of gummy peach ring as the wrapper I'd found at the house this morning.

I ask bluntly, "Were you looking at houses over the past few days?"

"No, why?" He looks confused.

I gesture at the candy. "I found a wrapper for one of those peach gummies at the open house I was supposed to help set up this morning. It was the same place where we found Lydia's body."

Nathan freezes in the middle of handing the pouch to Logan. Logan reaches out the rest of the way and takes it from Nathan's unresisting hand.

Nathan says, "Are you saying you think I was there?"

"Were you?" I ask.

"No!" Nathan takes a deep breath, then exhales slowly, trying to calm himself. "I don't even like those candies. They taste fake. But they match the aesthetic for some of the sweeter drinks. I put one on the saucer for my Have a Peachy Day Cotton Candy Cloud Peach Tea. Along with some other candy. If somebody's willing to pay nine bucks for a cup of tea, I try to make the experience worth their while."

"Nine bucks? For tea?" Logan asks skeptically. That's a lot more expensive than any of our drinks at Felicitations.

Nathan says, "It involves a setup with a cotton candy cloud suspended over the cup to sweeten it. I think most people buy it to Instagram it, so they don't balk at the price."

Nathan takes out his phone. He shows us a video of the beverage in action on his social media, the steam from the tea melting the cotton candy into the cup. And there, clearly visible on the saucer, is the wrapped peach ring. So while Nathan isn't necessarily our killer – it's likely that the killer has been in this shop. Unless the killer took the candy off of Lydia after killing her, which would just be awful.

"Interesting," Logan says. He's still looking at the number of the likes for the video. "I guess you got what you needed out of that business school."

Nathan laughs. "You could say that."

I ask, "Do you have any idea where Lydia was staying? We think she stole a goat, and now that she's dead, it is probably stuck somewhere alone."

Nathan doesn't look surprised by this information. He says, "Lydia didn't like hotels. She said they made her feel vulnerable. My guess is she would have rented a house somewhere."

Logan opens the marble pouch. He asks, "Did you look at these?"

Nathan says, "Just enough to figure out what they were."

Logan pours the marbles onto the counter, corralling them carefully with his other hand. There are a few other items mixed in with the marbles – including a key to a padlock. There's also the face of an old watch, a broken lipstick tube, and a keychain shaped like a dolphin. I take a picture of the random items.

Nathan says, "It looks like someone scooped up the leftovers from a sad garage sale."

Logan picks up the padlock key. "The question is – whose garage sale?"

I ask, "And where's the lock that goes to that key?"

Logan scoops the marbles and random junk back into the pouch. He says, "I'd like to hold onto this. And then, after I've examined it, I can pass it on to the police."

"Of course," Nathan says.

We nail down the details for our first order of his coffee, and then I take photos with him by the roaster, and then a close-up of him holding a cup with his logo on it. I need to social media about the upgrade to the Greetings and Felicitations coffee bar.

I start the post as soon as I'm in the passenger seat of Logan's car.

Logan asks, "Where to next?"

I tell him, "I don't know. There are so many directions to this thing – I'm not sure what to follow up on first."

Logan says, "Just take it one step at a time."

"The most urgent thing seems to be finding Patsy's dad. He could be in trouble. But I don't have a single lead on that. The next thing – we need to find that goat. Hold on." I text Ash, since he got contact info from Agnes and Esme. I ask, *Can you tell me where the goat farm girls are staying?*

He immediately texts back, *Did you find Princess Buttercup?*

No, but we're looking into it.

Ash sends me the address for an RV park. Logan puts it into the GPS for his phone, and we head that way.

While we're driving, Logan says, "Our friend Nathan is definitely hiding something."

"What makes you think that?" I'd found Nathan charming and confident.

Logan says, "I just find it hard to believe his whole *I didn't connect my kleptomaniac friend to the random theft* act."

"I don't know," I say. "Maybe he's just naive. Or maybe we're the ones jumping to conclusions. Just because Lydia had kleptomania, that doesn't mean she committed every petty theft in town."

"You have a point there." Logan drums his fingers against the steering wheel, thinking it through. "We just have too many clues that could point in one direction, without confirmation that any of them do. We could be starting to build the wrong puzzle."

"Maybe," I say, "but we have to put something together, just to get a place to start. Patsy is going crazy right now. Tiff could go to jail. I don't know what to do."

"Maybe Patsy has some idea where her father might have stopped, if he really was traveling towards Mexico. Her mom could pull his credit card statements, if she's on the accounts, and we could try to talk to somebody at the last place he stopped."

"That's a great idea."

I call Patsy. She sounds sleepy, but she gets her mom, and they access the accounts.

Patsy sounds surprised when she says, "The last time his credit card was used was right here! He stopped at a sushi joint on the bay side of Galveston, the day after he disappeared."

I say, "That doesn't make a lot of sense. If his phone location put him in Padre, then why backtrack all the way back here? If he's in town, surely one of us would have seen him."

"I'm going down to that restaurant," Patsy says.

Logan tells me, "Tell her we'll go, tomorrow afternoon. I know one of the chefs, but he doesn't work weekends."

I relay this information. Patsy seems hesitant about waiting any longer than we already have, but she agrees.

By the time we get to the RV park, Logan and I have talked through several possible theories. What if somebody from where Lydia and Tiff used to live had a grudge and decided to kill Lydia and frame Tiff to get back at both of them? Or a rival real estate agent killed her over the commission for the property on Mustang Island? Logan even suggested that maybe Nathan killed her, before she could bare any more of his secrets in another book.

But none of it really matches up.

Jokingly, Logan says, "Maybe Patsy's dad killed Lydia as some kind of insurance scheme."

A shudder goes down my spine at the thought – which feels more plausible than anything we've come up with so far. "That's not funny."

"Sorry." Logan puts on his blinker and turns into a long driveway. "Look, we're here."

It takes us a minute to figure out which RV we're looking for, but once we get close, the impromptu goat pen set up outside makes it obvious. The two goats look at us curiously.

I tell Logan, "We need to find out if Lydia had life insurance. Or something of value to be inherited. Just because she died here doesn't mean her killer is local." Then I knock on the door.

Logan starts texting someone. Likely, he's already following up on who inherits.

The RV door opens and Agnes peers out at us. "Felicity! Tell me you've found Princess Buttercup!"

I hate to dash her hopes, but I have to say, "Sorry, no. But I wanted to talk to you about where she might have gone."

Agnes lets us in. I've never been in an RV. This one is really nice, with a gourmet kitchen and upscale fake fireplace. From what I can tell, Agnes is currently here alone. She ushers us into a tiny living room that somehow has a loveseat and a triple row of theater seating. We sit on the loveseat, while Agnes takes the middle chair opposite us. She presses a button and her chair partly reclines. She says, "Tell me what you need to know."

I start with the hard question. "I know Lydia Dunning came by here last night, and you caught her breaking in."

Agnes asks, "What does that have to do with Princess Buttercup?"

Logan says, "We believe that Lydia may have taken your goat."

Agnes looks worried. "I heard on the news Lydia's dead. You really don' know where she took Buttercup?"

"Not yet," I say. "Since you had a disagreement with Lydia last night, we wondered if something might have escalated, if she refused to give you back Princess Buttercup."

"What? No. I didn't even know who Lydia was until I saw the news. I was home all night. You can ask Esme." Agnes pauses, taking a deep breath to calm the sudden panic showing in her eyes. "If everybody knows about me finding Lydia going through the RV, then why aren't the police here to question me?"

"They don't know yet," I say. "We just happened to find out about it."

I'm not about to give out Mrs. Guidry as my source. After all, Agnes could be a vindictive murderer. Though I doubt it, considering she just assumed that the murder took place sometime after her disagreement with Lydia last night.

Agnes says, "Lydia said something I didn't understand. She said, 'It's just like that time with Cal. Nobody believes me.' Of course I didn't believe her. She claimed she had broken in to leave me a jar of honey. Which is just weird. But then I found out her step-brother Cal was a killer. So maybe it wasn't the break-in she was making a comparison to. Maybe something else was going on."

Logan asks, "What else did she say?"

"She said the goats were cute. That they reminded her of a farm she used to visit before her mother died. That's the main reason I didn't call the cops – she looked so sad. But I assumed she was talking about Thumbelina and Spiderchick. If I had even imagined that she'd taken Princess Buttercup, I would have called the police, then and there. Goats have to be milked daily. Otherwise, it causes a lot of discomfort. Do you think Lydia knew that? Do you think she milked Princess Buttercup this morning?"

I hold out a hand to stop Agnes, since she's getting worked up. "We don't even know for sure if Lydia had her."

Logan says, "You named your goat Spiderchick?"

Agnes manages a smile. "Esme's son wanted it to be Spiderman. But it's a lot more complicated to keep bucks and does in the same place, so when we went to the rescue, we just got girls."

"Why not go with Spiderwoman?" Logan asks. "Since she's in the comics."

Agnes half-laughs. "He said he didn't like the costume."

I ask, "Are all your goats rescues?"

"Most of them are." She gestures towards the pen outside. "The three we brought are part of a group of six goats that were surrendered to the rescue after the person who originally bought them realized he didn't really have room or time for goats. Like I said, you have to milk them every day. And they can make a lot of noise. An upset goat can sound like a screaming girl."

Logan says, "Then it's surprising that nobody's found Princess Buttercup yet."

Agnes says, "That's right. Especially because goats are herd animals. Being on her own is likely causing stress."

I know how Princess Buttercup feels. I'd tried isolating myself, after Kevin had died. But I'm an extrovert, and feeling isolated had caused me stress too. We have to find the little goat. And with her, hopefully some clue as to what happened to Lydia.

My plan is to spend the rest of the day sorting through the clues we have so far and contacting everyone who might be able to give me information.

I pull up the list of Pete's investigations. Nothing on this list relates to the theft of jewelry. But he did have one case that was in Texas. It's the one involving the social media cat. Maybe there's something about this cat that only comes across in person. At least – maybe Pete initially came to Texas to see, and there's some clue we could find of how he wound up heading for Corpus. The cat and its owners are in Austin, but with Logan's access to a private plane, I'm sure he can get us there in an hour or two.

I tell him my plan, and then get in touch with the people I want to talk with. Once the plan is sorted, Logan and I head to the hanger where Logan keeps his planes. It's funny, I've known him all this time, and this is the first time I've ever ridden with him while he's flying. I knew he was a practical, no-nonsense kind of guy, but the amount of care he puts into a pre-flight check is something else.

But once we get up in the air – there's something about his face that just looks so free. I've never seen him that relaxed before. He tells me, "I have literally dreamed of taking you flying."

I like the fact that I'm showing up in Logan's dreams. I know I shouldn't – not if I'm planning on rejecting him. But it's still flattering. I tell him, "This is fun."

He says, "I can give you a flying lesson, if you want."

"That's okay," I say quickly. It's incredibly noisy inside the six-seater plane, even with the headsets, and the idea of controlling the craft is a bit intimidating. I point out the window at the scenery speeding by – ribbons of highway, stands of pines, rocky terrain. "I've driven this route more times than I can count – but I've never seen things from quite this perspective."

"That's one reason I love flying. You get a sense of clarity about the big picture in life."

I tell him, "I can see the appeal in piloting a plane like this – though it's not something I'm sure I would be able to do."

"Fee, you can do anything you put your mind too," Logan says. But he doesn't push for me to take the lesson. Instead, we sit in comfortable silence, occasionally broken by one of us remarking on a passing landmark.

Logan says, "I thought about bringing Cindy with us. I have a harness for her that buckles into the seatbelts. But it didn't seem right, since we're meeting up with a cat."

I laugh. "I'm sure the cat's owners appreciate that."

Logan says, "I hated to leave her home alone again, especially since I'm not sure how long we're going to be gone. So I dropped her off with Tracie, for a play date."

Tracie has a schnauzer, so that makes sense. I tell Logan, "I'm sure they're going to have a great time."

It's adorable that he looks worried.

Soon enough, we put down on a small airstrip, and we take an Uber into Pflugerville, a small town outside Austin. The driver drops us off outside a large house, one of the cookie-cutter tract homes lining the street.

I knock, and a girl comes to the door. She's maybe seventeen, bleached blonde, wearing pink – pink tee, pink jeans, pink sneakers. She takes one look at me and shouts back into the house, "Mom! The chocolate death lady is here!"

I give her a thin smile. It's not a description I would have chosen for myself. I hold out the "Box Set" collection of bars I've brough from my shop. "Well, the chocolate part is true enough."

She takes the bars. "Are you wanting me to do an unboxing video? I don't have a hole in my posting schedule for a couple of weeks, but I think I could fit you in."

"I was just trying to thank you for your time," I say.

A woman appears in the doorway behind the girl. She looks like a lot like her – only twenty years older, and wearing a less monochrome outfit. She says, "Don't mind Chloe. She thinks of everything as a marketing opportunity. It's going to pay her way through college, so I can't complain."

"I'm not opposed to an unboxing video," I tell Chloe. I have seen a few of the chefs I follow on social media do them for brands they appreciate. It's just a short piece where the vlogger takes things out of a box, talks about what they appreciate about each one, and sometimes tastes things live. I have a lot of products I'm proud of. "I could send you a bigger box."

Chloe smiles and says, "Consider it done. I looked at your social media while we were waiting for you. It has potential. You might be able to find some sponsors in the true crime market." She gestures us into the house. "Have you considered writing a book?"

"Remind me to hire you when I'm ready to step up my marketing," I say. I'm joking, but Chloe whips out a business card.

She says, "I can give you a couple of hours for free, because I love the concept. And in return, you can get me an interview with Autumn Ellis." She points a finger at me. "She's actually writing *her* books. I'm sure she could get you pointed in the right direction."

How is a high school kid suddenly making me feel inadequate?

I stand up a little straighter and say, "We're here to talk about Mr. Nash. I understand he was here a week and a half ago?" I look between Chloe and her mother.

Her mom says, "I told you everything I know over the phone. I hate that you made the trip out here."

Logan asks, "Did anything unusual happen while Pete was here?"

She takes a moment to consider the question. "I don't think so. The whole thing was a little surreal. He spent about an hour interacting with Chloe and Mr. Tunaface, trying to get Mr. Tunaface to act like his old jerk self. He seemed disappointed that he didn't even get scratched for his trouble."

Chloe says, "People used to love watching Tune-Tune scratch unsuspecting visitors."

The cat in question steps out from behind the sofa, letting out an inquisitive *mmmmrrrrp?* at the sound of his name. He's a big long-haired gray cat. I lean down and hold out a hand. Mr. Tunaface pads over and sniffs my hand, then licks it with a rough tongue. I say, "Hey cutie." Then I ask Chloe, "Did Mr. Nash stay in the room the whole time?"

Chloe says, "Actually, he didn't. He got a phone call about halfway through. He asked for a piece of paper to write a note, then he took his phone into the hall to answer. He was whispering into it, so I couldn't really eavesdrop."

"What did he do with the piece of paper?" Logan asks.

Chloe gestures over to an entryway table with a wide drawer. "I do everything electronically, but I keep a couple of cute notebooks for video props. So I let him use one of those. I offered him a gel pen, but he already had a cheap ballpoint."

"When he was done?" I prompt.

"He tore out the page and gave me back the notebook. I put it in the drawer, and he folded up the paper and put it in his pocket. Why is that important?"

"There could be an impression on the paper," I explain. "If you have a pencil, we could do a rubbing, which might reveal what he wrote down."

Chloe looks at me like I must be crazy if I think she has a pencil.

Her mom says, "I have one."

Chloe gets out the notebook. She says, "I guess Pete didn't have the tech to whisper into his phone and take notes at the same time. I mean, who's never heard of a headset?"

"A lot of people," Logan says.

Nodding in agreement, I place the notebook on the table, then make a rubbing of the top sheet. Sure enough, the message Pete wrote starts to appear. It's gratifying to see something I've seen before in fiction actually work.

The message when revealed reads: *She didn't pawn it. Just authenticated. Definitely belonged to the wife.* And then there's the word *library*, and then a phone number.

Logan calls the number. His eyes go wide as he hangs up. "It's Lydia's number." A few seconds later, he gets a call back. He checks the ID. "I guess I get to explain to Meryl what we're doing here." He steps into the same hall where Pete must have gone to take his call.

Meanwhile, I try to sort the implications of what we've just learned. That phone number means there was a connection between Patsy's dad and Lydia. Could he have been the one to arrange the strange meet-up after hours at the library?

If so, why hadn't he shown? Could it have been a trap? Maybe he had offered to buy the necklace. Assuming "it" had been the same object Pete had been scouring pawn shops for, the message implies that Lydia must have had it. But it hadn't been on her when she died, or the police would have asked me or Tiff about it. Maybe the necklace is safely tucked away in whatever room Lydia had rented. Or maybe Pete really did kill her for it, and absconded with it to parts unknown. But why? What could be so important about a piece of old jewelry that a respectable guy would kill someone over it?

And did the pawn shop necklace have anything to do with the piece the dead jeweler had been hired to re-create? There had been that picture of the vintage necklace I had seen at Vic's jewelry store. Roland had been commissioned to recreate that flower-shaped pendant, inlaid with peridot and rose quartz. It seems too much of a coincidence for there to be two important necklaces floating around. What if the reason the vintage piece had to be replaced was because Lydia had stolen the original? But the kind of thief she was, if someone had confronted her about it, or told her that the piece was important, she would have just given it back.

I started looking into all of this to help Patsy find her dad. Only now, it looks like he's a suspect. What will it do to Patsy if Arlo has to arrest her dad – after him arresting her brother broke them up?

My stomach hurts just thinking about it.

But we don't know anything yet for sure. Maybe there's another explanation. I hope so, for Patsy's sake.

"What do you think" Chloe asks.

I hadn't been paying attention. I realize she's showing me something on her phone. It's also a video of Mr. Tunaface sniffing violets and then sneezing. It's intercut with clips of edgy-looking ballet dance. It's all a little avant-garde. I don't really get what she's going for. I smile anyway and say, "That's interesting."

Chloe sighs dramatically. "You're right. It's rubbish. There's no way to salvage that sweet cat as an internet sensation. He's too cute to be mad at him for it, though."

"He is indeed," I say. "I'd watch video of just him with the violets. But I may not be your target demographic."

I start thinking about violets – and I gasp in a breath. Rose quartz is more pink, so I hadn't really thought about it, but from the shape of the necklace, that pendant could well be a violet. Or at least – Lydia might have thought it was.

I'd thought the dying message that Lydia had scratched into those cabinets had been Vic. But it is seeming less and less likely that Vic from the jewelry store had anything to do with Lydia's death. And Vic at the port has an alibi – he was at work. As does the Vic from McDonald's.

But what if Lydia hadn't been finished writing her message when her strength had given out? After all, it must have taken a bit of work scratching in those letters, all while bleeding out. What if that *c* was actually supposed to be an *o*? Could she have been trying to etch the word *violet*?

I know I've entered the world of wild conjecture. It's a lot of supposes to say that the pawn shop necklace was the same one the jeweler had been commissioned to recreate, that someone had killed Lydia over it, and that she'd tried to tell us. *Violet necklace* would have been quite an ambitious undertaking for someone in her state.

Even if she had been writing *violet*, it could have had other meanings. After all, Carmen's roommate's name is Violet, and she doesn't have anything to do with this case.

Still – it is one way the pieces of this puzzle could start to fit together.

Chloe is still watching videos of her own cat – this time without the cut-in art. She looks over at her mother and says, "Mom, how do you feel about starting a YouTube channel?"

Logan is still on the phone with Detective Beckman. I grab the notebook and the pencil and tell Chloe, "Excuse me for a moment."

I'm not sure that my comment even registers, because Chloe is busy explaining how the new hashtag #reformedjerkcat would appeal to her mom's demographic.

I flip the notebook over to the next page and write, *Ask her if they found a flower-shaped necklace in Lydia's car.* Detective Beckman probably won't share information with me, since I'm a suspect – but she might respect Logan's law-enforcement-related past.

Logan quirks an eyebrow, but does as I ask. He listens for a minute, then shakes his head.

I write, *Has she talked to the Insurance Inspector attached to the missing stuff from the jewelry store? The inspector's name is Hailey.* She probably hasn't – since there's not real link to show any of this is connected – but it never hurts to ask.

Logan asks my question. He listens for a lot longer this time. Then he says, "I'll let you know." Then he hangs up.

"Well?" I ask.

"Hailey has her out of office message on her phone, and her email. Her boss said she took a couple of personal days."

That's odd, right after being assigned a new case. I feel my eyes widen. "You don't think – Logan, is she dead too?"

Logan puts a hand on my arm. "We don't know that. For all we know, she has a sick kid who had to go to the hospital. Or she needed a mental health day and went to the beach."

Still. The coincidence of her being gone while all this is happening feels ominous.

My phone rings. It's Enrique.

When I answer, Enrique says, "I had some ideas for an appetizer course involving savory chocolate. What do you think of an earthy chocolate mushroom arancini? And a curry stuffed fried bread with a hint of dark chocolate?"

"Well, hello to you too," I say.

Enrique chuckles. "Hi Felicity! I was hoping to talk to you about changes to the menu for Autumn's wedding, if you have a moment."

I can't help but laugh too. "You are aware that this event is in four days? You can't just go changing everything around. If you mess with Autumn's budget, it might be the one more straw that she can't take, and she'll set the hay bale on fire."

"What's happened? Is Autumn okay?"

I'm not supposed to mention the missing ring. Even though everybody else already seems to know. "She'll be fine. Just a few things not going to plan, and she's trying her best not to turn into a bridezilla."

"Gotcha. But I'm not trying to replace anything in the current menu. I just want to add a course. I won't even charge her for it. Now that I've had the idea, I just really want an excuse to test the recipes."

I tell him, "Come by the shop, and I'll have Carmen give you some of our 90% dark Ecuadorian chocolate to work with. I'll square everything away with Autumn."

"Isn't the 90% part of your Sympathy and Condolences line?" Enrique asks. "You know, that could be part of a selling point for a new menu offering for the pop-ups."

I'd been reluctant to even agree to do the Sympathy and Condolences chocolate bars. All of my bars have wrappers with pics of my lop Knightley on the front and a place to write a message on the back – except for the Sympathy and Condolences Bars, which have a stylized image of Carmen's German Shepherd, Bruce. (Yes, since Carmen's a surfer and a master of irony, she'd named her dog after the shark from Jaws.) When I'd first been asked to do a 90% and 100% bar that people could eat on a dare – due to the murder-associations with my grand opening party – I had nearly said no.

But I've stopped freaking out about such things. "Sure," I tell Enrique. "We can discuss your ideas for a death by chocolate dessert *after* Autumn's reception. I don't want to go giving you ideas that will distract you from the project at hand."

"Sure," Enrique says. "I'm laser focused. Consider me one less thing you have to worry about." Then he adds, "How many other deserts do you think there are out there called Death by Chocolate?"

"Please don't look that up," I say. "That's a deeper rabbit hole than we have time for." I've always had problems with change. Enrique on the other hand is nothing if not adaptable. I ask him, "How are you managing to grow your catering business, while staying in school and keeping your football scholarship?"

He says, "It's all about not shying away from opportunities, and finding ways to say yes while staying sane by delegating. And by being very, very organized."

That's exactly what I need to be doing with my own business. Even if it is very, very difficult for me.

Chapter Eleven
Monday

By now the news has broken that I'm part of another murder investigation – and might even be a suspect this time. And for once, it isn't Ash's fault. I'd asked him to hold off on mentioning that I'd been second on the scene to find Lydia's body, and surprisingly, he'd agreed – although, he had begged me for details he could use in an expose on Lydia's last day. I didn't give him much. I don't want to compromise the police investigation.

Carmen is over at Greetings and Felicitations, baking like crazy, in anticipation of another wave of true crime aficionados visiting the shop. It's almost become a tradition, with many of the same people coming back each time I wind up involved with another murder. On one level, I dread it. But on another, I can't deny that it's good for the cash register.

Tracie is coming in to help out, and Logan plans to be there by the time we open.

However, with the shop being crowded, it's not a conducive place for following up on leads. So I'm at Tiff's office, since she volunteered to help me track down Princess Buttercup. Tiff knows practically everybody on the Island, so I'm grateful for the expertise.

I've got my phone and my laptop, and I'm contacting every short-term rental I can find. Unfortunately, a lot of the listings are through third party sites, so I'm emailing a lot of the hosts. Who knows how long it will take them to check their email, if they even choose to respond. But it's the best idea I've got. Nothing we tried yesterday panned out.

Tiff is calling all her contacts. She hangs up her phone. "I'm surprised how many people I've known for months who never showed the least bit of sympathy about making a deal – who are brokenhearted that there might be a goat out there somewhere upset about being alone."

"People are suckers for all things cute," I point out.

Tiff says, "You seem pretty invested in finding Princess Buttercup."

"I'm a sucker," I quip. But then, in a more serious tone, I add, "I think one reason I'm working so hard to find this goat is because I can't figure out how to find Patsy's father. Last night, I tried calling his coworkers, but most of them wouldn't even talk to me, because I'm not with the police. And I'm not actually a detective. Despite what everybody seems to think."

"You're putting in a lot of work into not being a detective. It might be easier to just give in and get licensed." Tiff opens a drawer on her desk and pulls out one of the mini chocolate bars I did for her clients. She unwraps it and pops it into her mouth. "But you have plenty of time to worry about that. Right now, the important thing is to clear your own name – and mine. I'm sorry I got you mixed up in this."

Before I can think of an appropriate response, my phone rings. It's a number I don't recognize. Ordinarily, I wouldn't answer it, but I did just send out a dozen emails inviting folks to call me.

When I answer, a woman says, "I'm Farrah Cantor, with Beachside Bungalows. You said it was urgent to find out if Lydia Dunning is staying at one of our properties."

Farrah isn't stating anything that might be violating the privacy of one of her guests. But she might as well be saying Lydia had rented from her, just by calling me back.

"Yes," I say. "I regret to have to inform you, but Ms. Dunning has passed away. She had a pet with her, and I'm trying to find it."

"We have a strict no pet policy," Farrah snaps. "You'll need to remove the animal as soon as possible."

I ask her which property, and – after she verifies that Lydia is indeed dead, and that I'm a business owner on the island who could reasonably be Lydia's friend – she gives me the address.

I call Arlo and ask him to meet me there, since it would probably be better to have someone from the police there with me, lest I get accused of evidence tampering. Assuming that there is any evidence at the bungalow to be found. Arlo doesn't sound happy about it, but when I explain about the goat, he reluctantly agrees to show up. He says that he will have to pass the information about the place Lydia was staying on to the detective actually handling the case. Which is fine by me. I'm not trying to hide anything from Meryl Beckman.

I ask Arlo, "Why didn't they already have the information on where she was staying?"

"Meryl was complaining yesterday that there hasn't been activity on Lydia's credit card in months. Apparently, she's been using cash, staying off the grid."

I say, "That's weird, considering Lydia's lifestyle. Was she afraid of something before she even came here?"

"Maybe?" Arlo says. "Look, wait for me outside, before you approach the rental agent."

The door to the real estate office opens. The whole jazz band troops in. Flip is carrying a vase full of red roses. Starsky has a big cardboard box with a teal crepe streamer sticking out of it.

"What are y'all doing here?" I ask.

Boone says, "Autumn just told us we're supposed to decorate the stage. So we thought we could run some ideas past you."

"How did you even know I was here?" I ask.

Charlie says, "Autumn pulled your location off her phone. She said you wouldn't mind us coming by." He looks more relaxed today, wearing jeans and sneakers and a navy and hunter green sweater.

"I wouldn't mind," I stammer, "except that I'm about to leave."

"I can probably help you," Tiff tells the band guys. "I have a good eye for design."

"That would be great," Flip says. He adjusts the vase of roses.

I tell him, "It's a bit early to be buying fresh flowers."

He holds out the vase, saying, "These are for you, as a bribe for helping out." Then he looks towards Tiff. "Or I guess for you."

Tiff gets up from her desk and takes the vase. She puts it on top of her filing cabinet, saying, "I wouldn't want to get water on the surface of this desk. We just redecorated."

Charlie steps closer and runs his hand across the wood. He says, "This is such a magnificent piece. You know old Baroque desks like this sometimes have hidden compartments?" He fiddles with an edge of the molding, and it pops open. There is a narrow drawer – but it is empty. All of us look vaguely disappointed – most of all Charlie. He says, "Maybe I can take a closer look at this while we're here."

"I guess." Tiff sounds hesitant. But her papers are in the filing cabinet, so what's the harm? Tiff turns to me and asks, "Will you be coming back? I thought we were driving to the bachelorette tea together later."

I say, "Logan and I are going to lunch, then I should be back. The tea isn't until four thirty, so there should be plenty of time. We have a lead on Patsy's dad. We know he was in Galveston a couple of days ago, so we're going to the restaurant he stopped at. Want me to bring you back some sushi?"

"Yes, please," Tiff says. "Can you bring me a dragon roll and tamago sashimi?"

"Hey, if you're going," one of Tiff's coworkers says, "I'd love a spider roll."

"Me too," another says.

I hadn't realized that they were all listening in to our conversation. There's one guy, sitting at a desk in the middle of the room, who is starting very intently in this direction. When he catches me looking, he looks down at his desk. I can't tell if he's embarrassed, or maybe upset about something.

I'm going to have to ask Tiff what's going on with that guy, when we have more privacy to talk. It was a long-shot theory that Logan and I had come up with yesterday, that Lydia might have been killed by a competing real estate agent in search of a big commission – but considering how little of this makes sense, it's something I can't discount completely. I may have been too comfortable talking around all these people. If they've been listening all morning, they know exactly what I'm about to follow up on about Lydia.

Not that any of them could easily do anything about it, considering it would be conspicuous if they left work. But still. It makes me feel a little bit itchy as I get into my giant catering truck to head over to the bungalow where Lydia spent her last night, with a giant order for sushi in the notes on my phone and a cup of cheap coffee at my side.

Before I can put the truck into gear, my phone rings. It's Patsy.

"Felicity, my dad's okay!" She's almost sobbing with relief.

"That's great! Where is he?" I'm overcome with relief, myself. Not that my attempts to find Pete had been any help. He must have been holed up in a hotel somewhere in Galveston all along.

"Mexico," Patsy says. She sounds a bit less excited, since obviously he's not with her. "He emailed from an Internet café and asked us to send his passport. He said he needed some time to think, about his job and his marriage. And then he explained there had been a mix-up, and gotten arrested, but his passport card got lost in the shuffle."

As Patsy is recounting this, a chill dances down my spine. This midlife-crisis scenario doesn't sound at all like the man Pasty's mom or Pete's coworkers had described. Maybe it's just because of that copy of *The Thin Man* – but I wonder if Pete was really the one who sent that message. And if someone sent it in his place – then we're not talking about someone asking for ransom or a simple misunderstanding. We're talking about someone trying to cover up a crime.

I say carefully, "So you didn't actually get to talk to him?"

"Well, no."

"I think you should try to," I tell her, in a more ominous tone than I had intended. I don't know what else to say. I want the far-fetched story to be true. Maybe Patsy's dad really is drinking café de olla at a little café, regretting having left home. I hope so.

"What are you trying to say?" Patsy asks.

"Nothing," I say. "I'm happy things are turning out okay. Say hi to your dad from me when you see him. I know we've never met, but I feel like I've gotten to know him while helping look for him."

"I'll do that," Patsy says, but she sounds shaken.

I hate that I'm the one that deflated her sails. But there's a good chance her dad is dead. And if he's not, that he may well be in trouble – potentially for having killed either Lydia or Roland the jeweler.

I can't think of a good reason why Pete would have come to Galveston. This was the place where Patsy's brother had gotten arrested for murder. Unless – maybe he had wanted to have it out with Arlo, either to finally get some twisted sort of justice for his son – or to patch things up between them. Which gives Arlo motive, if something sinister has happened. I know he wouldn't hurt anyone, any more than Tiff would, but being suspected in a case wouldn't look good for his career.

Still, I need to talk to Arlo about Pete, when we get to the rent house. I have no reason to believe Arlo would withhold information. But what if he's trying to protect someone here, maybe even Pete himself? After all, Patsy's mom called Arlo, and he seemed pretty hands-off about getting involved.

I get the catering truck in gear and on the road. There are so many pieces to all of this – if it all is even connected. Like that pouch of marbles. What does that key we found open? Could whatever that padlock is protecting be what Lydia had been killed over?

I keep trying to sort the pieces, all the way to the bungalow.

Despite the delay with Boone and with Tiff's coworkers, I still get there first. It's a cute little house at the end of a cul-de-sac, painted sky blue with a yellow door. I get out of my car and go up onto the porch. I don't hear any noise coming from inside. I could be wrong. Princess Buttercup might not be here at all.

I peer in the window to the right of the door. There's a charming living room, with fleur-de-lis patterned tile on the wall, and a blue sofa fronted by a long coffee table. There's a laptop sitting on the coffee table. Unfortunately, there's a large hole in the upholstery of the sofa, with some of the stuffing pulled out. And there's a pile of cloth on the floor where the bar holding the drapes has been pulled down. Things have been knocked off the mantle, with glass left to shatter on the floor – and the flatscreen TV is hanging on by one wonky support.

I don't see the goat – but she's definitely here.

Arlo and Farrah show up at practically the same time, with Arlo parking behind me in the narrow driveway, and Farrah pulling to the side under a detached carport. Farrah strides over to join me on the porch, while Arlo takes his time.

Farrah says, "I'm sorry to hear about Lydia. I realize I was rude on the phone earlier. It's always hard to lose a friend, and I just wasn't thinking."

"It's okay," I say. I can't admit that I'm not really Lydia's friend, not after what I'd implied on the phone. She'd never let us into the bungalow after that. "I'm a business owner. I understand how frustrating it can be to have guests who break the rules." I gesture towards Arlo, who is just climbing the steps. "This is Detective Romero."

Arlo explains, "Try not to touch anything. We want to leave this space as is until the CSI team has a chance to go over it. We're just here for the goat."

"Goat?" Farrah looks like she's unexpectedly sucked on a lemon while getting punched in the gut.

I realize I hadn't mentioned what type of pet Lydia had taken with her.

I brace myself as she unlocks the door. At the sound of the key, from inside there's loud bleat and the sound of something falling over. The door swings open, and there's Princess Buttercup perched on a narrow ledge separating the entry area from the kitchen. She'd gotten the pantry open, and there's flour and cornmeal scattered all over the floor.

Farrah looks like she's going to pop. Her lips have turned into a pale thin line, and her hands are balled into fists. "Why you little."

Princess Buttercup recognizes the tone in Farrah's voice and quickly retreats into one of the two bedrooms.

"Let me help," Arlo says. He takes a zip-top bag of cut apples out of his jacket and starts talking soothingly to the goat, following Princess Buttercup into the bedroom. He's a lot more prepared for this than I am. But while he's busy, I take the opportunity to snoop.

There's a big dog carrier in the middle of the kitchen. So at least we're going to have a way to get the goat out of here. Aside from the mess, there's not much of interest in there. In the living room, Lydia's laptop is sitting there, tempting me. Could there be emails or files that would clearly state why she'd really

come to Galveston, what she had wanted to talk to Tiff about –
even name suspicions about the person who would become her
killer? But Arlo wouldn't forgive me if I touched it. On the floor
under the coffee table, there are ragged parts of pieces of paper,
and half of one flap of a manila folder. It takes me a second to
figure out what I'm looking at.

Seriously – the goat has eaten most of the files Lydia
took with her to the library. The scattered pieces that are left have
writing visible on them. I snap a couple of pictures. Hopefully
they're clear enough that I will be able to zoom in and study the
information later. From a cursory glance, some of the documents
were travel itineraries, but there's no name on the parts the goat
didn't eat. One was for a flight from Chicago to somewhere
starting with "N." There are pieces that look like transcripts –
maybe meeting notes? Or telephone calls? Somebody's
unpublished play? I don't know what to make of it all. One phrase
stands out: *the disappearance of his wife, during the course of the
burglary* . . .

What could the rest of that sentence possibly be? Had
someone else gone missing? Are we looking at a human traffic
ring, one that had taken both Patsy's dad and this mystery
woman? That wouldn't make sense. After all, who traffics a
middle-aged man? But that request for Pete's passport – while
still ominous – could mean he's alive.

What had Lydia been doing with this information? Could
she have come to Galveston looking for someone? I keep thinking
about the port, and all those boats. Even the marinas, with smaller
yachts and sailboats and fishing charters. If you wanted to get
somebody out of the country in a way that wouldn't be easily
traced – this is a perfectly located town to do it.

Of course, looking at the evidence a different way, if
Patsy's dad had possessed a reason to kill Lydia to keep her from
revealing whatever was in the files, pretending to be stuck in
Mexico provides a hard-to-verify alibi. That is still assuming the
cases are even related.

I can't help but edge one of the larger remnants of paper over to one side, to see what is under it. It's a roughly printed photograph of the guy who held up the jewelry store. I snap a picture of this, too.

"Lis, what are you doing?" Arlo asks.

"Nothing," I say as I shove my phone into my pocket.

Arlo is leading the goat out of the bedroom with what looks like the sash from a terrycloth bathrobe tied around her neck. Princess Buttercup could probably chew through the cloth easily if she wanted to, but she's happily munching apple right now instead. She jumps her front legs onto Arlo's knee, balancing there as she begs for another piece.

I glance into the bedroom, but there's no sign of a necklace – violet-shaped or otherwise – on the dresser or the nightstand. Arlo's not about to let me go rifling through the drawers, so I turn back to the little goat.

We get Princess Buttercup loaded into the crate, and the crate out of the house and into my catering van – since it is never going to fit in Arlo's car. We leave Farrah on the porch of the house, already on the phone with her insurance company.

Arlo walks me over to my driver side door and plants a kiss on my cheek. When I don't respond to the affectionate gesture, he asks, "Everything okay?"

"Yeah," I say. "Patsy finally heard from her dad. Apparently, he's stuck in Mexico."

Arlo grins. "That's great news." He arches an eyebrow at me. "So why does that make you sad?"

If you love someone, you should be able to just talk to them, right? About anything? So I lay out my concerns. "Be honest. Tell me you didn't hear from him when he came through town. That there wasn't still animosity between you two. Tell me, and I can put this doubt out of my mind."

Arlo looks extremely disappointed in me. "I hate that you even have to ask that. No, I didn't hear from Pete. And I certainly didn't hurt him." He hesitates, then looks vaguely surprised. "But come to think of it, I did have half a dozen blocked number hangup calls the day he went missing. I put it down to a persistent telemarketer – but what if he was trying to get ahold of me? If he was in trouble, and I didn't just pick up the phone. Man, that's awful."

There's an unhappy bleat from inside the catering van, and the noise of Princess Buttercup moving heavily inside the plastic carrier. I remember what Agnes had said about the proper care of goats. The poor doe is probably uncomfortable.

I take out my phone.

"What are you doing now?" Arlo asks.

"I'm about to Google how to milk a goat. Want to help?"

"Sure," Arlo says. "There were actually a couple of goats on the property when I was working keeping bees. But we shouldn't do it here. Farrah is likely to have a fit if she sees Princess Buttercup again."

"Agreed," I say, and I start to get into the van.

But just then, Detective Beckman and Officer Price turn into the driveway, their car taking up the last of the space right up to the street. Detective Beckman gives me a disapproving look as she gets out of the car, and I can tell that she's going to want to have a chat with me. Princess Buttercup is going to have to wait a little longer.

Chapter Twelve
Monday

We stop a little way down the island, to regroup. We park our vehicles at a turn-in for the beach, with Arlo's car next to my catering truck. I zip open the backpack that Logan gave me. Surely something in here will come in handy for the task at hand. Probably the Thermos. And the hand wipes.

I take a moment to consider some of the other stuff that's in there. In what situation does Logan see me needing a UV flashlight? Or a fishing lure?

Arlo comes over and taps on the window. I open the door so he can see what I'm doing.

"What's all that?" Arlo asks.

"Logan wanted me to be more prepared, since I keep getting involved in crazy stuff."

"Makes sense," Arlo says. I can tell he wants to say more.

"What?" I ask.

Arlo says, "He wants to make sure you're okay, even if things change between you two soon. I feel the same way. Though, I still think you need training if you're going to keep putting yourself in danger – instead of giving you a tool kit for getting yourself into more trouble than you know what to do with." He holds up a piece of wire with little teeth in it – which I can only guess is a lightweight saw.

"Thanks for the advice," I say, brushing off the more emotionally uncomfortable aspects of what Arlo is saying. I may be coming to terms with change – but I still don't have to like it. I admit, "There's stuff in this bag that I don't know what to do with." I pull up a roll of canvas strips with rope wrapped around it. "I'm guessing this isn't for towing a car."

Arlo laughs. "That's lightweight climbing equipment. So the next time you find yourself stuck halfway up a mountain, you'll be fine."

"I'll keep that in mind. Come on, let's help out Princess Buttercup."

Milking the goat is a bit awkward – but reasonably straightforward. And I am rewarded with a full Thermos of goat's milk. Not that I know what to do with it. At least the catering truck has the ability for me to get it refrigerated. I ask Arlo to get the goat back into the crate, which is still inside the catering truck. Meanwhile, I text Logan the pics I snapped of those fragments from the files. I add, *Any idea who the guy in the pic is? He's obviously the same guy in the sketch from the jewelry store.*

If the police managed to ID the guy, they certainly weren't going to share that information with me. Not even Arlo, assuming the break-in dovetails into his murder case. It's frustrating – but I can understand his ethical boundaries. Arlo closes the back doors of the catering truck and moves around to where I am standing. "Everything okay?"

"Considering? Just peachy." I check the time on my phone. "But I need to return a goat, meet Logan at a sushi joint to follow up on a clue about Patsy's dad, and get to a tea party, where I'm supposed to be leading silly party games, all in the next five hours."

"I should probably let you get to it," Arlo says. "I'm a bit busy myself, with the murder of a guy who likely got carjacked by some bored thug. Makes it really hard to narrow down the suspect pool, with both the car and the jewelry long gone."

Now that's more information than I expected him to share. Maybe it was unintentional, just because we're bantering. But it helps put things in context. I didn't realize Roland had been carjacked. It's probable that Roland didn't even have his wallet when he was found. Autumn's posey ring gift to Drake is long gone – and it was purely random. Contemplating the tragedy of a loss of human life over a few material things – it makes us both somber. Even though I never met the jeweler, I empathize for the fear he must have felt in his last moments. I've had more than one murderer try to kill me, when I'd gotten too close to the truth. I still have nightmares sometimes, about the multiple times when I have been convinced my life was going to end.

I get a text back from Logan that says, *That guy's not in the system. Either he's never committed a crime before – or he's just never gotten caught.*

He's referring to the picture I had texted of the guy who had busted open the safe at Vic's jewelry store. It makes more sense that he was careful enough not to get caught. After all, the guy had gone through the trouble of killing the cameras at the jewelry store. But there's something that's been bothering me. Why had he gone during open hours? It doesn't make sense. It almost guaranteed that someone would notice the theft right away. If he was so cautious, and the theft was planned – why demand the piece, first?

Arlo gestures towards my phone. "Did you tell Hanlon that Pete showed up alive? Maybe you can just skip the sushi place."

I tell him, "I haven't had a chance. And something still feels wrong about that whole situation. If Pete isn't in trouble – then why did he run? I keep thinking maybe he's on the other side of this. He could be guilty of something."

Arlo blinks. "Are you suggesting Pete might have killed Roland? But why? Where's the connection between the two? Except that they both were coming to Galveston from out of town . . ." He's looking off in the distance, thinking to himself. "The timing does line up."

"I don't know if it counts as motive," I say carefully, "But Patsy's mom did say Pete had gone to a number of pawn shops looking for a specific necklace. Maybe it was a piece Roland made?"

"Maybe. Maybe you're a genius." He cups my face in his hands and plants a warm kiss on my lips. "Call me when you get done at the sushi place. I want to go check out a few things. Maybe solve my case before Logan solves his."

"It's not a competition," I chide.

"Tell him that," Arlo says.

I can't help but laugh, and it lightens the mood.

I still feel the impression of the brief kiss as Arlo turns to get back into his car. These ease and rightness of that kiss helps me hold onto my decision to choose Arlo, even as I'm heading off to meet Logan.

I have to go by the RV park first, though. There's no way I'm leaving a crated goat in the back of my catering truck for half the day. That just seems cruel.

I get the catering van into gear and pull out onto the road. I glance towards the back. "Okay, Princess. Are you ready to go home?"

There's an answering bleat.

"I'll take that as a yes," I say.

The weather is clouding over, and soon there is a soft drizzle against the windshield. I hope it blows over before Thursday. Autumn is planning a ceremony at a huge rented auditorium, before her reception at Wobble House, a historic home with a beautiful ballroom. It's going to be the best of both worlds – simple and elegant and overflowing with people, followed by grand with modern touches. And she's going to have a horse-drawn carriage take her and Drake from Wobble House to the hotel where they're staying, before they leave Friday for their honeymoon. All of it is very Autumn. But a carriage ride would be miserable in the rain. And all of our dresses would be in danger in a downpour.

Pavement is dangerous when it's first damp, so I drive extra careful, but I'm having a hard time not distracting myself with my own thoughts, which keep bouncing from problem to problem, from something as trivial as a rainy wedding day to solving multiple murders.

Is it possible that Patsy's dad was going to meet Roland the jeweler here, in Galveston? Maybe they were plotting insurance fraud, and something went wrong. Pete decided to flee to Mexico to escape the consequences – only he didn't have his passport. Somehow, he snuck across the border and wound up in trouble – maybe because of whoever helped him cross. It's all unsettlingly plausible – especially considering everything that had happened with Patsy's brother. Her brother had been a complete narcissist. Wallace had almost killed me, despite wanting to date me. I've never met Pete, and his coworkers had nothing but nice things to say about him, but it's possible that father and son are more alike than anyone realized. After all, narcissists often come across as charming – right up until you cross them.

I hate that Arlo is the detective in charge of this case. If he and Patsy are just now getting over each other, he's going to be the worst possible person having to ask Patsy questions about what her father might or might not have done. I don't want to see either one of them in that kind of pain.

I wind up driving past the RV park entrance and having to backtrack. Despite my resolve, I'd been driving on autopilot. I drive slowly to the back of the park, where the cul-de-sac widens out the space between vehicles. Only – the spaces back there are empty. No RV, no goat pen, no sign that Agnes and Esme were ever here.

Maybe I've driven to the wrong RV park. Surely I wasn't that out of it while I had been driving, but I still go back to the entrance to check the sign. Nope, I'm in the right place. They've just left.

I park and look in the net pouch behind my chair, designed to allow a passenger to store items – although the way the truck had been put together, there's only a fold-out emergency third seat, making the pouch seem out of place. But there in the

pouch, I find all the fliers and information from the bridal expo –
including the one from Daydream Hills. I call the number printed
on it and get their office recording, with open hours from
Wednesday through Sunday. I should have gotten Agnes' cell
phone number yesterday. Agnes hadn't said anything about
leaving. You think she would have wanted to make sure we had a
way to get in touch with her, since she knew we were still looking
for Princess Buttercup.

Honestly, it makes Agnes look guilty, leaving
unexpectedly while she's a suspect in a murder investigation. I
don't know. Maybe Detective Beckman doesn't consider her a
suspect. After all, Agnes and Lydia had no connection prior to the
theft of the goat. But even if her motive is weak – it's still motive.
And sometimes people do stupid things.

I want to give Agnes the benefit of the doubt, though.
Something about her just seems so non-threatening. Maybe she
and her sister just moved the RV. After all, they could have
booked another event, here or in Houston – or even Corpus –
while they are in town. The beauty of an RV is that the whole
thing can just roll up to a new venue, without having to be packed
and organized every time. If they're doing another goat yoga
class . . . maybe Ash would know.

I call him to ask, but he doesn't have any leads on where
they are. He tries the number Agnes gave him, but calls me back
to say it doesn't seem to be working. Completely changing the
subject, he asks me, "Do you think I could have a look at the
murder book this time? I have an idea for a blog post."

"I don't see how that could hurt," I say. "Come by the
shop when you get a chance."

He sounds very happy when he hangs up.

Well . . . dang. What am I supposed to do now? I can't
very well leave a goat in the middle of my aunt's half-remodeled
hotel. I'd seen what Princess Buttercup had done to the bungalow.
There's nothing for it – I'm taking her with me.

I do a quick Google search for, *Can you put a pigmy goat
on a leash?* The results make it clear that I'm going to need a goat

harness, as a collar can be dangerous for the goat. I have no idea where to find a harness. Still sitting there at the RV park, I start calling stores that could conceivably sell such a thing. The guy at the pet store laughs at me. All the feed stores are on the mainland, so I really don't have time to get across the highway into Houston or the ferry to Port Bolivar and back in time to meet Logan. I'm starting to eye the climbing gear and the industrial stapler in my backpack for a temporary solution, when the woman at one of the local building supply stores says she has just what I need.

The store is actually on the way to the restaurant where I need to meet Logan. I purchase the goat harness, plus a leash, and the shop owner helps me get it onto Princess Buttercup. The goat doesn't resist, which means she is probably leash trained – a big deal according to Google. I had hoped she was, considering she hadn't given Arlo any trouble, when he'd been holding onto her with a flimsy piece of terrycloth. At least one thing is going improbably right today.

When I get to the sushi place, Logan is already standing outside, waiting for me under a long awning. He has Cindy on a leash. I guess she's had enough of being alone at his apartment all day. The dog is small and cute, so there's a chance Logan won't get kicked out for taking her into the waiting area of the restaurant. I'm not sure what I'm going to do.

Logan gives me a questioning look when I gesture him over to the catering van. Ignoring the drizzle, Cindy jumps up against my leg, exploring the denim I'm wearing for the source of the unfamiliar goat smell. I lean down and pet her as I explain the situation to Logan.

Logan says, "The goat will probably be alright in the van, with ventilation, for long enough for us to ask questions. Then we can come back outside to eat and wait for the to-go order."

I love that he's being understanding about this.

Together, we walk across the parking lot and enter the restaurant. There's a host stand, and a cluster of a dozen wooden chairs for people waiting to be seated. When the woman behind the host stand sees Cindy, her eyes light up, and she says, "Kawaii wanchan!" enthusiastically. She is in her twenties, clearly Japanese, and has a colorful decorative clip holding back her long hair. She's wearing a black sweater and jeans. She comes around from behind the stand and leans over to pet the dog. "I love Bichons," she says, "but dogs are only allowed on the patio."

I hadn't noticed a patio. I guess it is on the other side of the building. Maybe it would be goat-friendly, too.

"That's fine," Logan says. "Actually, I wanted to know if Seth is working today."

"Chef Seth always works Mondays." She gives Cindy one final scratch between the ears and straightens back up. "Can I tell him who's asking to see him?"

"Logan," Logan says. "He's booked a couple of flights through my puddle jump service."

The woman says, "Oh. You're the one who gives my boyfriend cheap rides to California. It's the only way he can afford to see his family."

Logan straightens the cuffs of his pilot's jacket. "It gives me a good excuse to stop and see the beach."

We're all standing not far from the beach right now, but the beach in California is very different from the beach in Galveston. The water is bluer. It's better for surfing. We all understand exactly what Logan means.

The woman introduces herself as Ami. She goes to get Seth, then Seth waves to Logan as he approaches the waiting area. Seth is a tall, lanky white guy wearing a short sleeve white chef's coat with blue piping down part of the front, and a baseball-style hat with the restaurant's logo on it. The woman had called him chef, which means he's probably had a five-to-ten-year apprenticeship, plus formal culinary training, so he wears the coat with ease and confidence.

"Hanlon!" he says, going up to Logan and giving him a hug.

Huh. Maybe I was wrong about Logan being slow to make friends.

Logan introduces me. I get a hug from Seth too. So maybe Seth was the extrovert who made friends with Logan?

Seth says, "If you're not here to eat, then what can I do for you?"

Logan says, "Oh, we're going to eat. We'll have to take it to-go though. After we ask a few questions."

Seth grimaces. "I hate doing to-go. If you don't eat it when it's fresh, you lose a lot of the nuance of flavor. Plus there's the ambiance. We went through a lot of trouble to get all of this right."

I say, "It shows. I love all the dark wood and black granite."

"Thanks." Seth looks like he wants to hug me again.

I pull up a picture of Pete on my phone and show it to Seth. "We're trying to find out what happened to this man, after he left here. I don't know if you remember him?"

"Yeah. Nice guy. He sat up at the bar, where customers can watch us work. A lot of people like to do that, when they come in alone." Seth gestures at the photograph. "Is he okay?"

I tell him, "We hope so. But we're trying to follow his steps and talk to him."

"You can't just call him on one of his cell phones?" Seth's tone is joking – but it doesn't match the worry in his eyes.

"What do you mean phones?" I ask. "As far as I know, he only had one."

Seth says, "No, there were two. He was texting on one of them the whole time he was here. I assumed it was a work phone and a personal phone. He took a couple of calls on the other phone."

"Were you able to hear any of the conversation?" Logan asks.

Seth nods. "He was talking about meeting someone on Pelican Island. Something about an old railroad car near the university. It sounded like he was going right then, because he left right after."

Logan and I exchange a significant look. So far, there's been nothing in the news about where Roland the jeweler was found. But if it happens to be near an old railroad car – then Arlo will have some significant questions to ask Pete, once we finally catch up to him.

"You didn't think that was odd?" I ask. After all, Pelican Island is an island between Galveston and the mainland. There isn't much over there except a university, and some industrial stuff.

Seth purses his lips. "I mean, I guess. But I didn't think much of it at the time. The guy looked like a college professor, so I just assumed it was near his place."

Logan turns to me and says, "I'll call and ask around. Neither of us have time to get over there before the parties."

Drake is planning a low-key fish fry with the guys at the same time as Autumn's tea. Neither of them wanted a wild party. They want to go into their marriage with clear minds and no regrets. I can't blame them. My bachelorette party, all those years ago, consisted of a couple of bottles of champagne and a bonfire on the beach. I've never been much of a wild party person either. Though I did get a pink sash, and a matching tiara. Which I still have stashed away somewhere.

Logan already has his phone out and is talking softly to someone.

I ask Seth, "Is there anything else you can remember?"

When he says there isn't, I present him with Tiff's giant sushi order and start to add rolls for me and Logan.

The door behind me jangles open, and Patsy strides purposefully in. I can see Arlo in the parking lot outside, getting out of his car and trying to catch up to her.

Patsy steps up very close to me and says, "My father did *not* kill anyone. And I'm going to prove it."

"I didn't say he did," I protest. Though, I did give Arlo the idea that that might be a possibility. I wince mentally.

Patsy asks, "Did they say anything about the night he was here? Was anyone with him? Did he have a suitcase?"

"I think he was alone." I turn to Seth for confirmation, but he has already gone back to his station at the sushi bar. It's hard to tell from here, but it looks like he's already starting on Tiff's order. Which is great, for me. "I didn't ask about a suitcase. One of the chefs gave us some information we're going to follow up on. Have you still not been able to get ahold of your dad in person?"

Patsy's shoulders slump, and a little of the righteous anger goes out of her. "No. I tried, but the hotel where he's staying keeps saying he's gone out for the day. Maybe he's at the consulate, trying to find a way home."

"But someone at the hotel has seen him?" I ask.

"I described him," Patsy says. "The description seemed to fit."

I nod slowly, considering what to say next. I don't know what's worse – if he father really was dead, or if he's involved in a murder.

But before I have to come up with an answer, Patsy turns to Logan. "Can I talk to you for a minute. Your puddle jump service can fly people across the border, right?"

"With the right flight plan and paperwork," Logan says.

Patsy gives Arlo a dirty look, then pulls Logan into the restaurant and towards an empty table.

Arlo says, "I guess she didn't want to share her plan in front of me."

"Maybe it's for the best," I say. There are too many emotions involved for Arlo to tell her how impractical her plan obviously is. Logan will at least come off as a credible third party.

Ami says, "I can take the rest of your order."

Arlo orders some to-go sushi too.

I tell Arlo, "I need to go check on Princess Buttercup. She's in the catering van."

"I thought you dropped her off with her owners at the RV park."

I scrunch up my nose. "Her owners left town without a word. I thought maybe the police had heard from them."

"Not as far as I know," Arlo says. "But I can ask around."

I go outside. Arlo comes with me. It's still sprinkling rain, but the sky looks blue again.

I open up the back of the catering van. Princess Buttercup looks excited to see us, bumping up against the side of the carrier as she does a little sideways dance. I never would have thought I'd describe a goat as adorable, but she is.

"Now that's adorable," Arlo says, voicing my thought.

I step up into the truck so I can get her leash on without having to open the carrier door all the way. Suddenly, the truck doors swing shut.

Arlo shouts from outside, then there's a hand over my mouth and a chemical smell. I fight it for almost a minute, but the smell is making me woozy, and the hand is strong, and eventually, I slide into darkness.

Chapter Thirteen
Monday

I wake with a pounding headache. I'm lying on the floor in a dusty warehouse, and there's a weight on my chest. For a split second, I'm afraid I'm dying. Drugs can make your body fail, right? There's a reason chloroform was discontinued as an anesthetic. But then I realize the weight is the goat.

I heave a sigh of relief. Princess Buttercup shifts her weight on my chest and makes a soft questioning sound.

I realize there's a scraping sound when it stops abruptly. Arlo comes into view, leaning over me. He puts a hand on my cheek. "Oh, thank goodness, Lis. You're awake."

I must have been out for a really long time for him to be that worried. I blink up at him. The ceiling above us is thick metal. The space is maybe three stories tall. I ask, "Where are we?"

Arlo says. "This warehouse a really old building, so we could be somewhere in the historic district. But I'm guessing we're closer to the port. I keep hearing gulls up there."

I follow where he's pointing. There's a catwalk going around part of the building, leading to a bank of windows on one side, and a large rectangular door. It's a lovely way out – except that it is far too high to reach.

Arlo moves Princess Buttercup off of me, and I manage to sit up. I look around, but there's not enough debris in this whole space to stack high enough to get up to the catwalk. Not even if we dismantled the set of cabinets and the work counter over in the corner. "Do you know who brought us here? Or why?"

There's a thick plexiglass partition across part of the space, and I see movement on the other side.

Arlo says, "Don't freak out, okay? They kidnapped the wrong girl."

"What?" I blink in still-bleary confusion. "This isn't about Lydia's murder? Or Roland's?"

"It still might be," Arlo says. "They didn't say much to me. I'm just extra collateral. But you have to-"

A door opens in the plexiglass, and a guy walks through it, closing it carefully behind him. He's about twenty years old, sporting a thin mustache and spiky hair. He's wearing a white tee-shirt and looks like a goon from an old gangster film. Which reminds me again of *The Thin Man*. Only – in that book Nick never lets Nora get kidnapped.

The guy brandishes my phone at me. He says, "Why do you have a picture of Creed Macintosh?"

"I'm sorry. Who?"

The guy glances at the phone screen, then taps it. He obviously didn't realize it had faded to black. There, right in my photo roll, is the picture I took of the photograph from the file the goat had partially eaten. It's obviously a picture of a picture, with a slightly odd perspective.

I don't know what answer the guy is looking for here, so I go with honesty. "I think he might have information about a friend of a friend who died."

"Not likely," The guy says. "Creed doesn't have friends. Or dreams, or motivations. He's a thief for hire, who works with dangerous people. Which means he doesn't run in the same circle as you, Patsy Nash. Unless there's something you want to tell me."

My first instinct is to tell him I'm not Patsy.

Arlo grabs my hand and squeezes it, tugging a bit to remind me of what he said about not freaking out. "It's okay, Patsy, honey. You can tell him that you're helping me with a case." Arlo turns to the guy. "I know it's against protocol, so I told her it had to be a secret. She's been researching at the library. Archives and newspapers and such."

The guy tilts his head and stares hard at me. "Creed's photo was in the newspaper."

I shrug. "It was in the background of another pic. I blew it up. I didn't know who he was until you just told me."

I don't like lying, but that doesn't mean I can't do it, when necessary.

The guy starts to say something, then closes his mouth and looks at me skeptically. He drops my phone on the floor and steps on it, cracking the screen. "Maybe it would be safer for you to mind your own business in the future. Assuming you have a future." He takes his own phone out of his pocket. "I'm about to make a call to your father. Once I give you the phone, tell him to sign off on the checks for all five building fires. Don't try to give him your location, or anything else that would get the police here."

"Too late," Arlo says. "You know I'm a cop, right?"

The guy sniffs derisively. "You're a two-bit sheriff of a Podunk island. And I have your gun, so pardon me if I'm not worried."

Arlo stiffens, but he doesn't point out that almost all of the guy's statement is incorrect. Except the gun part, apparently.

"So that's what this is about?" I ask. I have to pretend I'm Patsy, to say *my* instead of *her*. "My father is the investigator on your cases. And since the pattern makes it obvious it's arson, you're leveraging me to make him push the claims through."

Arlo says, "Can I just say – that's not a great plan. If you let us go, Pete is just going to turn around and report you. And if you kill us, then Pete is going to report you – and you'll wind up in jail for murder. But let us walk away, and we can all just pretend this never happened. I'm a homicide detective. What do I care about arson?"

I don't know if Arlo is *trying* to make the guy angry – and thus deflect attention away from me – or if he really thinks this negotiation tactic might work. But the guy takes Arlo seriously.

He waves the phone at us and says, "See, he's not just getting the paperwork pushed through – he's getting the checks deposited. Once we re-route those checks into our offshore account, then we leave here and Patsy's father gets a text with her location. By the time the police figure it out, we're on a flight to a country without extradition. It's beautiful really. And nobody has to die – if you all just cooperate."

I gesture at Princess Buttercup, who is standing close to Arlo. "Why bring the goat?"

The guy squints at me. "What was I going to do? Leave it in the truck? Or let it go to wander into the road? Don't worry – if I have to eliminate you two, I'll take it with me."

I don't know what to make of this guy. I get the feeling that he's mostly bluster – that even if Patsy's dad doesn't do what he wants, he won't really hurt us. After all, someone who cares about animals has to have a softer edge, right? Of course, there is Tiff's theory that some people care more about animals than people. But in this case, I don't think so.

Of course, that's a huge gamble on my instincts about human nature. And it is about to be tested. Because the minute Patsy's father hears my voice on his phone, he's going to know I'm not his daughter. And who knows what happens after that. Who knows? Maybe the guy just lets us go.

Maybe it's pushing it, but I ask, "What does all of this have to do with Lydia Dunning's murder? Or the dead jeweler?"

The guy looks at Arlo. "What is she talking about? Like I said – we do arson, not murder."

Arlo squeezes my hand again. He says, "Honey, we seem to have stumbled into a completely separate crime."

Giving us an odd look, the guy taps the number in his phone. I wonder which one of Pete's phones he is calling. The guy says all the things kidnappers say on TV, like, "We have your daughter," and, "If you want to see her alive again."

When he hands me the phone, I say, "Daddy, I'm so scared!"

To my surprise, instead of demanding *Who is this?* the voice on the other end of the line says, "It's okay, button. We'll get you through this. Put the man back on the phone."

Huh. I sound nothing like Patsy. Our accents come from different places. So why is Pete covering for me? If that even was Pete. If not – I get the cold feeling that I might have been talking to Pete's killer. Because who else would have his phone?

We hear the guy's end of the conversation about how long it will take Pete to get the guy's demands sorted. It doesn't sound like we're going anywhere anytime soon. The guy seems to have planned for this. After he hangs up, he says, "There's food in that cabinet and water in the mini-fridge. Use the empty bottles to – you know."

Ewww. Well, that's going to be awkward.

The guy goes back through the door, leaving us alone in the room. He left my phone behind. The screen may be cracked – but there's a chance it still works. I scoop it up.

The guy comes back into the room. He says, "I knew I was forgetting something," and snatches the phone out of my hand. He looks skeptically at me, and then at Arlo. "What's up with you two? My intel said you two broke up."

Arlo puts an arm around me and pulls me close. He gently kisses my forehead. "We just got back together. Recently."

The guy rolls his eyes. "Let's hope it's not a short-lived reunion." Then he leaves again.

The goat tries to follow him out, and winds up getting the door shut in her face. She lets out a sad little noise.

Arlo says, "What just happened?"

I shake my head. "I'm not sure." I explain my suspicion that I probably wasn't talking to Patsy's dad. Which tracks for his story about not being able to communicate personally from Mexico. But why on earth would someone who had stolen a phone pretend to be the owner? Especially when blackmail is involved?

"Look, Lis," Arlo says. "We have to get out of here. That guy was the nice one. The other guy wanted to shoot me instead of taking me with them. With my own gun."

"That means the nice guy is the one in charge," I say. "That's good, right?"

"Don't count on that." Arlo's voice sounds calm. Which is helping me not panic. He makes his way over to the cabinet – he's hobbling and favoring his left leg – and looks inside. There are boxes of granola bars and pouches of nuts, cereal and fruit snacks. It's enough to last us for days. "When they figure out that you're not Patsy, you become just a loose end. And if you weren't talking to Pete, but some imposter, there's no way whoever that was is going come through with the demands. Or send anyone to rescue us."

I say, "At least we found out about Creed. Logan said he wasn't in the system. Yet he seems to have a reputation as an excellent thief. So good his fingerprints aren't even on file." Logan has a lot of contacts. If they were on file *anywhere*, he would know. "So why would that kind of guy have committed the clumsy encounter at the jewelry store?"

"I don't know," Arlo says. He knocks on a nearby crate. It sounds empty. He leans against it to rest. "It's almost like he wanted to get caught. The bigger question is – why would Lydia have his photograph? I've been trying to stay out of Meryl's investigation, but I looked into Lydia as a potential suspect in mine. By all accounts, she was a real estate agent, nothing more. She has a record for a few petty thefts – but other than that, not even a parking ticket."

"It doesn't make sense," I agree. I make my way to the plexiglass and look through. There is no one in the space on the other side. There's a door there – though who knows where it leads. I try the handle, even though I know it is going to be locked. "You put it together with the files, and it's like Lydia was conducting an investigation of her own."

There is a desk in the other room, and from the other side of it, I can see the distinctive pink straps of my backpack sticking

out. If we can get access to that, there's a Taser and a flare gun –
both of which would be helpful if we make an attempted exit
through the mystery door.

Arlo says, "I guess you were right, Lis. If we had pooled
our resources, we might have had a shot at solving this thing." He
half laughs. "In time to go bowling, even. I was really looking
forward to that."

"Hey," I say. "Stop sounding like we're not going to
make it out of here."

"Were you really looking forward to bowling?" Arlo asks.
"Or were you just humoring me, letting me pretend that things
weren't going to be different after you finally make up your
mind?"

"Honestly? I was planning on going more to hang out
than anything. I haven't been inside a bowling alley in years." I
start walking around the perimeter of the space we're stuck in,
looking for anything that might help.

"That's not strictly true." Arlo says. He starts hobbling
slowly in the other direction. "What about the prohibition era
speakeasy slash bowling alley we found? That absolutely counts."

I counter, "It does not count. That wood was so warped
from floods, there's no way you could have thrown a bowling ball
down one of those lanes."

Arlo laughs. "Fair."

I ask, "When was the last time you went bowling? You
said you wanted to feel like nothing has changed, but wouldn't
going bowling actually *be* a change? For all of us?"

Arlo hesitates. "Patsy and I used to have a weekly
bowling night with her friends and some of the guys from the
precinct. Though you know how it is being a cop. I wasn't able to
go every time – but I always made it up to Patsy, when she had to
go alone. It was something that worked, you know?"

"And now you want to do that with me?" I don't know
how to feel about that.

"You can't expect me to come up with all new hobbies," Arlo says. "I was with Patsy a long time. Most of the stuff I like, we did it together."

There's a sting to that. "Did you ever take her diving?" I ask.

"Oh goodness, no. Patsy hates the water." Arlo's expression brightens. "Assuming we live through this, do you want to go diving next week instead? That can be our thing. That and sailing. It's not as low-key as bowling, or as likely to increase our group of friends. But I don't want you to think that I feel you and Patsy are interchangeable."

"Even if we're similar enough that a kidnapper looked through my phone and didn't notice a difference?"

Arlo's face takes on a skeptical expression. "I don't think you look that much alike."

"Admit it, Arlo. You have a type."

"Okay, I admit it. I think you're beautiful. I always have. Ever since high school." He shrugs. "If beautiful is a type, guilty as charged."

I feel myself blush. I tell him, "You know I had the biggest crush on you, long before we actually got together."

Arlo says, "We have to find a way out of this. We finally have our timing on the same page. We can be together, like we were supposed to be all those years ago before we let a stupid misunderstanding break us up." Arlo has his fists clenched with determination or frustration or simple passion. "I see you, Lis. Not some type. Not an ideal. But the girl who loved me despite my flaws, when I was a kid on the wrong path. The one who gave me a second chance, even though I'd been stupid. The one who loves the ocean at sunrise, and dancing in the living room, and lazy Saturday afternoons reading thick books."

I feel tears glitter in my eyes. "Yeah? I see you too. And you don't give yourself enough grace." I spot a sliver of metal on the floor and pick it up. I make my way back over to the partition. The door in the plexiglass has a manual lock. I slide the metal sliver into the keyhole. I've seen Logan do this a couple of times, but I have no idea exactly how. And what I'm doing jiggling the metal obviously isn't working. I should have paid more attention.

"Here, let me," Arlo says, as he gently takes the makeshift lock pick out of my hand.

"I thought lock-picking was Logan's thing," I say.

Arlo replies, "He may have taught me a thing or two. Just because we're competitive doesn't mean I don't listen to my friends."

I laugh. Arlo really is a good guy. And we both care about our friends. Which is why we're such a good match. "And what did you teach him?"

"How to make flan." He shifts the sliver, and there's a soft click. The door swings open. We move through into the space, and I spot my phone sitting on the desk.

Arlo moves over to the next door, semi-hopping as he favors that left ankle. He says, "There's no way a lockpick is going to get us through this one. The door requires a swipe key. And it's reinforced, so we're not going to kick it down."

"That's disappointing," I say. I pick up my phone. "It still turns on." The screen is so cracked, though, that it won't let me access the keypad. I try holding down the button that should send a SOS to 911, but that doesn't seem to be working either. I look closer at the phone and realize it has zero bars. Which is about par for my day today. "No signal."

Princess Buttercup starts chewing on one of the straps of my backpack. I shoo her away and shoulder the pack.

There's a loud noise from the other side of the door. Startled, Princess Buttercup rushes away and jumps at the wall, landing about four feet up on the uneven brickwork. She then proceeds to climb the wall, moving from one spot of protruding brick to the next. At some point it seems that she's gone from being scared to just curious. From a perch about halfway up the wall, she looks back at us, clearly pleased with herself.

Arlo and I exchange a glance, and I don't like the look on his face. He has an idea for a way out of here.

I say, "Don't even think about it."

He says, "Logan gave you that climbing gear in case of emergencies. I would say this counts." He pauses. "Assuming you're up to it. I know your asthma is in remission, but climbing really taxes your respiratory system. And it's crazy dusty in here."

I'd undergone an experimental treatment. Most of the time I'm fine now, but I have been in several life-threatening situations where bad air quality has triggered attacks.

"I'm guessing you're not up to going?" I ask. It's obvious that he's hurt, from the fight he must have put up to try and avoid being abducted.

"I can try, if you need me to. I'd have to free climb, since I'm too big for that harness. My ankle is shot from when the less nice guy stepped on it. And I still have a bad shoulder, from the car accident when we were kids. That weak joint got re-injured for the umpteenth time when I hit the pavement. But still – I might be able to make it up there and then pull you up." He holds out his hand for the climbing rope.

"I can do it," I say. "I'm lighter, so it will be easier." I also don't want to be responsible for him getting hurt even worse, should he fall. "But I've never climbed before, so you're going to have to tell me what to do."

Arlo rummages in the backpack and pulls out a compact device that turns out to launch a grappling hook. Who does Logan think I want to be? Batman?

Arlo attaches the climbing rope to it and shoots it over the railing of the catwalk. When he's sure it is secure, he helps me into the harness and hands me a piece of chalk for my hands. I'd wondered what that had been for. My guess had been for leaving marks on rocks and trees if lost in the wilderness. It would probably work for that, too.

Princess Buttercup looks at me curiously as I grab onto the bricks and push myself up. She bleats, sounding like this is the most exciting thing that has happened to her all day. I can already feel how hard this is going to be on my muscles, and hope I can make it to the top. As I move from handhold to handhold, I try to use my legs as much as I can, since they're less likely to wear out. I'm not sure if that is how you are supposed to climb, but the technique seems to be working for me. Princess Buttercup keeps climbing too, staying a bit ahead of me, looking back frequently to make sure I'm keeping up. She's decided this is a game. I imagine she's never seen a human being trying to play goat before.

Still, I find her presence encouraging. I slip, once, and there is a heart-wrenching feeling of inertia as I fall a few inches before the rope catches me.

Arlo – who has a tight grip on the other end – calls out, "You okay?"

"Yeah, I just need to be more careful." I manage to get myself back against the wall and climb the rest of the way to the catwalk. I pull myself up onto the stable surface. My legs are shaking. My breath is coming hard and shuddery. But it doesn't feel like an asthma attack is imminent. I take a hit off my emergency inhaler anyway. Then I pocket it and trade it for my phone. "I have two bars up here."

The screen still isn't letting me type – but it does call Ash, who answers on the first ring. I explain the situation.

Ash says, "I can get you help, as soon as I know where you are."

Arlo had said we were either in the historic district or near the docks. I look out one of the windows. "I don't know where we are exactly. This building is taller than the ones near it. And there is a two-story gray one across the way, with a sign on top that says JiffyPrint. But it looks like it has gone out of business."

"I know exactly where you are," Ash says.

"Of course you do," I say. If there's random information to be had, Ash has it.

"Hey, don't sound like that when I'm rushing to help you."

"It was the site of one of your LARPs, wasn't it?"

"I can neither confirm or deny that. Look I'm getting in my car. I'm on my way."

"Call the police first," I say. "And Logan."

"Of course," he says. Then he hangs up to do that. Which makes me feel bereft of the lifeline of connection to the outside world.

Arlo says, "Go ahead and pull the rope up. You can thread it out the window and rappel down the outside."

"No need," I tell him. "There's a ramp and a fire escape. Do you think you can make it up here?"

"I can try." Arlo starts climbing, carrying my backpack. I can see him wince as he moves his shoulder, and again when he has to land his left foot on a foothold. About six feet up, he stops, then climbs back down. "There's no way I'm going to make it to the top. Look, Lis, I want you to go. I love you too much to watch you get hurt."

Part of me wants to climb back down and stay with him. Who knows what happens if the arsonists come back in and realize I'm gone. It can't be good. Still – staying won't help. I say, "Ash is on his way, and hopefully so are the police. I'll let them know where you are in the building."

"If something happens-" Arlo's voice cracks and he starts over. "If something happens, tell Patsy I'm sorry, okay? I hate that the last thing that I said to her was to accuse her father of murder."

From the pain in his face, I can see that he still cares about her. He acted like he was over her, like he was ready to move on. Maybe he really believes he is. But now – I'm not so sure.

"Tell her yourself," I say. "We'll get you out of there. But you need closure with Patsy, if any relationship between you and I is going to move forward."

I grab the end of Princess Buttercup's leash and make my way through the window, out onto the fire escape. She comes along with me, happily enough. I've just given Arlo a monumental emotional task – with an implied deadline. And then left him alone with his thoughts. Sometimes I suspect I'm not as nice of a person as I could be.

But it could be the worst mistake of my life give up Logan if Arlo isn't really ready. First, though, Arlo just has to make it out of the building. I can't lose somebody else I love to a senseless death.

Chapter Fourteen
Monday

It doesn't take long for the police to arrive. After I give the cops the information, there's little more that I can do besides wait. For once, Logan is stuck on the sidelines too. He doesn't look happy about it, standing with his arms crossed, tapping his foot.

"It's going to be okay," I tell him. "At least one of the bad guys can be reasoned with."

"You telling me that, or yourself?" Logan asks.

"Both." I put a hand on his arm, touched by his worry over his friend.

Logan says, "Things can go wrong, even on the simplest op. Believe me. I know."

Logan had been a cop once. He had blamed himself for something that had gone wrong during an op, and that burden of guilt weighed on him so much that he had quit. He's dealt with a lot of the aftermath, finally coming to terms with it emotionally, accepting that some things are out of his control. He really has come a long way since I met him.

"I'm sorry to just disappear on you like that," I say. "How long did it take you and Patsy to realize we had gone missing?"

Logan says, "We talked for maybe twenty minutes. Mostly about her father. I talked her out of going to Mexico. Whatever's going on in that town, it wouldn't be safe. I told her I'd go."

My heart squeezes with sudden panic. "Logan, you can't."

"Why? Because you need me here?" Logan uncrosses his arms. "You know Patsy still has it bad for Arlo. But he's made it clear to her that he doesn't plan on giving you up – no matter what he still feels for her. I just want to make sure she doesn't get the short end of this from everyone involved."

Which is exactly what he feels like is happening to himself, too.

"Okay," I say. "Just – wait until after the wedding. I do need you here. And so do your friends."

Sudden emotion comes into his face. For a second, I think Logan Hanlon might actually cry. But then he crosses his arms, the picture of a tough guy once again. Still, he quirks his lips into a wry smile. "You know all I want is to be needed."

I want to kiss him more in that moment than in any other moment since we've met. But somehow, that doesn't seem fair. I clear my throat and ask, "Now, this is just hypothetical, and I'm not trying to imply I'm changing my mind, but if you did have someone in your life to come home to – would that make you more careful?"

Logan considers my face for a long moment. "Are you saying would I skip going to Mexico? Probably not. But you wouldn't respect me if I did. But it might make me think twice about how I handled myself, sure. You've already lost one person you cared about. You don't deserve to go through that again." An unexpected blush crosses his cheeks. "Though nothing is ever sure. Look at today. When I woke up this morning, I never expected that I wouldn't be able to keep you safe."

I ask, "What happened once you realized I was gone?"

Logan says, "I tried to figure out where they had taken you. When it seemed you'd dropped completely off the grid, I went to Tiff's office and dropped off the sushi order."

"Really? You cared that much? I rate the same as sushi?" I'm teasing, but it doesn't seem like sushi should be that urgent.

"It wasn't the sushi itself, per se – although I did eat that spicy tuna roll, and it was amazing." He pauses to get a laugh. Then he says, "You had mentioned a suspicious real estate agent eavesdropping on you talking about your investigations. And then you disappeared while following up on a clue. It felt like a big coincidence. I expected that guy to be gone, with a trail to follow to find you. But he was still there, still awkwardly watching Tiff and those band guys making paper flowers for the stage. So I guess he's not our guy."

"Not everything can be connected," I point out. "The arsonists had no connection to Lydia's murder, or what happened to Roland. They called Pete. If they knew Pete was in Mexico, instead of at his office, they never would have done that."

"True," Logan says. "But their connection to Pete says something. What does it mean about Patsy's father that these arsonists targeted him? Did he just randomly get attached to the arson cases?"

"Maybe he noticed a pattern," I say. "Maybe he was going to deny all the cases because he had figured something out. Patsy did say he was good at his job."

"Interesting," Logan says. "We've assumed Pete murdered Roland because Pete is a corrupt investigator. But what if he isn't? What if he was investigating Roland for some reason?"

"It's possible," I say. I think about how that would re-align the events we know happened. It doesn't make Pete's flight out of the country make any more sense. I can see why Logan wants to go find him, to figure out what happened. But we haven't exhausted our clues here. "Maybe Pete was meeting someone who had information on Roland. When you're done with Drake's bachelor party, I want to pull up some maps and look for this abandoned railroad car."

There's a commotion at the front of the building, as the two arsonists get led out in handcuffs. The one I hadn't met before has a black eye. There's a moment of triumph in seeing justice done, and these arsonists being hauled off to jail. I'll happily testify to the fact that they confessed to setting the building fires.

This is followed by a moment of panic, as I realize Arlo isn't with them. We're waiting across the street, but I keep my gaze glued to the door. Which seems intent on not opening.

I exchange glances with Logan. He starts heading across the street, and I follow. Princess Buttercup trots amiably alongside me.

They still won't let us inside the building. Nobody seems to know if Arlo is okay. It feels like a lump of raw bread dough has fallen into my stomach. All I can do is wait. Princess Buttercup looks up at me and makes a questioning noise. All this tension has to be making her nervous. I lean down to pet her. I'm not sure whether I'm comforting me or her.

The door opens, and there's a guy carrying medical equipment. And behind him, Arlo slowly makes his way to the door, leaning on a uniformed cop. There's a brace on his ankle and a bandage across the knuckles of his right hand, which explains why it had taken so long for him to leave the building. It also explains something about how the bad guy wound up with a black eye.

The uniformed cop helps Arlo down the stairs, then Arlo spots me. He says something to the guy who has been helping him, drops my backpack on the ground, and then he rushes as fast as his braced ankle will let him over to me and wraps me in a huge embrace. He needs reassurance and comfort, and my hand on his back seems to help him keep standing. After the hug goes on for a long time, Logan clears his throat.

Arlo lets me go. He turns to Logan and says, "Those guys couldn't tell between Lis and Patsy. You know they weren't all that bright."

"Good to see you too, man," Logan says.

Arlo says, "I got my gun back." Beyond that, he doesn't seem to want to talk about the details of what happened inside the building. The man who had helped Arlo brings over my backpack and hands it to me. As I take it, Arlo says, "I guess there's something to be said about being prepared."

I wonder which of the items Logan had selected had come into play during that tense situation. But I don't ask, because Logan already looks a bit smug.

Now that Arlo is safe, I can worry about how late I am for Autumn's tea. I pull out my phone. The tea was supposed to start at 4:30. It's already close to five. I ask, "What happened to my catering truck?"

Logan says, "They're going to have to process it as evidence."

I groan. "I forgot to call Autumn. She's going to kill me."

Logan pulls his keys out of his pocket. "Take my car. Arlo and I can find somebody to drop us off at Drake's."

"You ought to get somebody to drop Arlo off at the hospital," I say as I take his keys. Princess Buttercup bleats. I groan again, louder this time. "What am I going to do with this one at a hotel tea?"

"I'll take her," Arlo says. "After all, she helped save both our lives. Besides, Drake's party is an outdoor fish fry. I'm sure it's a much better fit for a goat."

"That would be a lifesaver." I hesitate in turning over the goat's leash. "Only – seriously, you should get checked out at the hospital."

"I promise I'll go after the party. The fact that we survived that experience is something to celebrate. I feel like being around friends."

"I get that." I give him the leash and turn towards Logan's Mustang. I turn back to the guys to say, "I still don't know why Agnes's phone is going to voicemail. And that's an improvement – at first it wasn't working at all. I'll try again to track her down after the party."

"While we're looking for the railroad car?" Logan asks.

"While we're looking for the railroad car," I assure him.

Arlo gives Logan a questioning look, but I don't have time to sort everything out between them. I drive to the hotel where the tea is being held, raising a few eyebrows from both staff and guests as I rush inside. I had been planning to change before the tea, but now I'm here in jeans and a tee, pit-stained from climbing and smelling vaguely of goat.

I burst into the room where the tea is set up. Autumn is standing in the middle of the room, covered in strips of toilet paper, which Tiff and Bea, another friend who recently moved to Galveston, are attempting to fashion into a makeshift wedding dress. Bea's dog, Satchmo, has a long strip of toilet paper cradled between his paws and his head as he watches the goings on with interest.

Kaylee, my former frenemy turned genuine friend, is holding up a large timer clock, counting down the seconds left in the game. That was supposed to be me. I'd bought that clock, just for this moment.

Only – everyone is staring at me in my raggedy clothes. The cake on the table is cut and half eaten. And I don't even have anything to add to the pile of girlie presents.

Autumn locks gazes with me, and I can tell she's upset, even though she tries to hide it, since she's the center of attention. She's not the only one being given the toilet-paper-bride treatment. Four other girls, including Autumn's friend Monique and Sonya, my friend who owns the yarn shop, are also adorned with various takes on dresses made by wrapping and hanging strips of TP. The clock finishes counting down, and Kaylee declares, "It's time for the bride parade."

I make my way over to where the girls are lining up.

Kaylee is busy trying to get the music started, so I take the opportunity to whisper to Autumn, "Sorry I'm late."

"Where were you?" Autumn asks vehemently. "I've been calling you for an hour. I know all the wedding stuff has been hard for you-"

I put a hand on her arm. The jostling causes a strip to fall from the makeshift paper skirt of her dress. It wafts to the floor and we both stare at it. I say, "I would have been here, only Arlo and I got abducted. My phone got smashed."

Autumn's mouth falls open in a shocked response. "Are you okay?"

"I'm fine," I say. "Arlo got a bit banged up. Not so bad he can't be in the wedding."

Autumn says, "That's not what's important here. If he needs to rest-"

"I don't think there's any way you could keep him from showing up on Thursday." Maybe now is the time to come clean about how I'm hijacking her big day. "Look, I know-"

The music starts, and Kaylee gestures for Autumn to lead the parade of brides around the room. It's silly, and everybody starts giggling as the improvised dresses start to fall apart. Monique is holding the bodice of hers up with her hands by the time they finish the circle back to us.

Tiff and Bea come over to help get the remaining TP off of Autumn. It hits me – I haven't actually interviewed Tiff, the way I have other people involved in all of this. It's possible that she knows more than she realizes.

Tiff is holding a large trash bag to gather up all the paper. I guess my expression gives me away, because she asks me, "Do we need to talk?"

I nod. "Just as soon as there's a break in the festivities."

Kaylee starts handing out paper for the Embarrassing Stories About the Bride part of the evening.

Autumn comes back over to me. "What were you going to tell me?"

I take a deep breath and just say it. "I told both of the guys that I would make a decision between them by the day of your wedding. The reason Arlo wouldn't miss your wedding isn't for you – it's for me."

I wince, afraid she's going to be mad that I'm complicating an already stressful day, adding in the potential for drama.

Instead, she hugs me. "That's great! Everything will be so much less awkward once we all know where things stand. So which one is the lucky guy?"

I start to say Arlo, but with everything going on with him and Patsy, I'm not as sure as I was a few hours ago. "I don't know."

"Felicity, we're talking about a decision you're making in three days." She looks worried.

Kaylee comes and grabs Autumn's hand. "You have to sit in the chair in the middle of the room and guess which of your guests wrote which embarrassing story."

I quickly scribble down a paragraph about the time Autumn and I were at a concert and the guy in front of us kept farting and trying to blame it on Autumn, until she had shouted, *I am not the fart bomber!* That one's always good for a laugh – and it's not really at her expense. I slip my paper into the pile.

Tiff pulls me over to the side of the room, where we can look like we're still participating in the party games without really being a part of it. She asks, "What's up?"

I say, "I'm just trying to fit all of these pieces together. Have you ever met Patsy's father, Pete?"

Tiff looks confused. "Should I have? I never hung out with Arlo, let alone his ex-girlfriend."

I nod. "You're sure?" I pull up a picture of Pete and show her. "This guy never asked you anything about Lydia? Or asked about a missing necklace?"

"I've never seen him before." Tiff studies me.

"So he definitely didn't come to the real estate office? No one there might have seen him?"

"I don't think so," Tiff stammers. "But I'm not there all the time."

I show her the picture of Creed. "And this guy? Do you think he could have been the person who attacked you at the house?"

She looks at the picture for a long time. Then she says, "I really didn't get a good look at the attacker. I know that sounds ridiculous, and that Meryl thinks I'm lying about it. She and Sabrina keep dropping by to chat about-" she makes air quotes, "one more thing."

"I hadn't realized that," I say. After all, they seem to have dropped the idea of me being an accessory to the crime. "It's just – this morning, right after I mentioned looking for Pete, Patsy suddenly got an email from him. It just seems a bit convenient. You didn't notice anything off about anyone at your office?"

Tiff closes her eyes and sighs. "I really wish I could help." She snaps her fingers and opens her eyes. "You know – it's been bugging me about how the guys from the band came to my office this morning. Don't you think that was a little bit strange? I mean, they could have just called you and asked for your opinion. And they were acting weird."

"Weird how?" I ask.

"Hold on, Autumn's reading my story." Tiff moves back into the group of girls all giggling as Autumn reads about the time she and Tiff accidentally traded purses and Autumn got to a book reading without her notes, and pulled out Tiff's client diary instead. That must be a recent story, since Autumn only started doing book events again a few months ago.

When Tiff steps back over to me, I repeat, "Weird how?"

Tiff says, "There was something going on between them. Starsky kept saying he might as well go home, since nobody was focusing enough when they had practiced to actually play, and Flip kept telling him to shut up, if he knew what was good for him. I don't think Charlie and Boone spoke to each other once all morning. I caught Flip looking in all the flowerpots in the office, and he said it was something about looking at soil types, since the plants were so healthy. But it is possible he could have been looking for something Lydia might have stashed when she came in that day. Come to think of it, he seemed awful disappointed when Charlie popped open that compartment in the desk and it was empty, didn't he?"

I realize I know absolutely nothing about Flip. Though he had seemed much nicer when I had talked to him. I say, "I wonder if Flip has ever been to Florida. Maybe he recently ran into Lydia there."

Tiff says, "I don't think Lydia still lives in Florida. I'm not sure where she moved. I didn't want to social media stalk her, mainly because I didn't want to get drawn into her life again."

"I get that," I say. "What do you think was the problem Lydia wanted her "logical friend" to help out with?"

Tiff raises one hand in a helpless gesture. "I have no idea. You were there. She just said there's 'something going on.' For her, that could mean anything."

"Do you think she was still having family problems? I know Cal's dead, but maybe somebody connected to her family or to that time in her life might have finally caught up with her."

"I don't think so. Lydia's step-mother went to jail for helping cover up what her son was doing." Tiff grimaces. "Lydia came back to visit her father after her stepbrother died in prison. I guess she finally felt safe. I was still living in Ohio at the time, but we never really talked. I didn't know then that she felt like she had been running for her life when she'd left town so abruptly. Or that she romanced Eli into helping her because she felt like she had no choice."

Eli must have been the boyfriend Lydia stole.

"So I guess you read Lydia's book?" I've been trying to skim through it myself, in case there are any clues to her murder hidden in her past. It's not an easy book to read, and I've skipped the worst bits. True crime is not my preferred reading – one more reason I haven't been on Ash's podcast. In the chapter where she talked about leaving, Lydia had said that the worst thing about what she had done to get out of Ohio had been taking Eli with her.

She had lied to him, had never even loved him. She had just been looking for someone to protect her. When they had finally parted, she felt that she had ruined his life.

"I bought the book yesterday. I just read the part that was important to me," Tiff says. "I had no idea Lydia had even written a book. I don't keep up with that kind of news."

It feels like Lydia had been trying to leave a message when she'd left a book with Tiff. But why leave a copy of *The Thin Man*, instead of leaving her own book, which would have done more to heal the rift between her and her former friend? That's something we will probably never know.

I ask Tiff, "Can I borrow your phone? I'm pretty sure Drake invited the band to his fish fry. I want to give Logan a heads up to keep an eye out for further suspicious behavior."

"Sure." She hands me her phone.

But then it is my turn to have Autumn read my story. And the way she reads it, she has all of us giggling. That's one thing I love about Autumn. She's able to own things, make them larger than life.

When they move on to opening presents, I take Tiff's phone out in the lobby and scroll down to Logan's number. I tell him to keep an eye on Flip.

This ease in asking him to help with investigations – that's something else that might change soon, too.

By the time I pull up at Drake's house, after having helped fold wrapping paper and pack gifts in the car, and then gone home to shower and change, I expect the fish fry to be over, but things still seem to be in full swing. Drake lives in a pretty beach cabin, and it is clear that he enjoys entertaining. There's a space off to one side with a sand pit, and a dozen guys are standing around it, playing horseshoes.

There's the gentle clink of metal on metal as someone scores, followed by cheers and groans. I'm supposed to be here picking up Logan and Arlo, since I have Logan's car. Then we're going to drop Arlo at the hospital and go grab me a new phone. It's a bit ridiculous – I just replaced my phone, during the last investigation. So I'm not in need of an upgrade.

Drake steps away from the group and their game. He walks over to Logan's Mustang and gestures me out of it. "Come on in, and I'll fix you a plate. We have plenty left."

"Are you sure?" I ask. "I'm not trying to crash your guy's night."

Drake laughs. "Things around here are pretty informal. I'm sure Arlo could use the company. We made him get off that leg and ice down his ankle about half an hour ago."

I have my tablet with me. I was going to use it do a bit of research about Flip while waiting in the car. It's uncomfortable to think there might be a murderer staying in the hotel with my aunt and my bunny. And he seems like such a sweet guy. I want to eliminate him as a suspect as soon as possible.

But I can do my research just as easily indoors. I follow Drake up the stairs and into the cabin. He gestures me into the living room, where Arlo is sitting, looking bored. I sit down opposite him.

It's an open space, with gray wood flooring and pale blue walls, very different from Drake's office, which has a warm red and gold color scheme. There are boxes stacked against one wall, with more half-packed ones in the middle of the floor. Drake brings me a plate stacked with fried catfish, waffle fries, coleslaw and glazed carrot coins – along with a glass of red wine. As I take the plate, I ask, "What are you going to do with this place after the wedding?"

Drake says, "We want to use it as a rental."

Arlo says, "It's in a good location. You should be booked solid."

I bite into the fish, which has been fried to perfection, with a thin crispy coating of cornmeal packed with spice. I tell Drake, "This is so good. Autumn is going to be so spoiled. You know she considers cheese toast cooking, because it has two ingredients, right?"

"I am well aware of that," Drake says. "I like cooking enough for the both of us."

We chat about Drake and Autumn's plans, for their honeymoon, and how their subsequent lives are going to fit together. It sounds like they're going to have fun.

Arlo tells Drake that he's going to the hospital to get checked out in a bit, and Drake looks relieved.

Drake says, "I don't know why you didn't just go there right away. I wouldn't have been upset about you missing the party."

"I wanted to be here," Arlo says. "You're a good friend, even if we haven't known each other that long. After Patsy left, I realized that most of our friends were actually her friends. And they seemed to blame me for the breakup, so I spent a lot of time feeling awkward. Remember that night at Chalupa's, when you and Autumn asked me to join you? I'd just had one of those awkward moments, and you didn't even ask what was wrong – which was what I needed at the time."

Drake says, "That wasn't pity. You've been a good friend too."

Apparently, this is all getting too mushy, because Arlo clears his throat and asks, "What are we going to do about the goat? I can't take it to the hospital. And Lis and Logan are going to do some investigating."

"You're asking me to keep it here," Drake says. He considers this, "It shouldn't be a problem. I can get PB back to you before the rehearsal dinner."

Yet another wedding-related event where I can't afford to be late.

When I'm done eating, Drake takes my plate and goes back to the rest of his guests.

Arlo says, "I had a lot of time to think, back at that warehouse. And I sorted through my feelings. I don't want to jeopardize what we have, Lis, just because I got sentimental over someone else. That's the past. I have no question or hesitation about committing to you."

I study his face. He looks sincere. I have no way to read what's actually in his heart, but he seems to have come to terms with some hard truths.

"Okay," I say. "That's what I needed to know."

He looks expectant, like he's hoping I will confess my feelings now, but I promised Logan I would wait three more days before I make my choice.

After and awkward silence, Arlo asks, "What are we going to do about the goat, long term? You can't ask Drake to keep it indefinitely. He's about to go on his honeymoon."

I flip open my tablet, which connects automatically to Drake's Wi-Fi. I say, "We have to track down Agnes. I want to talk to her anyway – I'm convinced she knows something more about all of this than she's letting on." Without a way to track her phone or her RV, I've been stumped. But then I have an idea. "Hey, is Ash here?" When Arlo nods, I say, "Can you text him and ask him to come in here? Tell him I want to do an interview for his podcast."

Arlo looks skeptical, since I've refused to be a part of Ash's true-crime cast in the past, but he does what I ask. Then he says, "What's on the tablet?"

I say, "It's about to be info on Flip. I hope. Any idea what his last name is?"

Arlo says, "Flip Trevino. I already pulled his basic information. Father of three, been married for roughly twenty years. His youngest has a chronic illness that is steadily draining their bank account. If the motive in all of this is money, then I think Tiff may be onto something."

I say, "I guess Logan filled you in."

Arlo just gives me a wry grin. "He should be in in a few minutes."

I say, "We need to find the necklace Pete was looking for. See if it was worth killing over. Though, that only explains Roland's murder. Lydia might have stolen many things since coming to Galveston, but she couldn't have stolen that."

I start looking at Flip's website. He is not only a gifted musician – but in addition to his bank job, he started a school for underprivileged children in the metropolitan area of Chicago, giving them a chance to study music. I flip through a photo album embedded in the page. There's Flip and his wife, classrooms with small children holding musical instruments that are practically bigger than they are, older children performing in concert halls, a colorful backdrop in a garden, where a choir of grade schoolers is singing, all dressed like ladybugs.

Huh. That garden seems to be part of the property belonging to the school. Which means Flip could well be a plant fanatic. So he might have been looking for something at Tiff's office – or he might be innocent, because he could really be that interested in soil quality.

I feel like this all keeps coming back to nowhere. Flip, Agnes, Nathan – even Patsy's dad. All of my suspects seem too nice to be a killer. Except for Creed, and I still have no idea how he fits into all of this.

I tell Arlo, "It feels like we're still missing a piece of the puzzle that will bring this all together. What haven't we considered?"

Arlo looks uncomfortable.

"What?" I ask.

His face tells me he's conflicted, and I'm pretty sure he's just going to say nothing and let it go, but then he says, "I really shouldn't be sharing information about an open case with an active suspect, but maybe look into that real estate agent from Tiff's firm."

I look up the website for Tiff's real estate firm. I find the guy who had been so awkward this morning. Creepy Guy's real name is Ray Casey. His photo and bio on the site make him sound like a dynamic guy, and a competent real estate agent. Which makes me wonder if there was a specific reason he was so awkward this morning. Could he have a history with one of the band members? Or maybe he just knows something about what happened to Tiff's friend.

Arlo made it sound like there was something more concrete. I do a Google search for his name. There's a ton of marketing and advertising stuff, and him doing ribbon cuttings in several cities. But none of that is really helpful. I do a search for his name paired with Tiff's. Again, not much help. I try his name paired with Lydia's. When the first image shows up, I suck in a startled breath. I say, "Ray Casey and Lydia Dunning were engaged?"

Arlo nods and gestures me back to my tablet. I pull up the article and keep reading. Lydia and Ray had worked at the same real estate firm in Florida, and were considered the up-and-coming power couple. Their wedding was slated for four years ago. So what happened?

I keep searching, start to put the pieces together. There are tell-all images of Ray with some YouTube star, that apparently broke up her relationship with a B-list actor. The photos are dated after the engagement announcement. So obviously, the scandal ended Ray and Lydia's relationship too. There's a vandalism claim having to do with his car. And then, last year, there was the announcement of him taking a job in Texas at – coincidence of coincidences – the same firm Lydia's friend worked for.

When Lydia had come back from Florida – had she been wanting to talk to Tiff because she was upset over a second failed relationship? Or had she been wanting to warn Tiff that her ex might be a stalker? Could Ray have killed Lydia? After all, he was one of the few people who knew that we were planning to meet her at the open house. And he could have used the lock box to get in before we did.

I ask Arlo, "Does Detective Beckman know about this?"

Arlo leans back against the corner of the sofa. "She's the one who brought Ray to my attention. She wanted to know if he had any connection to Roland or Pete, since the two cases might be connected."

"Oh," I say. I hadn't thought about Meryl's side of this, past her seeming to be fixated on Tiff.

Arlo says, "She's a good cop, Lis. I don't want you to think of her as the enemy."

"Even though she threatened to charge me as an accessory to murder?" I ask.

"She's just doing her job. Cops have to follow where the evidence leads. And if it doesn't feel like the whole story, we keep looking for more evidence."

"I get that," I say. "I'm glad she's still looking."

Ash comes into the room, looking wary. He's wearing a tee-shirt with a sea turtle stenciled on it in white. It's appropriate for the party – but I've never seen him dressed so casually. He looks at me and says, "Is this a prank?"

I gesture him into the chair next to mine. I tell him, "Since your podcast is pretty much only cases involving Felicity, I figure I'm a big part of what is making your following work. And I'd like to put that to use to help for once."

Ash blushes. After all, we all remember the time when an obsessed podcast fan had called me out to solve a murder that hadn't even yet been committed. He says, "I know I owe you."

I say, "It's about the goat."

Ash looks intrigued. He takes out his phone and says, "Usually, I'd do this with my studio setup, for the sake of sound quality, but it sounds like this is going to be time sensitive."

Arlo watches quietly as Ash asks me some preliminary questions about everything happening surrounding Lydia Dunning. I answer what I can, and for the rest simply say I can't speak about it at this time. Then, when he finally asks about the goat, I say, "Princess Buttercup is an adorable pigmy goat, who loves to climb on everything in sight. Lydia borrowed her from her owner, and I'd like to return her. Only – her owner has disappeared. I want to emphasize – her owner isn't in trouble. Though I am a bit worried. No one is answering her business phone, or what I think is her personal number. I will personally send a gift box of chocolate bars to anyone who can put me in touch with Agnes from Daydream Hills goat farm. And if you're into that sort of thing, I'll sign each bar."

Ash's eyebrows rise over the rim of his square glasses. He says, "Thanks for tuning in for this exclusive interview with Felicity Koerber. Hopefully, we'll see her more regularly on the podcast soon. But in the meantime, here's your chance to be involved in helping solve an actual true crime. I'll leave a way for you to contact me in the show notes below. Don't forget to like and subscribe – and remember WWFD my friends." Ash stops recording. He says, "Give me a minute to do the editing, then I'll get this up as a special episode within the hour."

Arlo says questioningly, "WWFD?"

Ash replies, "What would Felicity do?"

Because, of course, there's a whole group of people out there wondering just that.

Logan comes into the room. He says, "We can leave now. I finally won at horseshoes."

As we're getting into his car, me riding shotgun, Arlo carefully climbing into the back, I get a sense of déjà vu. I tell Arlo, "This is the second time in so many months that we're bringing you to the hospital."

"At least this time it's not a head injury," Arlo says. "There should be no need to keep me for observation. I'm not about to miss Autumn's wedding, for anything."

Logan's jaw flexes, so I know he has emotions about that, but he doesn't say anything, even though Arlo is being dramatic, since the wedding is still days away.

Once we get Arlo to the hospital, though, he insists on waiting by himself. He says, "There's too much still going on with both our investigations for you to sit around and waste the rest of the day. I have a couple of leads to follow up on. I still plan to solve my end of this first. Even if I did hand Felicity a bit of info that gives me a handicap."

"What does he mean?" Logan asks.

I say, "He gave me a heads up about a connection between Lydia and the creepy guy from Tiff's office."

Logan replies, "Well, we gave him the tip about Pete meeting someone at an abandoned railroad car, so I think that makes us even."

"Not entirely," Arlo says. "The murder I'm responsible for solving is Roland's. Finding out what is going on with Pete is just a bonus."

"Except that he's obviously the one who killed Roland," Logan says. "Which practically hands you your case."

"Maybe," Arlo says. "Which would be ironic, considering a lot of what he said when mine and Patsy's relationship was imploding. But – he just doesn't seem like the type. I'm more worried that he's in trouble than that he's guilty."

So we leave Arlo in the waiting room and head for the phone store. By now, since it's winter, the sun has gone down.

When we go inside the phone store, I recognize the girl who comes over to help us. She's in her late teens, and wears dramatic cat-eye glasses. She says, "Hey weren't you just in here?"

"Yep."

"Buying that phone?" She gestures at the phone I'm looking at, which is the same model as the crushed phone in my pocket.

I grimace. "I don't want to talk about it."

She laughs. "You know, you really should get the extended warranty, if you're that tough on them."

Chapter Sixteen
Monday

It takes a while to get everything transferred from my old phone to the new one. While we're waiting, Logan and I use my tablet – and the store's Wi-Fi – to pull up a map of Pelican Island. There really isn't much there. Large chunks of the island are completely undeveloped. And the 3D version of the map doesn't reveal an abandoned railroad car, or an area of cover thick enough to hide such a car, anywhere near the university.

I tell Logan, "This doesn't make any sense. Why would Pete have told his mystery caller that he wanted to meet somewhere that couldn't exist?"

Logan zooms in the map close enough that it goes fuzzy, but we're still not seeing anything vaguely train-car shaped, or any buildings on most of the island. "Maybe it was some kind of code?"

"Possibly," I say. "Wait." I point at a spot in the map with a construction vehicle captured in the view. "What's that?"

Logan zooms out. He says, "It looks like they're building something on one of the vacant lots. I have heard that the Port of Houston owns much of the land on Pelican Island, and that they've been holding off on developing it. But that's on a more industrial scale. Maybe someone is building a house."

"Maybe." I look at the shape of the rebar outline of the foundation that's going to be poured. "But doesn't that look about the shape of a railroad car?"

Logan leans in close to study the shape. I can smell the woodsy scent of his recently shampooed hair. Which is really nice. "It could be. The captures on these maps aren't updated all that frequently. Whatever was being built is probably finished by now."

"Then we should drive over and look at it." I gesture vaguely towards the counter inside the store where my new phone is doing its thing. "Once we can leave here."

Logan's phone dings with a text. He frowns at it briefly, then sends a reply. He tells me, "None of my contacts can find any proof that Patsy's dad ever crossed the border into Mexico."

Somehow, I'm not surprised. I say, "That's one thing I've been confused about. If he is asking Patsy to send his passport, then how did he get in? None of it makes any sense."

Logan says, "I've been talking with a friend of a friend of a friend in the town where Pete is staying. There's clearly someone there that looks like Pete, who rented a hotel room under Pete's name. I've asked my friend to send a photo of the guy."

Logan's phone dings again.

I say, "Your friend doesn't waste any time."

"She was already on site," Logan says. He turns his phone around to show me the image of a guy in a Hawaiian shirt, holding a beer. "What do you think?"

I say, "I mean, it could be him." I zoom the photo in, focusing on the guy's hand, which has a wine stain mark roughly the shape of Italy running across the back of it, up onto his wrist. "But nothing we've got about Pete mentions a significant birthmark. We'll have to ask Patsy. What's he been doing, other than shopping and drinking?"

Logan sends another text, and when he gets a reply, he says, "Apparently, looking into some kind of land deal."

"Well, that's just weird." I mean, what would an insurance investigator be doing looking for investment property while he's stuck in a foreign country?

"If it's not him," Logan says, "maybe the guy doesn't even know he's impersonating Pete. It could be that Pete's name is just the one the room was rented under."

I take Logan's phone and study the guy's birthmark. Then I use my tablet to study the picture we have of Pete. In our pic, you can't see his hand clearly, but you can see his wrist. So there's no conclusive evidence. I still say, "I don't think it's him."

The salesgirl waves me over to the counter, signaling that everything in my new phone is up to date. I pick up the phone. It looks and feels just like the old one. It rings in my hand. I look down, and the number is one I don't recognize. Hopefully, though, it's someone with information that will help make sense out of this mess.

I tell the girl, "Thanks for everything. I need to take this." Then I answer the phone.

It's Agnes. She says, "I wish you hadn't called all that attention to me on that podcast."

I say, "You didn't give me anything else to go on. What am I supposed to do with your goat?"

"You found Princess Buttercup?" Agnes's relief is palpable, even over the phone. "Is she okay?"

"She's at a friend's place right now. The question is, where are you?" I try to keep my voice light. Her fleeing Galveston after her fight with Lydia does still make her seem suspicious. But I want to hear her side of what happened.

Agnes says, "I'd rather not say."

I say, "Okay, why are you calling me, then? Is there something you want to confess?"

Agnes sucks in a loud breath. "You think I had something to do with what happened to Lydia, don't you."

I reply, "I don't know what to think."

Agnes says, "Esme is a wreck. Somebody broke into our RV again, looking for something. She was inside, taking a shower, and when she came out, the guy threatened her. With a gun."

"Did she get a look at the guy's face?" I ask.

"No. He was wearing a filter mask. But he demanded to know what Lydia had left us, and when Esme showed him the jar of honey, he was so mad he broke it." Her steadying breath is audible over the phone. "So if you don't mind, we're going to stay incommunicado until all of this blows over. I'm afraid that the guy might come back, if he runs out of other places to look for whatever it is Lydia took from him."

That's something I should have already considered. With Lydia's kleptomania, it's possible she was killed because she stole the wrong thing from the wrong person. Could she have taken the necklace that Pete had been scouring the pawn shops for? Maybe that necklace is different from the one the jeweler had made, after all. If Lydia had felt the need to have it authenticated, maybe it was expensive enough to kill for.

I know that is a long-shot possibility. None of Pete's cases had involved a missing or stolen necklace. Still, so far there's been nothing that connects Pete and Lydia, outside of the fact that he had her phone number. I think back to the message he'd written down. *Definitely belonged to the wife.* If that referred to the pawn shop necklace, maybe Lydia stole it from the wife of someone Pete knew.

"Felicity?" Agnes asks. "Are you still there?"

"Yeah," I say. "I was just thinking about what you said. I understand you wanting to stay off the grid until this gets sorted out. But I have to forward this number to the police. I'm pretty sure they have some questions for you. You okay with that?"

"I don't have much choice," Agnes says sullenly. Though if it's a burner phone, there's nothing stopping her from just changing her number again. Which seems like an overreaction, if she's not really involved in any of this. Agnes adds, "I want you to promise me you'll take care of Princess Buttercup. Don't let them put her in a shelter or anything. I'll come get her as soon as it is safe."

"I'll do my best," I say. Because really, how long can I take care of a goat?

After Agnes hangs up, I forward her new phone number to Detective Beckman.

Meryl sends me a text back, about how surprised she is to hear from me, and thanking me for the information. I guess I should have been more forthcoming about what I've discovered, the way I've been with Arlo. But there's nothing concrete enough yet to sum up in text. I want to give Beckman enough coherent information to clear Tiff.

I tell Logan, "Okay. Let's check out that spot we saw on the map."

We get into the Mustang and head out into the night. The bridge that arcs between Galveston and Pelican Island feels longer tonight, as though we are heading towards something momentous. The lights from shore reflecting on the water, the moon hanging low in the sky, feel poetic. I can tell Logan feels it too.

My phone rings, and the moment shatters. It's Patsy. I answer it.

She says, "I just heard that Arlo is in the hospital. Because of me. How is he?"

"He'll be fine. Though he won't be winning any basketball tournaments any time soon."

She says, "That's a relief. Can you tell him I'm sorry. I hate that I keep bringing trouble into his life."

I tell her, "I'll tell him when I see him. Or you can call the hospital yourself. We're following up on a clue."

"Oh," Patsy says. "If you're busy, I should let you go."

"Wait," I say. "I'm actually glad you called. We're still trying to sort a few things out. Does your dad have a birthmark?"

She makes a spluttering noise into the phone. "How could you possibly know about that?"

"There's a picture of the mark on his hand."

Patsy says, "My father doesn't have a mark on his hand. His is on . . . somewhere else."

Okay. That's more than enough information. Suffice to say, the man in the picture is not actually Pete. I change the subject. "How long are you able to stay in town?"

She says, "I've taken indefinite leave. I heard about the concert you're having at your place tomorrow. I was thinking I might come by – if it wouldn't be too awkward."

"You're always welcome at Felicitations," I say. It's hard how awkward all of this has become, everyone feeling like they're not welcome in each other's lives, all because of my hesitation to make a choice about my love life. I'd been selfish, trying to build up community around me, while at the same time putting others in untenable situations. "Patsy, I'm glad you like music, too. It gives us something to talk about."

Patsy says, "I like jazz well enough, but my favorite is classical. I'm a huge fan of Mozart. I've been listening to recordings of his work a lot, since my father disappeared, because I find it calming."

"I get that," I say. "So you're into old movies and old music?"

Patsy says, "Sometimes I feel like I'm always in the wrong place and time. But you have to live practically. Did you ever see *A Midnight in Paris*? It's my favorite film. It was Arlo and my favorite film. It's all about how you can't look back. No matter how much you want to."

Logan taps my arm. He says, "Are you seeing what I'm seeing?"

What Patsy is saying is important. She's telling me that she's okay with me winding up with Arlo, that she made her choices, and knows she can't go back and change things. But Logan is gesturing towards a couple of railroad cars, sitting in what was formerly the empty lot.

I tell Patsy, "Let's talk more at the concert."

She lets me go, as Logan pulls into the driveway leading to a small parking lot opposite the train cars. There's a sign: B&B

Railroad. It's a pun off B&O Railroad from the Monopoly boardgame, with a sign that looks vaguely like the game's property card.

I say, "When we heard old railroad car, we interpreted it as abandoned railroad car. But what Pete meant was repurposed vintage railroad car. It's like what they did with the Kettle House – that structure started out as a steel storage tank and now it's a popular Air B&B."

I should feel excited that we'd figured out the clue. But instead, I'm reluctant to get out of the car. The train-cars-turned-B&B-cottages are quiet, two of them with lights on, showing through the rows of small windows. The other two cars are dark.

Logan gets out of the Mustang, and I follow. We walk up to the closest lit train car, and Logan knocks on the door. A guy comes to the door, and Logan shows him the picture of Pete. The guy says he saw Pete a couple of days ago, staying in the car at the far end of the lot.

It's one of the cars with no lights on. I follow Logan over to it, our feet crunching heavily on the newly installed gravel path.

I ask Logan, "Why do I have a bad feeling about this?"

"I do too," Logan says. "No matter what happens, I want you to stay outside."

"Okay," I say, feeling a little bit the coward. But Logan has training that I do not – nor is it training that I would want.

I stand a little away from the door as Logan knocks, then when there is no answer lets himself in. He comes back a few moments later and says, "Call Arlo. We found Pete."

"Is he-"

Logan nods. "He's been dead for a while. Long enough he couldn't have killed Lydia."

"Aww, man." I don't know what else to say. Not only did I fail at finding a missing person, which is going to devastate the person who asked me to look into it, I still don't have a viable alternative suspect for clearing Tiff. I tell Logan, "We have to go get Arlo. Somebody needs to tell Patsy about this in person – and it should be him."

So I call Arlo, and Logan calls the cops. And once we've explained the actions and reasoning that led us to this lonely little B&B, in detail, to Detective Beckman, we head to the hospital, where we find Arlo waiting for us in the lobby. His arm is in a sling, but the brace on his ankle is pretty much the same – which means that at least it isn't broken.

We ride in silence over to the hotel where Patsy is staying. It's right on the beach. She comes outside to talk to him. Logan and I sit in the car and watch Patsy and Arlo walk towards each other by the light of the Mustang's headlights. They talk for a moment, then her body language collapses forward, her shoulders slumping her head bowing. Arlo catches her and hugs her with his single good arm. She buries her face in his shoulder.

I feel a wave of empathy, for her pain and her loss. Patsy is at that moment right when her world goes from okay to flipped upside down. I'm glad Arlo can be here for her – and it only makes me a little jealous. Okay, a lot jealous.

I don't like the emotion, but I can't deny it. My hands have balled into fists on my lap. Arlo chose me. He said he put his feelings for Patsy behind him, so we can move forward. Patsy even as much as said that she's okay with it. Dang it. Kissing Arlo makes me feel like I'm home, and he's promised to make me feel safe. Seeing him have this connection with someone else is making me feel territorial. I want to go out there and pull the two of them apart. But at the same time I just feel sad. Somebody has to get hurt in all of this. Probably several someones. So why do I feel bad for the girl who already ditched Arlo? Probably for the same reason I knew Arlo had to be the one to break the news to her. And that just makes me angry.

Logan looks at me, and it's a complicated expression. He's seeing what I'm seeing – that Patsy needs Arlo, the same way Logan needs me.

I look back at him, and I feel like the most selfish person in the world.

Chapter Seventeen
Tuesday

I'm making a much-needed pot of coffee, downstairs in the kitchen at the flip hotel. I was up all night, trying to figure out what I'm supposed to do. If Patsy needs Arlo and Logan needs me, it all lines up nicely, doesn't it? Only – that's only part of the equation. What about what I need? What Arlo needs? And what the two of us deserve?

If I settle for something just because it lines up neatly, Logan and I could wind up resenting each other later. Especially with Arlo still living in the same town. I have to be sure I'm making this decision for the right reasons.

And all I realized, after hours of staring at the ceiling, is that I've been focusing on what I want, and what feels nice, and not necessarily what I really need. And I have only two more days to figure that out. Despite the fact that both Logan and Patsy will wind up hurt, it seems like Arlo, who offers stability and ease and peace is the right choice. After all, I've always hated change, feared the unexpected.

But what if that's not what I need? Logan has pushed me out of my comfort zone, forced me to grow. Is that better? Maybe being with Logan wouldn't be settling, because he's an amazing person in his own right. Maybe I've been downplaying him, because I'm looking for some way to make an impossible decision. Is it any wonder I have a headache?

The coffee finishes brewing, and I pour myself a cup.

"That smells good." Logan says as he walks into the restaurant-sized dining room.

Naomi must have let him in. She said she'd come get pancakes in a few minutes, before heading over to spend the day with my grandmother, who lives in an assisted living facility here on the island. I haven't gotten as far as making the actual pancakes, just laid out a few ingredients on the counter.

"Want a cup?" I ask.

"Please," Logan says. He sees the dry ingredients lined up on the counter, and moves to the fridge to take out eggs and butter and blueberries. He starts making pancakes, while I just stand there bleary-eyed, sipping my coffee. He says, "You look wrecked."

"Yeah, you know, I have a lot on my mind."

He pauses, mid whisk. "Like what?"

He knows he's a big part of what I've been thinking about, contemplating and weighing. I ask, "What if I told you I wanted to quit the chocolate business, and just travel the world. What would you do?"

He looks stricken. "Do you? Want to give up the business, I mean?"

"No, I love Greetings and Felicitations. It's just a hypothetical question."

He goes back to mixing pancakes as he considers this. "I suppose I'd stay here and keep the home fires burning, so the business could finance your travels, and there'd be something stable for when you get back. Unless in this hypothetical you're inviting me to travel the world with you – in which case, I'd jump at the chance to see places and people through your eyes. Then I'd suggest leaving the business in Carmen's capable hands. Though you'd have to train someone as an official chocolate maker. Maybe Miles – unless he's too busy with school."

"What about your puddle jump business, if you were off traveling the world?"

Logan folds in blueberries as he works through what he would do. "I'm the only pilot, so that wouldn't work very well without me here. Besides, we'd need the main plane. I suppose I'd sublease the hanger, sell off some of the other planes."

"But you wouldn't abandon the business? Fly off into the sunset?"

"Now that wouldn't be very practical, would it?" Logan reaches into the cabinet next to the stove and grabs a pan. He puts it on the heat. "I've built a life here. It's been a lot more fulfilling than when I was moving around to suit my job."

Maybe Logan is offering more stability than I thought.

And yet, I sense hesitation in him. "Only?"

"This is horrible timing. Here I am, trying to prove that I can be there for you, no matter what. And I'm going to have to miss Autumn's rehearsal dinner." He winces at my shocked expression.

"What? Why?"

Logan says, "I got a call from my mom. My dad's in the hospital. They think he's going to be okay – for now – but I really need to see him."

"Oh, Logan, I'm so sorry to hear that." Logan's father has a chronic illness. Of course, he has to go to him. I say, "I hate that you're going to be traveling alone, with that much stress."

"I won't be alone. I'm taking Cindy with me. She may look like a cotton ball, but she's good company when I need somebody to talk to."

Logan starts pouring pancake batter into the pan. He says, "I can stay and help out with the extra business coming through during the concert, and I can do the chocolate making demo that we scheduled, but I'm flying out after that. I promise I'll be back in time for the wedding."

"You'd better," I say. "Autumn will kill you if there's an uneven line between the bridesmaids and the groomsmen."

Logan tilts his head. "There's that, too. But I don't want to miss whatever you have to say to me Thursday morning. I haven't come this far, just to bow out now."

I laugh and point to the pan, where bubbles are bursting on the batter. "Time to flip that pancake."

He does, and the back of it is a perfect golden color. Arlo had talked once about how making pancakes is one of those perfect, simple ordinary things to do as a couple. And it kind of is. I could see myself with Logan on a lazy Saturday morning doing just this.

But is it Logan himself, or just the simplicity of the activity that I really need?

Logan says, "I want to help with the investigation, as much as I can before I go. I already talked with my friend of a friend in Mexico. She says that the man registered as Pete Nash checked out of his hotel in the middle of the night and disappeared."

"That's not really surprising," I say. "It's just like in *The Thin Man*, once the ruse is up there's no point. Pete can't be framed anymore for murders he couldn't possibly have committed. I just don't understand – why leave the body in the railroad car? Someone was bound to discover it eventually?"

Logan says, "My guess is the killer intended to move the body before Pete's scheduled stay at the B&B is up. It was probably just a matter of finding a good time to do it."

"So you don't think Pete's killer fled with Pete's phone to Mexico?"

Logan says, "No, I don't. I think the same person who killed Pete killed Lydia. And I think there might be a clue to that person's identity in the train car."

"Do you think we could get in to look around?"

"I can get us in. But it's probably not going to be with permission. You okay with that?" There is something challenging in Logan's tone. He steps closer to me, like he's about to kiss me. We had started our relationship by breaking and entering. That had been the house of my murdered employee, Emma. And I'd been so much of a rule-follower at the time that I almost hadn't been able to do it. I've changed a lot since then.

"Get us into what?" a voice asks, breaking through the charged moment.

I poke my head out of the kitchen doorway.

There's Charlie, looking sleepy and rumpled. He says, "I smelled coffee." He follows me back into the kitchen, where I grab a third mug.

"What were you coming into the dining room for, anyway?" Logan asks, moving away from me to pour another pancake. "The hotel isn't open for business."

Charlie gestures out the door, vaguely in the direction of the far wall. I assume he means the piano. He says, "The band is supposed to meet down here this morning for a brief practice before we head over to your shop. Apparently, I'm the first one up this morning, which never happens."

"What are you planning to do for a piano at Felicitations?" I ask.

Charlie takes a deep sip from his coffee. "Flip knows a guy who is letting us borrow one. He should be dropping it off first thing."

"Did I hear my name?" Flip asks, as he walks into the dining room and heads towards us. "Somebody point me towards the coffee."

One by one, the whole band shows up. We wind up feeding them all blueberry pancakes, even though it necessitates making a second batch – and I have to set some aside for Aunt Naomi. While we're cooking, Logan and I continue talking softly.

I tell him, "There are still some clues here that I was hoping you could help me figure out. For instance, that key we found in the bag of marbles. It has to go to something, but we haven't even heard about anything that could be padlocked."

Logan says, "Just because it is a key doesn't necessarily make it important. I turned that bag of marbles over to the cops yesterday, so don't imagine you're going to go trying every lock in town while I'm gone."

"But it's a key," I protest. "What if the necklace we're looking for is locked up somewhere?"

There's the noise of musicians tuning their instruments, while chatting and cracking jokes.

"Then you should call Detective Beckman. That bag of marbles is the kind of evidence that could get someone convicted, and you don't want to be accused of tampering with it."

"But evidence we find in the train car is okay?" I ask.

Logan points with his spatula. "The police have already been over the space. We're looking for a different perspective. And if we find anything, we're not going to touch it. We're going to call Arlo, since it ties in with his case too, and let him report it."

Flip appears in the doorway, coffee cup in hand. "I'm hoping there's seconds?"

I pour him a second cup. I say, "I'm glad you like the roast. I usually do a Kona blend for home-brewed coffee, but I brought home something from a local coffee roaster."

Flip gestures at the bag, which is still sitting on the counter. "Global Seoul. That's a nice place. Boone and I went there right after we left the airport Saturday morning. Boone ordered a flat white, but they gave him somebody else's latte by mistake. The barista gave us a whole handful of candy to make up for it."

"Oh?" I say, trying to sound nonchalant, even though this places Flip more solidly in the suspect pool. "Was it those peach gummy rings?"

"Yeah, how'd you know?"

I shrug and shake my head, not about to tell him about the wrapper I found at the house where Lydia was killed. "Just a guess, I guess."

Logan asks, "Whose latte did you guys get?"

Flip says, "Actually it was Ray, from the real estate office. That man has a serious sweet tooth. I think he had double caramel in his latte. Boone spit it out into a napkin."

Huh. Lydia's ex must have also gotten a handful of candy due to the mix up. And it sounds like he might have been more likely to be snacking on a peach ring while waiting for Lydia to show up to her own murder than Boone or Flip.

Flip says, "I heard Lydia Dunning left something at the coffee shop. When you went, did you get to see what it was?"

Logan stares at Flip, frozen with his spatula halfway to flipping his last pancake. Flip just looks curiously back at Logan.

"Yo, your pancake's burning," Flip says.

Logan turns back to his pan.

I tell Flip, "What we looked through was the lost and found. There's nothing saying that Lydia's the one who lost anything."

Flip doesn't sound contented with this answer. But he still takes his coffee and goes back to the others.

Once we've got the musicians all squared away, and Aunt Naomi has a full plate of pancakes in front of her while she sits and listens to the practice, I go get more presentably dressed, and then Logan and I head out to his car.

As we drive, I look up the real estate firm Lydia Dunning worked with. It's a respectable-looking high-end firm out of New York. Lydia's face has a prominent place on the home page of the website, where they're creating a small memorial for her. In the photo, Lydia looks so sure of herself, so sure that the best in life is ahead of her. I can't imagine how the owners must have taken the news that one of their top performers was writing a tell-all book. On the one hand, a certain type of client would be drawn to that, happy to share a few seconds of someone's fifteen minutes of fame. On the other – being connected with scandal and murder, and being willing to bare all the family secrets, would probably give a lot of clients pause. Especially those who had secrets of their own to hide.

I dial the number for one of the friendlier looking agents, a Maggie Marrow. She answers her phone on the second ring, with a short spiel detailing her real estate services.

I tell her, "I'm not looking for a house. I'm a friend of a friend of Lydia Dunning, and I'm trying to find out who killed her."

Maggie sighs heavily into the phone. "If you're a reporter, just say so. I'm getting really tired of these games. Not that admitting it is going to help you, since my firm's official statement is, 'No comment.'"

"I'm not a reporter," I say, knowing I have no way of making her believe me. Given the circumstance, I'm not sure I'd believe me. "I met Lydia one time, on Saturday, when she came to visit my friend's real estate office. Now the police think my friend might have killed her, and I'm-"

Maggie interrupts me. "You're Tiff Henry's friend?"

"Yes." I don't elaborate. That would make the truth sound even less like I'm telling the truth. "I know this sounds weird, but I was trying to find out if maybe one of her ex-boyfriends had tried to come back into her life."

Maggie's voice drops lower. "Hold on. Let me go outside." There's the noise of movement, then the tinkling of a bell on a door opening. Then Maggie says, "I don't know if it was an ex-boyfriend or not, but somebody was giving her unwanted attention. I think Lydia received a threatening phone call just before driving to Texas. I couldn't hear what the guy was saying, but Lydia looked white as milk when she got off the phone, and she sounded shaky. When I asked what was wrong, she said nothing, just that she needed a change of scenery and a few days away."

So far, the gist of this supports my theory about Ray and his motive to kill Lydia. I'm not sure about his motive for Pete's murder, or Roland's. But maybe I need to dig deeper.

I ask, "Can you think of anything else that might have happened?"

Maggie says, "There was a guy – I'm not sure if it's the same one – who talked to Lydia a couple of times over the last few weeks. I don't think he was a client. It seemed a little clandestine, and she was giddy afterwards. So maybe the ex-showed back up, and it was going well at first – and then it wasn't."

"Maybe," I say, trying not to get stuck on that interpretation. "If she was in trouble, is there someone she would go to for help?"

"Tiff," Maggie says simply. "I know they were estranged, but Lydia was excited about getting to see Tiff again. I'd read about how their friendship ended in the book, and I'd offered her sympathy when so few did, so she really opened up to me about it."

I wonder if Tiff is taking this harder than I realized, too.

Maggie doesn't seem to have any other useful information, so I let her go, with the admonition to call me if she thinks of anything else.

I do a few searches for Ray, to see if I can come up with any more information. Apparently, he's in a band. There are headshots of him, highlighting various local venues his group will be playing. The main picture shows him with a guitar in his hands, head tilted like he's about to laugh. On the band's website, there are a couple of video clips of them playing live. The music is country-esque, but with some nods towards pop. It's not my favorite style, but Ray's band is not bad. I don't see anything that points to a connection between him and Pete, even when I search Ray's name plus *fraud*. Or *theft*. Or *scam*. If it wasn't for his connection to Lydia and that threatening phone call, he would seem totally innocuous.

I share this information with Logan, who says, "I'll admit, it's a lead we should follow."

We get to the train car, and there's still a band of yellow tape across it. Logan manages to get the door open and duck under the tape without touching it. We both have disposable gloves on – mine taken from the supply Logan put in my backpack.

This is a simple space, with a neat twin bed, and a love seat facing a flat screen. There are a few train-themed touches to the décor, including a line of railroad crossing signs on one wall. It's hard to imagine that we might find anything inside here that the CSI guys missed. And at first, I think we're not going to. But then I find the edge of a guitar pick sticking out of the cover at the bottom of the half-sized refrigerator. True to my word, I don't touch it, though I do lean in close to examine it. It has this year's date on it.

I ask Logan, "When you found Pete, was he near here?"

"Yeah," Logan says, coming over to see what I found. We both stare at the pick, trying to puzzle out if there's any other writing on the part shoved into the cover. Being so close but not able to pick it up is incredibly frustrating.

"Flip plays piano," I point out. "But you know who plays guitar? Ray."

Chapter Eighteen
Tuesday

The musicians are having their impromptu concert in the annex, and I find myself bobbing to the beat as I move through the shop, bringing people their coffee orders. It's not something we usually do, but I don't want to interrupt the flow of the concert by calling out names.

Patsy came to the concert – despite the way she's still reeling from her father's death. She is sitting alone at a small table we'd jammed in near the partition into the classroom space. She has an old-fashioned handkerchief in her hand. Her red-rimmed eyes are dry, but her body language is a little stiff, and her shoulders are drawn up towards her ears. I gave her a London fog, but it is sitting on the table in front of her, untouched.

We'll be doing a demo after the music, for everyone willing to stick around. Logan is in the fishbowl, as we refer to the plexiglass assembly line where people can watch us make chocolate. This space is directly behind the band. Logan is setting up for the roasting, but he can't turn on any of the machines yet, without disrupting the concert. Chocolate making is a noisy process, and we only do roasting in the fishbowl when we have the annex opened for announced tours. I still do most of my tests and roasts in the shop's original bean room, where I can feel comfortable at my work.

I set down multiple coffees and slices of rich chocolate cake on the table where Autumn is sitting with her parents, Drake and Drake's mom. The band is doing a rendition of Autumn

Leaves – the song Autumn was named for, possibly played in honor of her. They're surprisingly good, with Flip riffing easily on the piano, setting the tone for the conversation between instruments that good jazz often becomes. Charlie has his eyes closed, grounding the song with his bass, while Starsky is watching the audience from his drum set, showing off when Flip pauses to let him have a little solo moment. Flip bounces in again, then turns to Boone and Randall, as the two horns have a little conversation of their own.

When the song finishes, there's resounding applause from the forty or so people in here. We put as many tables as would fit in the annex, but even more folks are watching from the hallway, or listening from inside the main part of the shop. Carmen had stocked up on baked goods as fast as she could, but with the true crime crowd, and the unexpected concert, we're running low. She'd resorted to serving her test bake for Drake's groom's cake.

Her progress on Autumn's wedding cake has been spectacular, considering everything that has been pulling for her attention. She has the bottom two tiers stacked and frosted. They're lemon cake and classic white cake respectively. And the frosting has a light lavender tint to it – signaling that those are the tiers of the cake that have a lavender flavor, because lavender is one of Autumn's favorites. I've mirrored that same lemon and lavender flavor profile in one of the truffles for her guest bags. The double middle tiers of the cake are a traditional almond wedding cake flavor, so the other truffle is a white chocolate almond, to match that too. I'm glad all of those are already made.

Autumn's mom says, "Thank you for putting this concert together. It's a nice preview for the wedding. I haven't seen these boys play together in years."

I say, "You've seen them play before? I thought Denzel was the one who suggested and booked the act."

Mrs. Ellis nods. "He did. When my son first opened his restaurant, he had a standing jazz night, with a family friend's band. We've known Boone since just about forever. It was a great summer. I went down to stay with Denzel to help him launch the place, and I got to be like a second mom to the whole band – even though some of them are almost the same age I am."

"So what happened?" I ask. "It sounds like they get back together to play – but only sometimes?"

"Life happened," Mrs. Ellis says. "Boone moved back to New Orleans to help with his aging parents, and Charlie got married and moved to New York. Starsky still lives on Corpus – and he checks in on me like I really am his mamma, since his folks are dead. Starsky travels a lot, and Roland is a civil engineer, based in Houston. I don't think music is a main gig for any of them, but they all still love it."

"Obviously," I say, and we both pause, appreciating the bright notes of the alto sax. The band has moved on to "Satin Doll," one of Duke Ellington's classics.

Out of the corner of my eye, I notice Chef Seth sitting at one of the tables near the door. He's with his girlfriend, Ami. I wonder if Logan invited them, or if Miles' attempts to spread word about the concert via social media had gotten them here.

One person I don't expect has shown up: Ray, Lydia's real estate agent ex, who I still think might have killed her. He still has that broody stare going on. Which makes me shudder.

I come back to something Autumn's mom just said. Charlie had moved to New York. That's where Lydia had moved, as well. And then Charlie's wife had died. Could it be possible that Lydia had had something to do with that? I know it's a giant leap of speculation. New York is a big place, and it's statistically unlikely that Charlie and Lydia would have even met. Still, it's something I should at least ask him about.

I gesture at Logan to meet me back at the counter, and he gives me a thumbs up from the other side of the plexiglass. I thread my way through the crowd at the doorway, back into the main part of the shop.

Logan follows me through the doorway.

Once we meet behind the counter, where I start on the next order from the coffee bar, I tell him, "Your friend Seth is here."

"I know," Logan says. "I invited him. Because guess who plays guitar?"

I feel uncomfortable, but I give him the obvious answer. "Seth."

"Got it in one," Logan says. He turns to help the customer who is approaching the counter. She buys several individual truffles to take back to her table in the annex. This concert is going over really well. We should consider doing something like this regularly, since people are spending money without there being a huge crushing rush.

But I thought Logan and Seth were friends. I understand the concept of following the evidence wherever it goes, but it can't be easy for Logan to consider his friend a suspect. So it is a bit shocking that Logan would have invited him here to try and get information.

Still. Could the sushi chef somehow be involved in Pete's death? And if so, why would he have given us the clue that led to finding Pete's body? Logan had theorized that whoever had killed Pete had planned to move him away from the B&B when a convenient opportunity occurred. After all, the only way to make the disappeared-in-Mexico lie remain plausible would have been if Pete's body had never been found.

Still – Seth could have been working with whoever killed Pete and decided to double-cross that person. That's as plausible as anything else I've come up with.

Tracie appears in the hallway. She has been in the classroom space of the annex, setting up for a class she's teaching this afternoon, on basic 3D printing. They're going to be using our chocolate printer to make monogram chocolate plaques.

She threads her way out of the crowd and comes over to us. She says, "We have thirteen students lined up for this afternoon. I see several of them in the concert audience already."

"That's great!" I can't help but add, "Can I ask you something?"

"Fire away," Tracie replies cheerfully.

I'm not sure how to word this. I've come to rely on Tracie a great deal, for projects no one else in the shop has the skillset to complete. I say, "I know you're graduating next year. It probably sounds really early, but I was hoping to find out your plans. What comes next?"

Tracie says, "Don't worry – I'm not planning on going anywhere, not immediately at least. But I do know a couple of sophomore sculpture students who would probably jump at the chance to practice for pay. I know you set up this whole 3D printing service, and half of your chocolate as art classes around projects I've dreamed up. I'm not just going to abandon you – or the customer base I've started building."

I tell her, "I'm not trying to hold you back. You know that, right?"

Tracie says, "I know. Look, I know you're not great with change. So if I do decide to do something else, I'll give you plenty of notice. But I'm really happy here."

She gives me a hug. Which she's never done before. I'm glad I get a chance to feel better about something, at least.

Tracie moves over to get herself a cup of coffee.

Ash comes in. He makes a mock-disappointed face at me as he walks up to the counter. He says, "You found yet another body, and you didn't tell me. You should be setting up another appearance on my podcast – and not even a call. Or even a text."

"That interview was a one-off," I tell Ash. "I got the information I needed out of it, so thanks. But I have an ambivalent relationship with the true crime crowd, at best."

"You should lean into it," Ash says. "I've been getting all kinds of calls and emails after the goat interview. People are really sympathetic to you over that. Not to mention the leads in the comments. There are a lot of people out there who want to help solve Lydia Dunning's murder."

Logan says, "Those kinds of tips rarely lead to reliable information."

Ash pulls up something on his phone. "I know. I've been sifting through a lot of crazy comments. There have been a few people even taking credit for Lydia's death. I've collected all of those, in case they actually match up with what happened at the crime scene. Since the police have withheld the details of how she actually died, there's got to be something unusual, right? But Felicity, since you were actually there . . ." He hands me his phone. I peruse the messages. They're really creepy. Two separate people claim to have stabbed Lydia with a chef's knife – a reasonable guess, given that it was released that she was found in the kitchen. A few don't mention a method of death at all, so there's no way to eliminate them.

But one of the messages is clearly a threat, warning me and Ash to back off. It says, *Lydia's curiosity got the better of her, and look what happened to her. She should have stayed in New York, and you should have minded your own business. It's like the filter in a coffee pot – all that hot water flowing through, minding its own business, while the grounds get pummeled into something only good for plant fertilizer.*

It's a weird metaphor. What kind of person is that focused on both gardening and coffee? Rather coincidentally, the shop's front door opens, and Nathan walks in. And yeah, he's basically the answer to my question. There's those bags of coffee grounds in Nathan's shop – offered to local gardeners. And he knows that I've been investigating Lydia's murder. I'd even implied he might have something to do with it. But if he'd made that threat – why would he be here, at the show, smiling at me?

I mean, he could still be the killer. Lydia wasn't attacked until after she visited Nathan here in Galveston, and after she returned and took one of his Chemex pots. Maybe that symbolized something, or maybe it was just too much for Nathan, since she'd stolen from him before. Maybe the marbles and junk in that pouch weren't even hers, and they were just something random from the lost and found, and Nathan was just trying to see if Tiff knew Lydia was in town.

I really hope it's not him, though. He and Patsy have real potential as a couple. Which would solve one of my biggest dilemmas.

Nathan is still smiling as he approaches the counter. He starts to wait behind Ash, but Ash gestures him to go ahead. Nathan steps forward and asks me, "How is it going with the new coffee?"

"Everybody loves it," Logan says. He reaches into the case and puts a couple of individual truffles on a plate. He hands the plate to Nathan. "Here's a few things for you to try in return."

Nathan takes a bite out of a plain truffle, made with my Peruvian chocolate. He says, "This is delicious. I tried some of the bars when I first came into town, but this my first time trying one of your truffles."

I smile at the compliment, despite my misgivings. Hoping to ease my mind about him as a suspect, I ask Nathan, "Do you happen to play guitar?"

He looks embarrassed. "Not well. How did you even know that?"

Dang it. I say, "Just a guess." I had been hoping he would say no. Now I have to figure out where to go from there, since I can't very well ask him if he left a pick at a crime scene. Maybe I can try a bluff. I say, "We know you're hiding something about what happened between you and Lydia. Why wouldn't you want her to come here from New York?"

Now Nathan looks startled. He holds out his free hand and says, "It's not like that."

"Then why don't you tell us how it is," Logan prompts.

Nathan puts his plate down on the counter and wipes his hands on his jeans. "Okay. I did have more of a falling-out with Lydia than I admitted. We became friends, and I thought I could trust her. So I told her about this girl I had a crush on at work. Lydia went to see who I was talking about, and while she was there, she stole something personal to the girl from the coffee shop. It looked like I did it, and I got fired. So I had washed out of business school, because my mom was sick and I was too distracted to study. My current boss obviously wasn't going to give me a reference. I hadn't talked to Lydia in a couple of months, and I was at the point of selling my TV and game consoles to make rent, when out of the blue Lydia showed up with a check and information on a space for lease in Texas, of all places. I didn't ask where she got the money, or exactly why she was fronting me the cash to start my own place. I just assumed she felt guilty about tanking my life, and I took the opportunity to start over."

Logan says, "So maybe when Lydia showed up, it felt like she was checking on her investment. Maybe you were afraid she was going to ask for the money back."

Ash adds, "Maybe she did."

Nathan's mouth drops open. He says, "Are you suggesting I killed her? Seriously, no. She just wanted to do a book signing."

"Right," Ash says skeptically.

Nathan gives him a pleading look. "Don't say anything about this on your podcast, please. I didn't hurt Lydia, but I'll never get my reputation back if people think I did."

"I won't," Ash says. "Trust me." He's learned his lesson about unfounded accusations the hard way.

Nathan still doesn't look happy, but he walks towards the crowd, ready to shift gears and watch the concert. Just then, the band stops playing, and Flip announces a break. I see Nathan's shoulders slump. He's got horrible timing, all around.

Most of the band appears in the hall, Flip and Boone heading towards the bathroom. Charlie makes his way over to the counter and asks for a bottle of water. Logan goes to the fridge in the kitchen and gets enough bottles for each of the band members to have one.

I try to sound casual when I ask Charlie, "Did you ever meet Lydia Dunning? I understand she was a fellow New Yorker."

Charlie looks skeptically at me. "Does it seem like we would have moved in the same circles?"

I shrug, awkwardly. "It's possible. Maybe she was into music."

He laughs. "She was more after her big moment of fame. Even if it exploited the victims of her brother's brutal crimes. A lot of people just wanted to forget Cal Dunning – but her book wouldn't let them. I know how that feels. There was a lot of media attention when my wife disappeared."

I say, "I thought your wife was dead."

Charlie looks warily at me. He asks, "Who told you that?"

I feel confused and embarrassed heat coming into my chest and arms. I try to remember our earlier conversation. Had he actually used the word dead? I stammer, "I just inferred that from what you said. I offered my condolences."

Charlie says, "She's not officially dead. Just missing. But it's been three weeks. I know in my heart – she's not coming back."

Ash asks, "You left New York to come here, even though your wife is missing? What if there's new information?"

Charlie closes his eyes and rubs his fingers across the lids, towards his nose. When he opens his eyes again, he says, "If there hasn't been a ransom demand by now, there won't be. And any other information – I have a cell phone. Honestly, I needed the distraction of coming down here. Staying in a hotel full of people instead of in a big house all by myself."

"I get that," I say. I feel bad that we've touched on such painful territory. Especially since he's got to go back into the annex and play another set. I tell him, "If there's anything we can do to help, let us know."

He says, "Thank you. You've been very kind already. I guess I should have known better than to come here, if I wanted to get away from all thoughts of violence, considering your reputation as a mega murder magnet." He turns to Ash and says, "Right, Ash?"

Is he a fan of Ash's? After all, Ash is the one who called me a mega murder magnet, in his blog, after I kept stumbling over dead bodies at an improbable rate.

Logan asks gently, "I'm sorry if this is a painful question, but what exactly did happen to your wife? How did she go missing?"

Charlie grimaces. "There was a robbery. It was the second one in as many months. The first, time the thieves took an expensive musical instrument right out of its display case on the wall. The second time, they took Misty, along with all the money out of the safe. There was security video of the abduction, some guy carrying her out of the house. Which is why I thought there'd be a ransom." Emotion clouds his voice and he breaks off abruptly. He picks up the bottles of water to take to his bandmates. We watch him make his way back through the crowd, into the annex.

"Is he a suspect?" Ash asks.

Logan says, "I'm not sure his hatred for tell-all journalism burns deep enough for him to commit murder."

Ash quips, "If it was, I'd certainly be in trouble. But he seems to like my blog."

"That's the truth." I grab a bottle of water for myself and crack it open. When I come back, I tell Logan and Ash, "Ray, Nathan, and Flip all have a motive for Lydia's murder. And maybe even Agnes. But none of them seem connected to this missing necklace, so what about Pete's murder? Or Roland's? I still can't figure out how this all fits together."

"But it has to," Ash says. "Somehow."

Logan says, "It doesn't always. Sometimes cases just don't get solved. Like the one with Charlie's wife."

The band starts playing again. It's loud and somehow matches the cacophony of emotions inside me at the thought of Lydia's murder going unsolved.

Ash has to speak louder when he says, "You said I could see this copy of *the Thin Man*."

I had said that. "It's in my office. Not that there's anything special about it. Believe me, I've examined it closely. Come have a look."

Ash turns and walks towards the hall. I follow him. He says, "I wonder where Lydia got such a rare edition. That could be the important part about the book."

The door to my office is ajar, and the light is on. Only – it shouldn't be. I haven't been in there all day. I hesitate, but Ash doesn't. He opens the door, but he's glancing back at me to see why I've stopped. Gloved hands come around his shoulders and pull him into the room. Ash lets out a very girly squeak.

"Tell me where the pendant is," the guy holding Ash says. "Quietly. And this guy gets to live."

Ash lets out another squeak. Then he says, "Ouch. You don't have to poke me in the ribs."

I can't see the guy's face through Ash, but he sounds serious. He seems to be holding a weapon. And, of course, he wants the one thing we haven't been able to find.

I force myself to step into the office, which is a tiny space, with barely room for a guest chair and a bricked-over window that means no natural light. I get a little claustrophobic being in here on a normal day, so this takes all my resolve.

"I wish I could help you," I say. "I really do. But Ash didn't do anything. And if you hurt him, there's no way out of here once I start screaming my head off, not with all those people here for the concert. Or you could let Ash go, and we can talk."

The guy turns Ash around and pushes him into my office chair. "Stay there. Cause any trouble, and your girlfriend might not get a chance to scream."

Ash says, "Okay. I'm here."

I ask, "Why does everybody keep assuming we're a couple?"

Ash says, "You have to admit we look cute together."

Now that I can see the guy's face, I recognize him. It's the same guy from the jewelry store sketch. Creed Macintosh. He holds up the copy of *The Thin Man* and asks, "Where did you get this?"

I say, "Lydia gave it to me." Technically, she left it on Tiff's desk, but close enough. "Why?"

"Because this is the same copy I stole from a collector in Sweden. You can tell from the blue dot on the page edges. I took it for a client in New York."

Ash asks, "The same client that asked you to take the pendant?"

Creed gives him a withering look, and Ash shrinks back in his chair.

"Actually, no," Creed says as he places the book back on my desk.

Interesting. The person who hired him to get the book is not the same person who hired him to get the pendant. That means that Lydia likely took the book from someone other than her killer. Maybe it reminded her whatever she wanted to talk to Tiff about. Or maybe it was random, something she stole from somebody's house at a dinner party.

Creed adds, "That guy moved back to Sweden. I would have assumed he had taken his purloined library with him. But maybe there wasn't room, after he sold his house."

Is it possible that Lydia had been stealing things from the houses she's listing? Obviously, she stole the wrong thing – but from whom? If I had a list of her recent clients, maybe I could figure that out. But first, I have to get us all out of here with nobody getting shot.

My desk drawers are open, along with one drawer of the filing cabinet. But nothing looks out of place. If we hadn't happened to walk in here, I probably never would have known that Creed had been looking through my things. I ask, "Why come here when we're open? It's like you're trying to get caught."

Creed shrugs. "I was told to come during the concert, and to leave evidence that I had been here. It's weird, but I don't ask questions. I assume my employer needed a time frame to set up an alibi for the theft."

"What about the jewelry store?" I ask. "You came during open hours then, too."

"Same thing. I was supposed to trip an alarm on my way out of the back door, establishing a time for the crime. I wasn't supposed to be seen until I had the pendant and was ready to leave. Only, the safe wasn't the one I had been prepared for, and that employee came into the back room to make a phone call when she should have been watching the store. So things went sideways, and I wasn't even wearing a mask. I don't like feeling that sloppy. But I also don't like killing witnesses – unless I have to."

Clearly, that's meant to be a threat. And I have no doubt Creed has earned his violent reputation. I say, "It sounds like you were being used."

He shrugs, like he knows it and doesn't much care. "Smoke and mirrors, Koerber. That's what all of this is. Alibis and lies, and lies to create alibis."

"I think you've been reading too much poetry."

A grin takes over Creed's face. "I do write a bit of poetry. It's been in some magazines. I even made the New Yorker, once."

I tilt my head, genuinely curious. "Is it supposed to make me feel better, being threatened by a man of culture?"

"I'm not threatening you," he says. "Just let me walk out of here with the item I came for, and I'll tell you what I know about the person who hired me. It's not a lot, mind you, but it might be enough to help."

"You don't know who hired you?" I ask.

"Not entirely. I only deal in anonymous transactions, done over the internet. It's the safest way to conduct business in the modern era." He seems distracted for a moment, and I consider grabbing for the gun. But then he looks directly at me and says, "That line about alibis I said just now. I think I can start a poem with it. You don't mind, do you?"

"That's all you," I say.

"Good. Now, I have to have the pendant. Agnes didn't have it. Tiff didn't have it."

I suck in a breath as I realize he must have been at Tiff's place.

He looks at me curiously. "What?"

And it hits me. I've suspected that the necklace the jeweler had been commissioned to recreate and the necklace Lydia stole might have been the same design. Here's a chance to prove it. I ask, "Were you hired to steal the original pendant? Or the copy?"

"Both," he says. "But at this point, I will settle for one. Better that it's the original, yeah?" I don't say anything, so after a second he continues. "I have never not completed a job, so even though this one has gone a bit bonkers, I'm going to fix this. If you're hoping to convince me you don't have either pendant, you're going to have to try a bit harder."

"Okay," I say, taking a step closer to him. I've got to figure out a way out of this without getting Ash hurt. Creed has lowered his gun as he's been talking. And I don't think he sees me as a threat. "I just need my inhaler. Being in this space is making me feel claustrophobic."

Only, instead of my inhaler, I pull the pepper spray out of my pocket, and I spray Creed in the face. While he's flailing his hands, trying to figure out what to do, Ash knocks the gun out of his grasp, and it skitters under the desk.

Creed runs out of the room, this threatening man suddenly turned weak with pain and embarrassment. I feel bad for him – at the same time relief surges through me that I'm not about to get shot. I let out a hysterical laugh.

Nathan is in the hall, presumably heading towards the bathroom.

"Stop that guy!" I shout. But Nathan lets Creed get by him, while somehow bumping into Ash as Ash attempts to give chase, suddenly more courageous now that Creed is unarmed.

Creed makes it out the front door, pivoting onto the sidewalk, moving with confidence despite the residual effects of having been sprayed. I very much doubt we will see him again.

But what just happened with Nathan felt very suspicious. It was almost like he wanted the thief to get away. Did Nathan let him go on purpose? Was Nathan the one establishing an alibi? If so, it would be a bold way of doing it, trying to stop the thief, in order to prove you weren't a killer. Especially since the thief in question didn't know the identity of the person who had hired him.

Chapter Nineteen
Tuesday

As soon as the chocolate demo is done, Logan heads out, and I rush back into my office, Ash following at my heels. There was a thief in there. I know that Creed had no motivation to take anything he wasn't hired to – but there's one thing of value that I need to check on, before the police get here and kick me out of my own space. I should have looked immediately after we kicked Creed out, and secured the gun, but there had been damage control to do, and then everyone wanting to buy things after the concert wrapped – while we were one person short after Logan left for his flight. So I just now thought about it, in a moment of panic.

"What's wrong?" Ash asks.

There's one drawer on my desk that I usually keep locked. Currently, it is pulled half open. I open it the rest of the way. There, at the back is Kevin's old diving watch – right where it has been since the police returned it to me, after it had been evidence in a murder investigation. Next to it, there is a small box. I take out the box and open it. Inside, there is a simple silver band. I tell Ash, "This is Kevin's wedding ring. After he died, I wore it around my neck for a while, then I kept it in my nightstand. I wanted to still feel close to him, you know? But this place was something I originally opened in memory of him. So it felt like the ring belonged here."

Ash asks, "Are you worried about that ring right now, because you plan to give it to one of your love interests some day? Since it's got so much emotional attachment?"

I'm sure I look horrified when I say, "Are you crazy? I could never give Kevin's ring to anybody else."

Ash studies the box, curiously. He says, "I tend to forget you had a whole other life before you came back to Galveston."

I close the box. "Is it sad that I can have this box in my hand without tearing up? Like I've lost touch with that other life completely. I hardly even talk to Kevin's family anymore. It's like they're still stuck in one level of grief, while I'm not anymore."

"It's understandable," Ash says. He steps closer and awkwardly pats my shoulder. "None of them have a Logan."

I put the box back in the desk. "What do you mean by that?"

Ash says, "You've been through a lot, but who has been there every step of the way helping you work your way through it? Not caring if you didn't appreciate him? Backing off when you got scared, but never giving up on you? Admit it, most guys would have left by now. But not Logan."

I study Ash's face. "Forget the polls on your blog, or all that stuff you keep spouting about journalistic impartiality. I thought you were supporting my decisions moving towards Arlo. But secretly, you're team Logan, aren't you?"

Ash says, "I've studied your relationships, for the podcast. Of course I have an opinion. But my opinion doesn't matter, especially since they're both good guys. The big question is what do *you* want."

I say, "No, I figured it out yesterday. The questions isn't what I want, which could easily change. It's what do I need."

Ash says, "Okay. Let's make a list. That's what I do when I feel stuck."

He takes a piece of paper and a pen out of an open drawer of my desk. Apparently, we're both past trying not to disturb the crime scene.

He writes on the paper.
What Felicity really needs:
Someone who listens to her and supports her goals.
Someone who challenges her.
Someone who would take a bullet for her.
Then Ash asks, "Am I leaving anything out?"

I gesture at the paper. "You're phrasing all of those things in a way that would make me think of Logan. Sure, he's tackled a gun-wielding killer in the past, just to save my life. But I'm sure, given the circumstance, that Arlo would do the same thing."

"He probably would," Ash says. "I'm not saying that Arlo is not a protector. Just that he needs order in his life, and to feel like the people he cares about are safe. He might not say it, but he really needs a girl he wouldn't have to take a bullet for."

"What do you know?" I ask. "Shouldn't I be talking about this with Autumn and Tiff and the twins?"

Ash quirks his lips ironically. "Haven't you been talking to them? I know how girl talk goes. I've done enough eavesdropping over the years. You get caught up talking about feelings, and the fact that Arlo unquestionably has the better abs, while Logan's face is more ruggedly handsome. Now, you need to be honest with yourself."

I say, "Honestly, it's going to be hard to stop kissing either one of them, when one of them is off limits. So yeah, feelings factors into a lot of things."

"TMI, Koerber," Ash says, making a face. "TMI."

He hands me the list. I fold it up and put it in my pocket. I say, "I still think everything on this list could apply to either of them."

Ash says, "I still can't believe you pepper sprayed that guy. He had a gun."

I walk myself back through the moment. Part of me can't believe I did that either. I had been threatened by a cold-blooded killer with a gun before, right here in this room. He'd tried to make me write a suicide note. I'd been so terrified, so sure I was going to die. That feeling of absolute helplessness has been haunting me ever since, which is why I rarely do work in my office. There aren't any easy exits, so it makes me feel trapped.

But now – it feels like something has come full circle. I was still scared. I still could have died. But my confidence levels have changed, something I owe to everything I've been through recently, which has repeatedly pushed me out of my comfort zone.

And I'd gotten a clue out of the whole ordeal. I text Lydia's former coworker to ask for a list of clients from whose houses Lydia might have taken something. I get a message back. Maggie says, *I would love to help, but that information is confidential.* Then there's that series of dots that says Maggie is typing something else. They keep appearing and then disappearing, showing she's repeatedly typing and deleting what she's thinking of saying. Finally, a second message comes through. *Unofficially, if someone was caught stealing from houses that had been listed and lock-boxed, they might well have been reprimanded. Especially if several clients were to hypothetically report this to the police.*

Okay. So, Maggie is telling me that Lydia was close to losing her job, and possibly her real estate license. I thank Maggie for her hypothetical help.

I'm sure that Lydia's firm has probably turned the list of her recent clients over to the police. Only, the police aren't going to share that information with me. I can picture Detective Beckman laughing me out of her office. And Logan isn't here to ask his contacts to pull the info on my behalf.

It's going to be a lot harder investigating on my own. But that just means I'm going to have to think even farther outside of the box.

I've been telling myself that I want to be with Arlo, because I want life to go back to normal, so I can stop getting involved with these puzzles. But I suddenly realize that if that does happen, just how much I'm going to miss this. Not for Logan – but for me.

I hear Arlo's voice in the main part of the shop. I leave the office to meet him. When he catches sight of me, he wraps me in a huge hug and kisses me, in front of everybody. It's a nice kiss. When we break apart, he says, "When I heard what happened, I was so worried. I wasn't here to keep you safe."

His words echo almost exactly what Ash had said. I shake the thought away. Being kept safe is good. It's what I need, if I'm going to have a normal, functional life. I'm just letting Ash get into my head.

Arlo and I are still standing there in the hall, with Ash in the doorway of my office, acting like he didn't see me smooching Arlo, when Nathan and Patsy step into the hallway, lost in their own bantery conversation. Apparently, Patsy is trying to take steps in moving on. Good for her.

"Oh, hey," Nathan says.

I start to ask Nathan if he knows anything about Lydia's real estate clients – but then I catch the look bouncing between Arlo and Patsy. Patsy looks anxious and a little embarrassed. But Arlo – he looks jealous.

Which makes me feel jealous. And that's a feeling I don't like. But it does prove that my feelings for Arlo still run deep. I want to be with him, to the point where it physically hurts somewhere in my midsection to think of him with someone else.

I take a deep breath, try to force some of the tension out of my hands and shoulders. It's reasonable that it would be hard for Arlo to see his ex moving on, so I cut him some slack for it, especially when he puts his arm around me. He says, "Nathan, you need to stick around until Detective Beckman gets here. We need your statement about your encounter with Creed. Please."

"Sure thing," Nathan says. He heads for a table to wait.

Patsy says, "I should go." She strides quickly towards the door.

Autumn comes out of the annex and hurries over to me. "Lis, look at this."

I turn, and Autumn thrusts out her tablet to show me a picture of her and Drake, posed on a piece of driftwood at the beach. Autumn is wearing her wedding dress – she really isn't superstitious, so it's no surprise that Drake has seen it – and Drake has his tuxedo, minus the jacket. Instead his sleeves are rolled up, giving him a vaguely stuck-on-a-desert-island look. His bow tie is still smartly arranged. The photo is actually very sweet.

"That's awesome," I say. "I know the photographer said she wasn't sure if she was going to get the editing done in time. But look at her pulling through. Now we just need to get that to the printer."

Autumn says, "Look at this bird. It's in every shot."

She zooms in on a sandpiper, which appears to be looking quizzically at the camera.

"It's cute," I say. "People will find it charming."

"But it isn't what I wanted," Autumn says. "I wanted one thing to be perfect. One thing I could control. Look at this." She scrolls through the pictures, stopping at an image taken just off the strand, not far from my shop. She and Drake are standing in front of the Cornet sculpture, a giant white concrete instrument that was originally a stage prop for the New Orleans World Fair, and then transported to Galveston in the 1980s. And there, on the sidewalk at Autumn's feet is Photobombing Bird. Which is odd, because sandpipers don't often venture into paved areas. Autumn says, "I don't know whether to be charmed or creeped out. It must have followed us as we walked. Drake was feeding the birds earlier, on the beach, but there's no reason one would be that determined. Maybe I should try to get the photographer to re-do the whole thing."

"There's no time for that," I tell her. "Maybe we can just get Miles to just Photoshop it out."

"But I'll still know it's there," Autumn says. And from her bleak tone, I can see just how much everything that has been going wrong is getting to her. It's probably not even the same bird.

I give her a big hug. "Everything is going to be fine for your big day. I promise."

Though I don't know if that is a wise promise to make, considering I didn't even show up for half of her tea party. I release the hug, and Autumn looks more in control of herself.

"I am the bride," Autumn says. "I can choose not to get overwhelmed."

I hear the door open. Patsy already left, and Arlo is in my office, surveying the tiny crime scene, so it is probably a customer entering.

"Felicity Koerber?" A voice asks.

"That's me," I say, turning to face the girl who is striding towards me.

She is holding a 32-ounce souvenir cup from a local barbecue place. Her dark hair is in braids that trail down her shoulders, and her thick lips are in a resolute line. Once she gets close to me, she says, "Cal Dunning was innocent. I used to like the podcast about you, but now you're trying to solve the murder of his cheese stick of a sister? She's the one who was making up lies."

The girl pulls the lid off of the cup, and there's something dark and thick inside. She starts to hurl the goop at me, but her aim is wide and I can see it's going to hit Autumn. I push Autumn out of the way, taking the brunt of the attack on myself. Autumn has already been through enough. She doesn't deserve the indignity of being hit with a wad of liquid garbage. It's not as high-stakes as the scene in *The Thin Man* where Nick knocks out Nora to keep her from getting shot, and takes the bullet himself. But there's something about the choreography of what is happening that reminds me of it.

Only – the substance covering my clothes doesn't smell like garbage. Or barbecue sauce. Instead, it smells very familiar, like my workspace every day. I ask, "Did you just throw chocolate at me?"

"Ironic, right?" The girl snaps. "Look, Cal and I were going out when he got arrested. I was working to get him released

– right up until the day he died. In prison. And now Lydia gets to write a book about it."

"You do realize she's dead," I say, shocked that this girl could talk so callously about another human being's murder. "She was a real person, and she was in pain."

"She was a writer," the girl snaps. "That's not the same as being a real person at all."

I blink in confusion. Autumn makes an anguished noise and runs into the annex. I want to follow her, to comfort her, but I have to deal with this unbalanced person first.

"What's her problem?" the girl asks.

"She's a writer," I say. "And she was already having a horrible day, so thanks for that."

Arlo comes out of my office, looking very official, letting his jacket drape open to reveal his badge. When the girl realizes there's a cop there, her mouth gapes open, then she turns to run. Only, Arlo bars her way to the door.

I go after Autumn. She's sitting at a table, just staring at the empty stage, where the piano still sits.

"You okay?" I ask.

"This was my favorite shirt," she says. There's splatters of chocolate across one side of it, and also on her face.

"I can take care of that. I've gotten pretty good at getting chocolate out of clothes. Not this much chocolate, of course." I gesture down at myself. I'm covered in chocolate, from the chest down. "But that doesn't look too bad."

Autumn says, "I'd forgotten how people view writers sometimes. They can say the most hateful things – but if they call it a review, or if they say the person deserved it for putting their thoughts out for open consumption and criticism, they can feel it is justified."

"I hadn't realized that happened to you," I say.

Autumn waves a dismissive hand. "It happens to everybody. Even if you write the most innocuous stuff, there are going to be trolls and haters. Usually, it doesn't get to me. After all, most of those people wouldn't put in the time or energy to create something positive themselves. But Lydia Dunning was killed. And to know there are people out there applauding her death – it's enough to make you want to stop creating."

"Don't do that," I say. "You have too many fans applauding your comeback." I take a napkin and wipe off her face. "Let me get the laundry wipes real quick. They're in my backpack."

I may not have Logan with me today – but at least I have his supplies, and he seems to have thought of almost everything.

Ignoring the awkward scene of Arlo questioning the hater girl, I go into the kitchen and wash my own hands and face. I blot off as much chocolate as I can, then I pull the backpack out from under the counter. I plop it onto the countertop. I have just about had it with this day.

I unzip the pocket of the backpack that has the stain wipes. Only – there's something in there that wasn't there before. It's a chocolate bar. The wrapper is pink, and it *says Limited Edition Bar – Strawberry Dreams made with 65% Single-Origin beans from Macoris, Dominican Republic*. Logan has signed the back, *With much love, Logan*.

I can't believe what I'm holding in my hands. The other day, when we were working on the Jamaican chocolate, and Logan had said he wanted his first bar to be from beans he chose himself – he'd already chosen them. When had he had time to fly to the D.R.? I've never made a bar from there, so he must have come up with the contacts himself. And he had to have used the roaster in the middle of the night, or I would have known about it.

Careful not to tear the wrapping, I open the bar. The front has artistically arranged flakes of gold leaf molded into the squares at irregular intervals. And the back has a dusting of freeze-dried strawberry powder. It's gorgeous to look at. I break off a piece and take a bite. It's a sweet dark chocolate, creamier than most because of the lower cacao content. There are flavors of berries in the beans themselves, which are accented by the strawberry dust, along with a tannic element that is somehow reminiscent of champagne.

I feel tears coming to my eyes, because this bar is so perfectly me. It must be how Logan sees me. And he's not even here for me to tell him how spectacular this gift is.

Tiff, Autumn, and I are back at the real estate office. It's after hours, so we have the place to ourselves.

I ask Tiff, "How are you holding up? I know it was complicated, but Lydia was still your friend."

Tiff says, "I'm sadder than I thought I would be. But knowing everything I know now – holding a grudge over a boyfriend seems a bit petty. If Eli had been willing to go with her, then he wasn't really in love with me. In the long run, she probably did me a favor. Because otherwise, I wouldn't have met Ken."

Autumn says, "That's a philosophical way to look at it."

Tiff says, "I just wish I could have gotten to that point while she was still alive. Obviously, she needed a friend. And I didn't even make time for her, the day before she died, even after she said she needed my help. I'll never know what she wanted to tell me. And I have to live with that."

I ask, "Did you figure why she was here?"

Tiff says, "She really was working on a land deal on Mustang Island. She was representing an investment group called Molten Entertainment. They want to build a theme park. Something called the Candy Craze Safari Party."

I ask, "Why on Earth would they put something like that on a barrier island?"

Tiff gives me an *I know, right?* look. She says, "Apparently, Lydia talked them into it. She pointed out the success of Moody Gardens, here on Galveston, and presented the right property at the right price."

Autumn says, "She must have not pointed out all the restoration Moody Gardens needed after Hurricane Ike."

Tiff says, "I would have led with that. I always want my clients to be happy in the long term. But Lydia – who knows? Maybe she did, and they were willing to take the risk. After all, we all live here, despite the finicky weather."

"True," I admit. "But that doesn't help us figure out who killed her."

I think about that exhibit Lydia had been examining at the library. There had been something about weather models. Presumably, the information could relate to land values. Had Lydia determined that the seller might be hiding something?

Autumn says, "Lydia sounds really impulsive. She made somebody unhappy enough that they sent a dangerous thief to retrieve what she stole."

"I'm still in shock about my little encounter with Creed," I admit.

Tiff says, "I'm still creeped out, too. Creed was at my house – and probably here too."

Autumn gestures at Tiff's filing cabinet, which she had been sifting through. "Then what are we doing here? If a professional thief couldn't find where Lydia hid something, what hope do we have?"

"Probably none," Tiff admits. "But I need to be doing something. What if I had run into Creed? What if Ken had?"

She holds up a flower pot, looking for any sign Lydia might have hidden something in the dirt. Lydia might have been good at sleight of hand, but she had never even been on that side of the room.

"What exactly are we looking for?" Autumn asks. She had decided to come with us because, as she had said, she didn't want to be alone. Which was an odd way of putting it, with all her family in town, and her fiancé home babysitting a goat. But, after that verbal attack on her as a writer, I get what she meant.

I describe the pendant, and then add, "Lydia might have left something else. Some clue as to what this was all about. That necklace didn't have any precious gems. It certainly wasn't worth killing over."

Autumn says, "I wish I could see a picture of it. Maybe it's something historic."

Autumn sells vintage jewelry on Etsy, so she might be able to see something in the piece that I hadn't. I can't believe I didn't think to ask her about it sooner.

"I took a picture of a picture," I tell her, reaching to pull the image up on my phone.

Autumn takes my phone and studies the image. "It's a nice piece, but you're right. Assuming it's not a reproduction – which would be worth even less – I'd say the value would be maybe five or six thousand dollars."

Autumn duplicates the picture and crops it down to just the pendant. Then she uses the image to do a Google search – which rewards her with similar images. I didn't even know Google could do that.

Some of the images are of necklaces that aren't even close to the one we're looking for. But when I finally spot one that is identical – Lydia is wearing it. I click on the thumbnail to get the related website, and it takes me to a feature about Lydia's book. She's wearing the necklace at a book event, holding a glass of wine while standing near a blown-up poster of her book cover.

How did she wind up with that pendant? Is this picture how her killer knew she had taken the necklace? Is she somehow taunting the killer by wearing it? I study the people in the background of the photo. It's hard to tell for sure, but that could be Cal's obsessive girlfriend, in profile at the very edge of the photo. She seems to be talking to someone I can identify clearly. Ray Casey. What was Ray doing at Lydia's book event? Had he been stalking her? And if he had met Cal's girlfriend, still pining over her beloved's death – could they have decided to work together to rid the world of the one person who had been causing both of them pain?

It would make some sense, considering this book event took place near where Lydia grew up. Which means that if the girl dated Cal in Ohio, before he went to prison, she might well still live there. If that's true, she probably traveled across multiple states just to throw chocolate at me. It would make more sense if she was already in town for some other purpose – like killing Lydia, perhaps.

But that still doesn't explain the import of the necklace itself.

I try calling Hailey, the insurance investigator in charge of the jewelry store robbery. I have so many questions, and it seems like she would have at least a few of the answers. Only, I get her *out of office* message again. I'm beginning to worry that if this killer has already dispatched one insurance investigator, they might not have compunctions about hurting another. But if something had happened to Hailey, surely someone would have reported her missing by now. But there's been nothing in the news.

I go back to the Google search of the necklace, scrolling through the images, looking for any others starring Lydia, maybe even another one showing Ray in the background.

Instead, I find one with Lydia in the background. It's a gala for some investment firm, at least a month before Lydia's book party. I don't recognize the woman in the foreground, the one who's wearing the necklace. She's laughing, holding a glass of champagne in her hand, her pose not that different than Lydia's in the later image. She has curly brown hair, pink cheeks, and a button nose, and she's in her mid-forties, with wrinkles just beginning to blur her good looks.

I click on the picture and read the related article. The woman is Adriana Shelton, wife of Preston Shelton, of Shelton Investments, LLC. Adriana apparently helped organize the gala, as part of her many aspects of volunteer work.

I do a search about the Sheltons. Preston Shelton seems a bit camera shy. What pictures there are of him have been taken from a distance, or with his face half-obscured. His wife appears to be the face of the company. Or more accurately – appeared. According to several of the article titles, Adriana Shelton has disappeared.

I skim through one of the articles. There was a home invasion, and a kidnapping. No ransom demand ever made. It sounds eerily similar to what happened to Charlie's wife, Misty. For a second, I wonder if we're talking about the same case. But Charlie is short for Charles, not Preston. So more likely, we're looking at a pattern, a kidnapper executing multiple crimes with the same M.O.

Lydia had seen Adriana shortly before she disappeared – as had Ray. And when Lydia had come into the real estate office that day, she hadn't even acknowledged Ray's existence. Why?

What if Ray knew she had some connection to the home invasions? He is obviously comfortable with travel. Maybe he's been kidnapping women on his day off. Could that pendant everyone seems to be looking for have been one of the pieces that had been stolen in the Shelton home invasion? Could Lydia have been flaunting that she knew what Ray is up to?

"What did you just figure out?" Autumn asks.

"How do you know I figured something out?" I ask.

Autumn says, "You just did that little thing where you lick your teeth. You do that when you make a leap in reasoning."

"I do?" I am utterly confused.

"You have, ever since we were kids. Apparently, you just don't notice." She gestures at the phone. "So what is it?"

"I think Ray might have killed Lydia," I say, still thinking about my teeth. "But I have no idea how to make sure I'm right."

I glance over at Ray's desk. Surely he wouldn't keep anything incriminating at work. But it never hurts to have a quick look.

Tiff asks, "What are you doing?" when she sees me move over to Ray's desk.

"Seeing if he's a kidnapper," I say.

Ray is definitely into country music. He has several coffee mugs from Nashville on his desk, all recently used but empty. He also has a magnet collection on his filing cabinet, with magnets from all over the country – including one of that sculpture from Rockefeller Center in New York.

I open the drawer at the center of his desk. There's a stack of manilla folders. I take them out and start looking through them. They're contracts, mostly for houses here in Galveston, though there are two in parts of Houston. And then, on the bottom of the stack, is one for a piece of land on Mustang Island.

I wave Tiff over and ask her, "What am I looking at here?"

Tiff flips through the pages of the contract, then she says, "This is the contract for the amusement park site. See – the buyer is listed as Molten Entertainment. Ray was representing the seller. One Seth Harper."

My first thought it to wonder if this is the same Seth as Chef Seth, from the Japanese restaurant, who Logan obviously thinks is a potential suspect in all of this.

My second is to consider how Lydia and Ray had wound up representing the two sides in the same agreement. Could they still have some kind of relationship? Or had it been a total coincidence? I reevaluate the picture of Ray at Lydia's book event. Could Lydia and Ray have been in on the home invasions together? And maybe she had been flaunting it by wearing the necklace? I don't like to think of Lydia as a bad guy in all of this – but it is possible.

I take the contract, trying to make sense of what I'm looking at. The signature areas are still blank. I ask Tiff, "So what happens to the commissions, since Lydia died before all this got completed?"

Tiff says, "The buyer could seek representation from somebody else at Lydia's firm. Or since everything has been hammered out, Ray could wind up with both the buyer's and the seller's commission.

"What exactly are you doing with my desk?" a deep voice asks.

I look up, and there's Ray. I'd been so absorbed in my theorizing that I hadn't noticed him come in the front door. My first instinct is to hide the contract.

But at this point, I might as well confront him. I show him the open folder. "Do you care to explain your connection to Lydia Dunning? I was under the impression that you had broken up years ago."

"We did, but once her book came out, I realized I had misinterpreted a few things. I reached out to reconnect," Ray says, moving over to take the folder. When he does, the papers get jostled and the contract falls to the floor. The paperclip comes off, and I wind up helping Ray pick up the pages.

That's when I notice a signature on one of the preliminary documents. Preston Shelton has signed off on the request to have the land surveyed. Huh. Preston must represent Molten Entertainment. Maybe it's a subsidiary of his own company. I show the page to Ray. "Have you ever met this guy?"

"Nah, he always worked through Lydia. He isn't even scheduled to show up for the closing."

That tracks, considering Preston's reclusive nature.

Tiff asks, "What are you even doing here?"

Ray says, "I forgot my phone." He pushes his way around me to retrieve it from a drawer. Too bad – I hadn't gotten to take a look at it.

Tiff says, "I don't mean right now. I mean, what are you doing living in Galveston? It's a huge coincidence that you moved here what – six months ago? To the same town – the same agency – that your ex's old friend moved to. It's a huge coincidence, don't you think?"

Ray's cheeks go crimson. He says, "That wasn't a coincidence. I was trying to figure out how to get back in touch with Lydia. I thought you might still be in touch with her."

Tiff looks horrified. "And so you *moved* here? That's a stalker-y move, don't you think?"

Ray says, "I'm harmless, I promise."

"Tell Lydia that," Tiff says.

Ray blinks, then his eyes widen as he realizes what she's saying. "I did not kill her."

I tap the paper in my hand, over Preston's name. I say, "And I suppose you had nothing to do with the disappearance of Preston Shelton's wife, either."

"What are you talking about?" Ray asks. His confusion looks genuine. "Like I said, I never met Preston. Or his wife."

"And Lydia?" I ask. "Where were you Sunday morning?"

"I was asleep. I'd been out late the night before." Ray leans back against the edge of his desk. "Look, I was working with Lydia on this deal, because it was beneficial to both of us. But she didn't want to get back together with me. At least not yet. But I behaved badly when we were together, and I wanted to try and make some things up to her, whether it changed anything between us or not."

"I believe him," Autumn says.

"I don't," Tiff says. "He seems willing to go to extremes over Lydia. That's not a trustworthy personality."

I want to believe Ray. He sounds sincere. But once Ray heads to the break room I still take pictures of the contracts and pass them, along with a brief text summarizing the information about Ray and Lydia's relationship – and the coincidence involving Preston Shelton – along to Detective Beckman.

She sends me a text back, saying, *Be careful, Felicity. You should know by now that poking your nose into this type of investigations can get people hurt.*

And Meryl should realize that I'm far too enmeshed in this to give up now. She should be happy I'm sharing information. Especially since she hasn't asked for any. I don't mention that I'm texting her right in front of one of the potential suspects. Even if Ray seems distracted talking to Tiff.

Tiff asks Ray, "So what now? Lydia's gone, so are you planning to stay in town?"

Ray says, "I like it here. There's a cool music scene, and my new band already has been getting gigs. I know it's weird how I wound up here, but I'd like to stay." He gives Tiff a hesitant look. "If it's not going to creep you out."

Tiff says, "Assuming you don't turn out to be a murderer, I'm okay with it."

"Or a kidnapper," Autumn points out.

"Or a kidnapper," Tiff repeats.

My phone rings. It's Logan. I go into the break room to take the call.

"How's the investigation going?" Logan asks.

I explain this newest development. "I think we've uncovered more than one crime. This is outside the scope of anything I've dealt with before."

I remember Flip looking into the flower pots. I never did figure out if he had a motive for murdering Lydia – beyond potentially taking an expensive necklace to defray his money woes. But we're talking about an investment group, and Flip said he is an investment banker. I ask Logan to help me do a bit of research. I starting with finding Flip on his business page. He manages a number of group investments. Logan contacts one of his resources and texts me a list of the investments Flip offers. Flip manages a mutual fund which includes stock in Molten Entertainment. I point this out to Logan, saying, "If there was something wrong with the land for the amusement park, his investors stand to lose big time. But, in that case, why not come forward opposing the purchase, which still hasn't been finalized? It seems a bit extreme to kill the real estate agent – unless there's something bigger being covered up."

Logan says, "You need to talk to Flip. Go with Arlo, if you need to. We both know he'll keep you safe."

I can tell it pains Logan to say that. "Hey," I say, "Are you okay?"

"Yeah, I'm fine. Only – my parents are going to move into a one-story house. It'll be easier for my dad. I'm still coming back for the wedding. But after that, I'm going to need to spend about a month in Minnesota, helping them pack and get moved. I'm leaving Cindy here for the time-being."

He doesn't say it, but what if his parents need more help than that? What if he decides he needs to move back to Minnesota to be there for them?

"That's understandable," I say, despite the lump of emotion trying to close off my throat. "You have to take care of family."

"Are you really okay?" Logan asks. "Did you get your catering van back?"

"Yeah, Autumn took me by the impound to get it." I don't mention that we had gone by the hotel first, for me to change clothes. He will just worry if he knows I was attacked – even if it was with chocolate.

"That's good." He sighs heavily into the phone. "I wish I could do more to help."

I don't tell him that I found the chocolate bar he left for me. I don't want to talk about it when his worry is divided between what's going on here, and what might happen with his father in Minnesota.

Chapter Twenty-One
Wednesday

The next afternoon, I'm still thinking about Logan while I'm packing up the truffles and hearts we made into cute two-piece boxes. The boxes have clear rectangles in the tops so you can see the chocolates inside. The hearts had been a great idea.

It's been pouring rain all morning, so I'm grateful for the shop's humidity control system, which allows me to work without worrying about the finished products.

Flip walks into the space, looking around curiously. "You wanted to see me?" he asks.

I know Arlo isn't here, but Flip seems so mild mannered that I'd just asked the musician to come to the shop. He has a motive for wanting the necklace – or for blackmail – in order to solve his money woes, but it feels like there's more to it than that.

I hand Flip one of the chocolate hearts. "Try this," I say.

He samples the rum-accented chocolate. "This is nice. Like a drink I had once in Saint Thomas."

"Not Florida?" I ask. "There's lots of rum drinks there, too."

He squints at me. "When would I have been in Florida?"

I shrug and pack another box. "Just checking. So much of what's been going on ties back there. Patsy grew up there, Lydia and Ray both worked there."

"Well, I've never been there." Flip finishes the chocolate and wipes his hands on his pants. "So if there's some kind of conspiracy, you can count me out."

"I was thinking maybe it had something to do with a land deal," I say, deciding to be honest about what I've figured out. "We know Lydia was trying to confirm something about amusement parks, here at the library. But the only amusement park I know she was related to was the one tied to Molten Entertainment. I think maybe something was wrong with it, and she was killed to cover it up."

Flip's eyes go wide with shock. "And you think I had something to do with it?"

I point at him with the box I just closed. "You do manage a fund that includes Molten Entertainment."

"That was a favor," he sputters. "Including a friend's company might not have been the most ethical thing I've ever done, but there's nothing wrong with the investment. Lydia might have been researching Preston's other foray into theme parks. A kid got killed on one of the rides, but it was because the construction company cut corners, and Preston was later cleared. Lydia may have had legit questions about Preston's judgement. Frankly, so did his wife, before she disappeared. She was planning to pull the plug on the whole candy entertainment park thing and quietly unload the land. Which was hard for him. He loved her, but it put him in a weird place, having to defer to her on the important decisions. Especially since in the beginning, she'd started the entertainment company because she was supportive of his music. But when it didn't go anywhere – she wanted him to be entirely a corporate guy."

I'm surprised that Flip knows so much about this. I say, "You and Preston Jennings must be pretty good friends."

Flip looks at me oddly. Then he says, "Yes and no. There's a lot of times when we don't get along. He always has to have his way."

I ask, "But you didn't know Lydia, even though she was representing him."

"I never met her," Flip says. He casts a longing look at the beer and sweet potato truffles. I give him one. It was imperfect, so I wasn't going to box it, anyway. After savoring the truffle, Flip says, "I had nothing to do with Lydia Dunning's death, or any real estate scandal."

"I think I believe you," I say.

"Good," he says, and swipes another truffle before leaving me alone to finish my work.

Logan had made the truffles yesterday, at some point before he had left for Minnesota. It had been a close call getting the chocolate processed in time, but I had tasted one and the chocolate, the jam and the ganache had all worked together beautifully. The sour of the beer and earthiness of the sweet potato had complimented each other, and the shells had been glossy and even. Logan really does work hard to become competent at whatever he turns his hand to.

But now that he's back in Minnesota – what if his priorities change? I can't fault him for taking care of a parent. My mom and Aunt Naomi put a lot of time into checking on my grandmother, so I've seen how much work can be involved.

Honestly, I probably wouldn't respect him if he just left his dad in need. After all, Logan has finally made progress in reconciling himself to his past, and realized that his father didn't blame him for the tactical mistake that had cost lives and made him leave the police. And if his father's health is in decline – that could mean being forced to retire from the force himself. There's a lot more at stake than just a house, or a change of address.

I can see Logan deciding he needs to put his all into helping his dad make the needed adjustments. I don't know – maybe this isn't the right time for him to want to start a serious relationship. Maybe I waited too long. After all, he hasn't called since yesterday.

My phone buzzes, and I think it's him. I'm disappointed to see a number I don't recognize. The last four digits are 7121. And for some reason that seems familiar.

I answer the call, and it turns out to be Hailey, the other insurance adjustor, the one I'd half convinced myself must be dead.

"Hailey! Hi!"

I must sound more excited than the situation warrants, because she doesn't say anything.

I say, "Can you hear me?"

That gets me a timid, "Hi, Mrs. Koerber. Can I ask what this is about?"

How do I approach this? She's not likely to give me a ton of information, since I'm not a cop. I say, "I'm friends with the daughter of one of your fellow insurance investigators, Pete Nash."

"I am aware of that. Shame about Pete. Ours usually isn't a dangerous line of work."

I stifle a laugh. I mean, I'd just recently been abducted to use as leverage, because of that line of work. But what I say is, "Did you know Pete?"

She says, "Not personally." She doesn't elaborate.

I ask, "Then how did you know his daughter?"

Hailey says, "I don't. But I do watch the news. And when I realized it was you who had called me – curiosity got the better of me and I called back."

I say, "I'm so glad you did." But I'm thinking, *how did I make the news in another state?*

Hailey asks, "What was it you wanted to ask me?"

I'm just glad she's alive. But now that I've got ahold of her – she might have more information. I say, "It's about the jewelry store, here in Galveston. One of my other friends lost an antique posey ring, and I got caught up trying to find it."

"That's all been a bit of a mess," Hailey says. "Now that we can't verify the dead guy's identity."

"Can't what now?" I ask. I feel like there's something important here that Arlo neglected to tell me. Probably more of his not-sharing-information-with-civilians policy.

Hailey says, "They identified the dead jeweler off his wallet. But they couldn't find any dental records to match. Now, it is looking like the dental could match a car thief who went missing over a week ago."

I gasp, quickly putting my hand over the phone to hide the noise. There's only one car thief that I know – albeit a reformed one. Carmen's boyfriend, Paul. Who has been out of town at a computer security conference. For over a week. But he's not in that business anymore, because he wants to be a better example for his kid. So surely, it's not him. Still, my voice is timid when I ask, "What's the thief's name?"

"Gregor Emil," Hailey says.

I let out a sigh of relief. That's not an alias Paul would choose. I ask, "Do you think that means the jewelry got stolen, along with the guy's car?"

"That is a possibility. I'm still waiting to get looped in on some details of the case. I was out with a cold for a few days, and I didn't realize any of this had escalated."

I assure Hailey that her health is important, and wish her the best with the case. Then I hang up and text Paul. I know he isn't involved in that world anymore – but his dad is. If he can find out anything about the whereabouts of Drake's ring, Autumn would be grateful – which would go a long way towards winning her over, since she's never really warmed to him. I'm not sure how much Paul cares about that – but I know Carmen has been a good friend to Autumn and would love to see the two getting along. I caveat my request, *If it won't put you in an awkward position with your family. Or in danger.*

Paul texts back, *Let me see what I can find out.*

I finish getting the chocolate boxes assembled, and then I tuck them into the special gift bags for the guests at the rehearsal dinner. I puff up the pieces of teal and purple tissue paper and arrange them on top.

I check my phone. The rain has slowed to a drizzle, and even that should be stopping soon. There are still hours before the party starts. Which gives me time to think about the case. I still want to talk to Seth, the sushi chef who also happens to play guitar – and has a possible connection to Ray, and therefore Lydia. Logan seemed to consider him a potential murder suspect, which means he might be dangerous. But if I have a chat with him at the restaurant, it's at least a public place.

So I let Carmen know I'm heading out, and I bring a couple of chocolate bars with me over to the restaurant. It's a quiet time of day. Ami is at the host stand again, reading a thick novel. I can't quite see the title, but the edge of the cover is blue.

She waves me into the restaurant, where Seth and two other chefs are joking as they organize things behind the bar. There are two customers at a table in the corner, but otherwise the dining room is empty.

Seth puts down the towel he had been using to wipe down his station. He comes around and gestures me over to a table. I offer him the chocolate bars.

He grins. "You know, I wanted to buy a few of these after the concert, but everything was so busy. And then that crazy girl showed up, so I figured it wasn't the best time."

I feel my face going red. I hadn't realized Seth had witnessed the chocolate throwing. I say, "I'm sorry you had to see that. Things are ordinarily a lot more tranquil at Felicitations."

"That goes without saying," Seth says. "But I'm sure you didn't drive over here just to share these." He taps the chocolate bars.

Trying to ease into everything I want to ask, I say, "Logan tells me you play guitar."

Seth's grin gets even wider. "You want to book another concert? I've got a couple of demo tracks you can check out on my website. I mostly do acoustic stuff, both classical and flamenco."

I hadn't intended any such thing – but I'm not opposed to the idea. Assuming Seth doesn't turn out to be the murderer. I say, "That sounds great. It would be such a different musical style from the concert we just had."

Seth says, "I saw that Patsy was there. I just wish there was something I could do. Being the last person to see her father alive – it makes me feel responsible, you know? Like, if I had done something different, offered some kind of help, he might have been okay. I know that doesn't make complete sense."

"I get it, though," I tell him. "I've felt the same way myself, a couple of times." And one face in particular flashes into my mind – Mitch, the art collector who had asked me for help not so long ago, shortly before he had been murdered. I'd found his killer, but it still feels like too little, too late. I say, as much to myself as to Seth, "You have to remember, the only one responsible for what happened is the person who killed Pete. You couldn't have known."

"I guess," he says.

I can't really read the look on his face. Could it be actual guilt? Or just more second-guessing the chain of events? I ask Seth, "Is your last name Jennings?"

"Of course," he says, looking at me like I should have known that already.

I ask, "Can you tell me about the land deal on Mustang Island."

"There's not much to tell," Seth says. He is making eye contact, doesn't look like he is hiding anything. He taps his fingers on the table and explains, "I inherited the land recently, from my father. Some of the land was beachfront, and I figured it was worth more in the hands of a developer. I had met Ray at a couple of different open mic nights and music festivals at venues here on the Island, so when I decided to sell, he seemed like the right guy for the job."

"That makes sense," I agree. "So there wasn't anything wrong with the appraisal, or the history of the land? Anything Ray might have asked you to cover up?"

"What?" Seth looks alarmed. "Is something wrong? Do I need to cancel the deal?"

"No," I say as soothingly as possible. "I'm just looking for possible problems, since Lydia was representing the buyer." He looks relieved – but still skeptical. I've already upset him, so I might as well ask the hardest question, the one that is always to most difficult to put tactfully. "What happened after Pete left? Later that night, into the next morning."

Seth's questioning look sharpens. "Are you asking if I have an alibi?"

I shrug. "I'm just sorting things out."

Seth laughs. "And an alibi is part of that. I'm afraid mine's kind of boring. I was here until close, then Ami and I went for a walk on the beach. After that, I caught a couple of hours sleep at my dad's place, then I drove him to the hospital in Beaumont to visit a friend. Dad's friend suffered an acute case of appendicitis while outside a fast-food restaurant on his way into Texas – and then the first person who stopped to help him-" Here Seth makes air quotes around the word *help*. "-decided to drive off in his car. Roland has been a friend of the family since I was a kid. But his wife passed away years ago, and he doesn't really have anybody. So my dad's staying with him. What?"

I realize that my mouth has slid open in shock. I close it so hard my teeth click. "Your dad's friend is Roland, the missing jeweler?"

"I wouldn't say he's missing, exactly."

"Seth," I say, leaning across the table. "The police are looking for him. Until recently, they thought he was dead. Nobody in his life could account for his whereabouts, so he's officially a missing person."

Seth looks alarmed. "Why would someone think he was dead?"

I explain about the dead car thief. It makes sense that the police wouldn't have checked hospital admission records as far away as Beaumont, which is a good two hours out from Galveston. At least Roland hadn't been carjacked, exactly. And he's reasonably okay. I ask, "Did Roland have a package with him at the hospital? Jewelry he was supposed to deliver once he got into town?"

Seth says, "I don't think so. But he was pretty out of it from the painkillers. I assumed he had reported the stolen car – but from what you're saying, apparently he didn't even do that."

"I guess not," I say. "Though it has been days since the incident. You would think he would be on the mend enough now to do so."

Seth asks, "What happened to the car thief?"

I say, "It's possible he was killed by the same person who killed Pete, in a potential case of mistaken identity. I don't have any proof to back that up – but it's the only thing that makes sense."

Seth and I reach for our phones at the same time.

He says, "I need to warn my dad there could be danger. You?"

"I'm going to text the cop in charge of the investigation into Pete's murder."

We make our respective texts. And Arlo texts back, *We will follow up on this immediately. Chances are that if it was mistaken identity, the killer doesn't know they failed. So Roland is safest if you don't go flying out over there advertising his location.*

I text back, *Got it.*

As if I was going to take a four-hour round-trip drive right before Autumn's rehearsal dinner.

I ask Seth, "Did Roland say anything else at the hospital? Maybe about an unusual pendant he'd been commissioned to make?"

Seth shakes his head. "He didn't talk about his work at all. Which in itself is unusual, since it is always his favorite topic. I know more than a reasonable amount about gems and settings. When I get engaged to Ami, I'm going to have no trouble discussing carat, cut and clarity."

I glance over at Ami. She doesn't appear to have heard what he just said. But I suspect she'll be happy when it happens. "Congratulations," I say softly.

Seth grins again. "I've never been in love like this before." Then his face sobers. "But I wish I could help you figure out what happened. I know it has Ami unsettled too."

I say, "Think back to the night Pete was here. Is there anything you might have forgotten to tell me? Anything he said? Any of those texts you might have accidentally read?"

He sucks his lips up against each other, thinking. Then he stands up and gestures Ami over to our table, saying, "Babe, help me go step by step through the other night. You were the one who first talked to Pete when he got here, right?"

Ami sits down next to Seth. She puts a hand on his. "That's right. I seated him at the bar. He seemed a little anxious, looking back out at the parking lot. I figured he couldn't remember if he'd locked his car or something."

The two of them go point by point through what had happened. It sounds like a million other interactions with a million other customers at a million other restaurants.

I ask, "What about after Pete left? Did anything unusual happen? Anyone else come in who might have been looking for him."

"I don't think so," Seth says.

But Ami looks hesitant. Finally, she says, "There was one odd thing. Though it's probably too insignificant to even mention. When we were closing up, I found an iPod on the floor, like somebody had accidentally dropped it. I figured it was some little kid, since those things aren't very popular anymore. I stuck it in the lost and found, but I don't think anybody ever came back for it."

"It's worth a look," I say, following Ami over to the host stand. She pulls out a box and rummages in it. I feel a pang of déjà vu. Is it possible that two important clues in this case wound up in the lost and found?

She hands me the iPod. A cursory glance reveals an archive of music files – mostly 80's music and 70's rock. Hardly the music choices of a kid.

But there's a folder of voice recordings, and one lone video.

I play the most recent audio clip, which is timestamped the day Pete died. Of course, that was the same day the device was lost, so I brace myself for some middle-aged guy's rendition of "Achy Breaky Heart" or "Don't Come Around Here No More."

But instead, it's a guy clearing his throat and announcing, "Investigation notes, arrival in Galveston." I never met Pete, but this could conceivably be his voice. It *has* to be him, right? The guy – probably Pete – continues, "I thought I had spooked the girl into running for Mexico, and I got as far as Corpus, following her trail, before I realized she never left Galveston. She's agreed to meet me. This could all be dangerous. We're talking about a guy who killed his wife. And now that the girl knows what she stole – what that pendant proves – I fear for her safety. For the safety of all concerned, honestly. I just hope he doesn't realize she has it. I'm going to get something to eat, and then check into the most out-of-the-way place I can find for a night or two, until the meet."

I click on one of the older recordings, from a few days before Pete's death. His notes start, "I'm heading for Texas. My first thought is to call the cop my daughter used to date – but I'm afraid I behaved badly. But who else am I going to tell my suspicions to? They're so outlandish, without the pendant to back me up. Because I have no real proof that the guy murdered his wife and kept a trophy, if that trophy has disappeared. I have to find the girl, get her to agree to testify that she stole the pendant, and the watch the guy's gardener used to own, before his supposed accident. It's a pattern I couldn't help spot, after investigating the first burglary. But if the wife hadn't called me, shortly before she disappeared, I'm not sure if I would have even thought to look into it."

There's a lot to unpack in that one message, most of it quite alarming. Yet, I wonder if Arlo will find that message comforting. It's the closest thing he will ever get from Pete to an apology for having broken him and Patsy up.

But a lot of things here aren't adding up. If Pete was only staying in town for a couple of days, how was his room paid up for a week? It must have been his killer who extended Pete's stay, wanting a better chance to move the body. A chill sparks down my spine at someone being that callous.

But the real revelation here is that Pete believed himself in danger, from the husband of the owner of that pendant. We have to be talking about Preston and Adriana, right? Pete had made the assumption that Preston had killed his wife and only claimed that she had been abducted. Pete had to be mistaken – there had been a pattern of kidnappings in the area, including Charlie's wife too.

But he wasn't mistaken about both him and Lydia being in danger – from somebody.

I click on the video file. It's the security footage from Adriana's home, on the day of the home invasion. The clip shows her sitting on an elegant settee, with a cup of tea in her hand. She looks startled as someone comes in from outside of the camera's view. She drops the teacup on the carpet, as she backs away. According to the reports, there had been multiple intruders, but only one of them is caught on this video. The guy is wearing a balaclava and holding a roll of duct tape in gloved hands. So he isn't likely to be identified from this clip. But more importantly – Adriana had clearly been wearing the rose quartz pendant when she'd been dragged out of the house. So – how had Lydia wound up with it?

It's possible Pete was right. Or it's possible Lydia has been involved in the kidnappings in some other way.

Chapter Twenty-Two
Wednesday

Drake shows up at the flip hotel an hour before the rehearsal dinner, with Princess Buttercup. The little goat is prancing along happily at the end of the leash, but Drake looks completely overwhelmed.

"Are you okay?" I ask.

Drake hands over the leash. "Goats really don't like being alone. I wound up sitting up half the night, keeping PB company. I finally fell asleep on the sofa, while she was chilling in the living room in that oversized dog crate."

I tell him, "It's okay if you want to head over to the restaurant. I just need to get Princess Buttercup settled, then I'll head over there myself."

"You can't leave her here alone," he says. "Upset goats sound like screaming little girls. I barely avoided my neighbors calling the cops last night."

"But Aunt Naomi will be home in an hour and a half," I protest. "I have a nice pen for her at the back of the hotel."

Drake gives me a skeptical look.

"Fine," I say. "I'll figure something out."

He looks a little sorry for me as he gets into his Honda and drives away. But he obviously can't be late for his own rehearsal dinner.

Arlo is supposed to be meeting me here at the hotel, so I can hand over the iPod. But he could just as easily meet me over by the restaurant. So I call Aunt Naomi to see if she can help with the logistics. There's no way she can get home sooner, so we arrange for her to pick up Princess Buttercup outside the restaurant. I update my plan with Arlo, then I get the goat into the carrier, and hop into my catering van.

I've never been to the restaurant Autumn chose for this event. I just know it's a seafood place, over on the bay side of the island. When I get there, I realize it's right next to a small park. Arlo's car is already there.

He gets out and heads towards me. He's moving slow, still favoring his braced ankle.

I take the iPod out of my purse.

Arlo takes out a plastic bag, but I tell him, "You're going to want to read what's on here, before you bag it up."

Arlo hands me the bag and pulls a pair of disposable gloves out of his pocket. He says, "The chain of evidence is already well broken by this being in the lost and found. And then in your purse." He sighs, then adds, "At least it isn't likely that the killer knows you have this. Otherwise, that person might have tried to take the device before you got a chance to turn it over."

Trying to ignore the chill that thought sends through me, I give him the iPod. While he's scrolling through the data, I get Princess Buttercup out of the catering van. Drake was right – she's not happy about being in there alone, and she's already starting to fuss. But the minute she's on the ground, she lets out a happy noise and starts munching on a dandelion that is growing up out of the crack in the sidewalk.

I move her over to the grass at the edge of the parking lot. Arlo follows us, still reading.

There's a small playground in the park, and near the equipment, there are a couple of benches. It's cold out, so the playground is empty. I move towards a bench and sit down. Princess Buttercup immediately hops onto the bench and tries to climb my shoulder.

"Hey," I tell her. "I'm all dressed up. This coat shows everything." I push her away from my shoulder. She climbs up onto the back of the bench.

Arlo reads through the notes, and watches the video of the home invasion turned kidnapping. When he's done, I say, "Pete was planning on coming to you for help."

Arlo nods slowly. "I wish he'd come to me directly, instead of going to that out-of-the-way B&B. We might have been able to protect him."

"I'm sure you could have," I say. After all, Arlo is big on protecting people he cares about. Even if I've found him overprotective at times, he's a really good guy. So why do I find myself distancing myself from him right now? It isn't what I expected to do.

"I have to say, Lis, you really have become quite the detective. This gives a real motive for Pete's murder. And the tip you gave us about Roland being in the hospital let us put a guard on him, until we figure all this out."

I tell Arlo, "You're keeping Roland safe, too."

"It feels like nobody in this case is who they say they are," Arlo says.

I say, "It really is just like in *The Thin Man*. All this misdirection, putting the puzzle together the wrong way. So how does my info on Roland play into the little competition between you and Logan?"

Arlo splutters a laugh. "Logan's not here." When I give him a pointed look, he says, "Technically, you're the one who solved it. And the guy's not dead, so it would be the murder of the car thief that counts – and it's looking more likely that the same person who killed him also killed Lydia, so there's not really a one case that gets solved first thing anymore, anyway."

I say, "At least that puts Tiff in the clear. She doesn't have a motive for any of these other crimes."

"True," Arlo says. "The only person who would have had a larger motive – assuming everything in Pete's notes is accurate – would be Preston. But as far as we've been able to ascertain, he's still in New York. His receptionist has him at a mental health retreat in the countryside through the end of the week, and part of the thing is no phones. So somebody would have to physically have to go out to the retreat to question him. Until now, we haven't had enough questions for him to justify doing that."

"That really does limit things." I absently tap a finger on my lips, thinking. Finally, I ask, "Did Detective Beckman ever figure out what the key went to?"

"What key?" Arlo asks.

"The one that was in the marble pouch. It feels like that pouch was important to someone. And I can't imagine what the significance of a broken lipstick tube or a dolphin keychain might be." I pull up the picture I'd taken of the items. It's an ordinary, unmarked key. There's no way to know where the padlock is. But why did Lydia have it? What if it wasn't because it was a key – but because it meant something else? And there's something about the watch. It's dancing at the edge of my brain.

Arlo quips, "Maybe it's the key to where Preston was keeping his wife."

It sounds like he's joking – but what if Arlo is right? I shudder. "Don't say things like that."

"Okay," he says. "There is something else I wanted to talk about."

He reaches into his pocket again, only this time, instead of bags or gloves, he takes out a ring. It's a very familiar sapphire, which Arlo had given to me many years ago as a promise ring. It had belonged to his grandmother, and I had selfishly kept it after we had broken up. I had only given it back to him after we'd re-encountered one another after the first murder I'd had to deal with – back at my chocolate shop's grand opening party. Arlo says, "You kept this ring all those years we were apart, even when you were married to someone else, even when we were both on different paths. I'm not asking you to make any big decisions today. But I do want you to have this back, as a promise that we will both try to make things work, despite the complications and despite all these years. I promise, I'm not going to hurt you again."

Which is sweet of him to say – since *I* was the one who had hurt *him*. He looks so genuine and sincere. So perfect. Emotion wells inside me, and I feel close to tears as heat bites at my eyes and nose.

I ask Arlo, "What do you think of my chocolate business?"

He looks confused. "I'd never ask you to give up a business that makes you happy. Unless you're worried I'd be jealous about Logan being there." Arlo makes a frustrated gesture with the hand that isn't holding a ring. "Honestly, I don't want to talk about him right now. This is about me and you."

"I know." Because at this point, I'm still not sure that Logan won't wind up moving halfway across the country. But even if he does, and Logan and I don't wind up together – this is about what Arlo and I both need out of life. And I'm afraid that it really is too different. I ask Arlo, "What would you do if I tossed the business aside and asked you to travel the world with me?"

Arlo takes the question seriously, spends a little time framing his answer. "I'd have to save up some vacation time first. And probably pull overtime to earn some extra money. But if it was important to you, one way or another, we'd go. If you really were giving up your business, liquidating it could fund a lot of the trip, and leave us stable when we got back. It might take a year or two, but I promise, it wouldn't be one of those someday things that never actually happens."

There's nothing wrong with his answer. It's quite reasonable, in fact. And yet, something about it makes me feel like Ash was right. Several tears slip from my eyes, running down my cheeks, as I instinctively reach for the list Ash gave me, which is in my purse.

"What's that?" Arlo says, looking into my bag.

I show him the list.

Arlo considers the paper for a long time. It still could be read as applying to him. Yet, he eventually says, "We just missed our timing again, didn't we, Lis."

"Something like that." I get Princess Buttercup down off the bench so that Arlo can sit down next to me. "I feel like I'm your past – but Patsy's your future. If you made a list, the type of person you really need – it would be her. Which is probably why you never really got over her. And she needs you, in a way that I never will. I need to let you go, so we can all be happy."

"You make it all sound so logical, so easy." He looks down at his grandmother's ring, so small in his hand. "But I never really got over you, either. And if you're asking me to now – it's hard to give up on something you've wanted for such a long time."

"Tell me honestly that you can't see that ring on Patsy's hand," I say. "You were practically engaged to her before I came back into your life and everything got all topsy-turvy."

Arlo says, "I doubt she would ever want to be with me. Not after I made it clear that I wasn't going to go back on my word to you. Would you want someone who made you feel like you were second best?"

Arlo does have a point. But I say, "I think you both might be able to get past that."

He grimaces. "I doubt it, especially now that I've been the one to deliver the bad news about her father."

I shake my head. "Now that's where you're wrong. That's when I saw how much Patsy still wanted to rely on you. I obviously don't know her that well, but I think you owe it to her to at least give her closure – whether you can work things out or not." I put a hand on Arlo's arm. "Imagine that trip again. It's five years from now, and you've been saving money. Can you look up from your deck chair on some perfect beach and see Patsy beside you?"

"I can," Arlo says sheepishly. "Does that make me a bad person? That I can see a future with two different people?"

I laugh, unexpectedly sharp in my own ears. "Only if I'm a more horrible one. I've been debating the future with either you or Logan so long that it became inevitable that somebody was going to get hurt. I want to let you know that I am so, so sorry for that. I really do want you to be happy. And if Patsy helps with that – it doesn't ease my guilt over putting you in this situation, but I'll do whatever I can to help make things right with her."

Arlo looks at me, such vulnerability shining in his warm brown eyes. He says, "Despite everything that's happened, once I get over being heartbroken, I think Patsy and I could be really happy together."

"That's great," I say. And as hard as it is to let him go, I mean it. "If you're already thinking about getting over me, maybe it won't be as hard as you think."

"I doubt I'll ever be entirely over you," Arlo says.

"Maybe you aren't ever supposed to get entirely over your first love," I say. It's corny, but I really believe it is true. "I know this sounds selfish, but I do still want you in my life – as a friend. You're one of the people who knows me best. You make a good sounding board – and an awesome Cuban sandwich."

Arlo snorts a laugh. "You don't think that might create a misunderstanding between you and Logan?"

"I hope not," I say. "He thinks of you as a friend too. We both know Logan doesn't make friends easily."

Arlo nods, acknowledging that. He says, "This probably sounds corny, but if I have to lose you to somebody, I'm glad it's somebody I can respect. Somebody I know will protect you, and be there for you."

I say, "You always were the best."

"Apparently not this time," he says. "If you're really sure about Logan, don't wait to tell him. None of us are guaranteed the leisure of time."

I know that, all too well. I'd nearly lost Logan, lest than a month ago, when he'd come seconds away from dying at the hands of a murderer. And yet I hesitate.

"What?" Arlo asks.

"Logan needs to prioritize his family right now. He's already said he plans to stay in Minnesota for a month. We all know he only came to Galveston as a self-imposed exile, because he felt he had failed, first as a cop and then as a bodyguard. Now he has a chance to get close to his dad again. Maybe the timing isn't right between me and him either."

Arlo says, "Lis, that's not fair. I don't think Logan is the type of person who can't balance love and family responsibilities."

I gesture helplessly, startling Princess Buttercup, who then hops back onto the bench, practically into Arlo's lap. I ask, "What am I going to say? I choose you, now let's go out on an actual date? Oh, and by the way, don't leave forever?"

At that moment, Aunt Naomi's car turns into the parking lot, saving Arlo from having to answer. When Naomi gets out of the car, Princess Buttercup bounds towards her. I realize that at some point during my and Arlo's conversation, I dropped the leash.

Naomi lets out a startled, "Oh!" as Princess Buttercup attempts to climb her knee. I still haven't caught up when the door to the restaurant swings open. Drake is standing there, holding the door, as Autumn's brother starts to cross the parking lot, carrying a box that looks heavy.

Starsky, the band member who used to work at Denzel's restaurant, comes out of the seafood place to take the box. The way the sound carries in this space, we can hear them talking from relatively far away.

Starsky says, "I wanted to talk to you, before everybody else gets here. I never did get to explain my side of what happened with that customer."

Denzel scoffs. "Seriously? My man, there is never an excuse for throwing crème brulee."

"I wasn't the one who threw it," Starsky says. "That lady's kid tripped me. On purpose. He's the reason it went flying."

Denzel hesitates. "She said she saw you throw it. That you were mad because she had said the clams stunk."

Starsky takes the box. "She did say that. And she called me the worst waiter she'd ever had. But you've known me for how many years? Am I the kind of person who would throw food? Especially at somebody who's being an idiot?"

"I guess not." The wind shifts and I can't hear the rest of what is said, but I assume that Starsky is getting his job back.

I return my attention to Princess Buttercup, only to realize she's on the move again, at a full out run towards Drake. I give chase, trying to catch the end of the leash, but I'm too slow, and Arlo, hobbling along, is even slower still. Princess Buttercup reaches Drake and pushes her head against his leg, begging for more affectionate pats. She really has taken a liking to him.

But when he tries to grab for her harness, she dances away – and moves into the building. Almost immediately there's a crash.

By the time I get there to survey what just happened, Princess Buttercup is trailing part of a flower arrangement, which is caught up in her leash. The chocolate fountain – which had been a central element of the dessert table, is on the floor, spinning like crazy, flinging chocolate, and a scared Princess Buttercup leaps away from the spray, winding up in an alcove above the wine display. One wrong move, and we're going to owe this place for every bottle she breaks.

Drake gets on one side of the alcove, while I get on the other, and after a bit of balking, Princess Buttercup lets Drake pet her, and then remove her from the alcove. He turns to me, holding the goat close to his chest like an oversized dog. The absurdity of the situation hits both of us at the same time, and we both start laughing.

The mirth of the moment fades when we look over at Autumn, sitting at the table where half of her guests have arrived. They all look vaguely in shock. One of the restaurant staff is approaching Autumn. There is a very unhappy looking exchange.

Autumn stands up and announces, projecting her voice to reach Drake, "We're getting kicked out."

I pull out my phone, and shout back to her, "I'll call Mrs. Guidry and make sure her offer still stands."

Autumn rushes over to me, and I think she's about to tell me off for showing up with the goat in the first place. Instead, she hugs me, and I realize how desperately she's trying to hold onto some sense of normality despite everything that has been going wrong in the middle of her wedding. She says, "You are the best matron of honor ever."

"I'm not sure about that," I say. "But at least I did clear one of your bridesmaids of suspicion of murder."

"Even if we didn't find the missing ring, Hon, it's all going to be okay," Drake tells her. He puts a hand on her shoulder, and she releases me from the hug to turn to him.

"You lost the ring?" Drake's mom asks loudly.

There are some anxious glances at the table.

"We have a replacement," Autumn says, making a *calm down* gesture with her hands.

I get a confirmation from Mrs. Guidry that she will close off half her restaurant for us, so I give Autumn a thumbs up. Somehow – we're going to salvage her special day.

I wake up the morning of Autumn's wedding feeling much more optimistic. The overcast weather of the past couple of days has cleared up – with a forecast now calling for a beautiful day. And everyone should be in a good mood. The rehearsal dinner had taken a while to get sorted, but once everyone had gotten to the new location, it had turned into an excellent party. Mrs. Guidry had really come through.

Even better – Ash had agreed to take care of the goat until after the wedding, and all it is going to cost me is his exclusive right to post any photos I take at the event at least 48 hours before me or anyone else. It feels like a small price to pay. After all, Aunt Naomi can't be here all day, and I can't very well leave Princess Buttercup in the crate where she had slept last night. Agnes and Esme are going to owe all of us big time, when they finally show up and take their goat back.

Knightley is hiding out under my bed, obviously unsure what to make of our visitor. I promise him extra parsley when I get back from the wedding to make up for the stress.

Ash shows up, right on time, and when he leaves with both crate and goat, I feel tension going out of my shoulders. I have a big morning planned, leading the bridesmaids through mani/pedis and up-dos and staying ahead of the inevitable fashion emergency. I'm a bit stuck on the murder-solving front, but I am going to put that aside long enough to be present for my friend on this important day. Who knows? Maybe a few hours of normalcy will let me come back to the problem with a fresh perspective.

My phone rings. It's Logan. Excitement bubbles through me. I've made my decision, but he doesn't know it yet. I want to tell him at just the perfect time. Which could be right now. Or I might wait until he gets here in person. In which case, what do I say now? He's going to know something's up.

I pick up, but while it's Logan's number, some girl says, "Hello? Felicity?"

I feel an instinctive pang of jealousy, thinking, *who is this girl*? But that is almost instantly followed by fear. What if something happened, and I'm Logan's last number dialed? I could be talking to a cop or someone who found his phone. I stammer, "That's me."

The girl says, "This is Dawn, Logan's sister. I was wondering if you had heard from him."

"No. Is he not there with you? I mean – that's his phone."

"Yeah, I think he forgot it this morning, don't you know. But someone called it, asking about his flight plan. Apparently, he had agreed to make a stop and pick up a passenger, only he didn't show up."

My chest somehow feels hot and cold at the same time. If Logan said he was going to be somewhere, he'd be there. I stammer out, "Last I heard, he was planning to be back before our friend's wedding."

Putting it that way with the *our* makes me feel like there is a lot more settled between us than there actually is.

"Okay." She sounds disappointed. "Well, then, I'll let you know if I hear anything, okay."

"Same here," I say, trying to sound cheerful and failing. I have a desperate need to hug my bunny, but he's probably not coming out from under the bed, even though the goat is gone. And I still have to go meet Autumn and the rest of the bridal party.

From the champagne breakfast to the post-spa tea, all of the events go perfectly. Everyone seems to be having a great time – except me. I jump every time I get a text. I worry and stare off into space. Twice Autumn asks me what's wrong. But what am I going to tell her that isn't going to derail everything? Surely Logan is fine.

But what if he's not? I don't know what I'll do, because I can't picture my life without him. Somewhere after the updo, but before the makeup, there's a moment where I'm looking in the mirror, at the anxious lines on my face, and I realize – all of this waiting and analyzing what's fair in a relationship is stupid. Even if I might get hurt, even if I'm not sure if I'm ready, and even if it winds up being long distance and complicated – if Logan gets off that plane in Galveston, I have to fight to hold onto him.

Finally, Autumn corners me, flanked by the twins, Sandra and Sonya, fellow bridesmaids and two of my best friends. Autumn says, "We know something is wrong. Are the police about to arrest Tiff or something? Because if so, tell them to wait until after the wedding, since we all know she's really innocent, and without her dress to tie everything together, y'all are going to look like you stepped out of different wedding catalogs."

"What? No! Tiff's in the clear." I flutter my hands around. I finally admit, "Logan is MIA. He went to the airport this morning, and took off in his plane a bit later than his flight plan suggested. But then he never showed up at his next stop."

The three of them all gape at me. Sonya says, "You poor thing. Your true love is missing, and you're getting ready for someone else's wedding."

Did everybody realize Logan was the one for me well before I did?

Her twin looks at her surprised. "Her true love? I thought she was set to choose Arlo."

Okay – so maybe not everybody.

My phone rings. It's a number I don't recognize. I answer it with dread – only to hear Logan's voice.

"Fee? Can you hear me?"

I blink around my heavy eyeliner and mascara, trying to keep tears of relief from destroying my makeup. "Yes. Absolutely. Are you okay?"

"I'm fine. But it's been an awful day. I forgot my phone in Minnesota, and then there was a problem with the plane, so I had to put down at a different airport. I sent a message to the passenger I was supposed to pick up, but apparently he didn't get it, and my sister has been convinced all day that I was dead. How was your morning?"

I don't tell him I'd been worried that he was dead, too. I say, "All the usual wedding stuff. Are you back in Galveston?"

"Finally. I'm heading out to meet the other groomsmen now. While you have been enjoying your spa day, they've been helping Drake finish moving, as a surprise for Autumn. I just have to get my tux."

"I'll see you at the ceremony, then."

Autumn, Sonya and Sandra look just as relieved as I feel. Sandra even brings me another cup of tea, to celebrate the fact that we are all alive and no longer being accused of murder – or accessory to murder – despite the fact that we had all sworn off liquids until after the ceremony.

We're getting ready to head to the venue when Autumn's phone buzzes. She answers it, hesitantly at first, then more excited. By the time she thanks the person on the other end of the line four times and hangs up, she is bouncing on the balls of her feet. She announces, "They found Drake's ring!"

"What?" I ask. "How?"

Autumn says, "The package with the missing jewelry just showed up at the store this morning. Somebody left it on the counter and walked away, managing to keep their face from getting caught on camera. Vic cleared it with the police – since Drake's ring doesn't appear related to the investigation, they are okay with letting us have it. We just have to go pick it up."

"Then let's go," I say. "Or I can get it, and just meet you at the building."

"Oh no," Autumn says. "I need to have that ring in my own hand. I trust you like a sister, but I'm not leaving this one to chance."

True. For all she knows, I could get kidnapped again on the way there. So all the bridesmaids head for the venue, while Autumn clambers into my catering van. Her dress is in a giant bag that takes up a good bit of floor space behind us. My own dress bag seems small by comparison.

I text Paul, the reformed thief, and ask, *The missing jewelry just showed up at the jewelry store. You have anything to do with this?*

He texts back, *I just shared the info that the jewelry could be important to the police in figuring out who killed Gregor. No idea if that information got to a friend of his or not.*

I thank him for his help, then we get on the road. When we reach the store, Vic comes over to talk to us personally, despite the fact that two of her employees are standing together, chatting, since we're the only customers. She says, "I want to apologize again for the inconvenience."

Autumn assures her none of this was her fault. Vic goes into the back room to get the posey ring.

I find myself drawn to the ring display I had looked at the other day with Ash. That black ring with the channel in it – the one that had made me think of Logan – is still there. It isn't so expensive that I couldn't afford it. If I really want to prove I want a relationship with Logan, it is conceivable that I could just buy it.

I realize Autumn has come up behind me when she says, "After all the flack you gave me about being impulsive with my engagement, I can't believe you're about to buy a ring for Logan, without even having been on a proper date."

It feels like the blush on my face is spreading down onto my neck. "I always thought you were Team Arlo for me."

Autumn gives me a half hug. "After watching you worry today – there's no question."

I say, "Don't make me cry, or I'll run my mascara and look horrible in your pictures."

"Girl, you better not." Autumn moves closer to the case. "Which ring is it?"

It feels weird having the little ring box in my pocket. When I'd gotten married the first time, Kevin had made a big deal of his proposal. There had been a hot air balloon ride, and about a million roses. I'd always assumed that if I did get married again, there would be a big moment like that. And that I'd be the one being proposed to – not the one proposing. I'm not even sure how you do such a thing.

As the bridesmaids rush us into the back room of the venue, and hurry us into our dresses, I try to make a plan. But people keep talking to me about other things.

Kaylee says, "I don't know how you thought of that Red Stripe truffle, but I think that may be my new favorite thing that your store makes."

"Mine too," Bea says. "I'm always in the mood for beer and chocolate – and you put them together in perfect balance."

"I can't take credit," I say. "Logan actually made the beer and sweet potato truffles. I just made the Jamaican chocolate and rum crystal hearts."

"Those were so good too!" Sandra says. "You know I'm a sucker for anything with rum."

I say, "Logan and I do make a pretty good team."

Autumn gives me a significant look. She says, "You know, it won't hurt my feelings if you go talk to him now. If you wait until after, you might pop."

"Really?" I ask. Unexpected relief washes over me – followed by fizzy anxiety. I'm about to be vulnerable in public. And excited yet nervous to finally tell Logan how I feel. But it's okay. Because one way or another, I am finally ready to see how this plays out.

I find Logan chatting with Starsky, Charlie and Arlo in an anteroom where about a dozen people are waiting. I wasn't expecting to have to do this in front of Arlo. I almost turn around and walk right out – but Arlo gives me a look that lets me know that it's okay. Then he arches an eyebrow, making it clear that he's going to tease me if I don't go through with this. Although, he doesn't know that I'm doing more than just asking Logan for an official date. He will probably tease me for being crazy impulsive, instead of cowardly.

Logan doesn't see me at first. He's listening to the guys.

Starsky says, "So I start back at the restaurant next Tuesday. I'm actually going to start working in the kitchen, since that's what I really wanted all along. Eventually, I'd like to be a chef."

"That's great," Charlie says. "I wish we had time to hang out, but I am getting on a plane tonight. I'm on my way to the Philippines, instead of flying home. I'm taking my startup overseas."

Oh, boy. If they start talking airplanes, I might not get to talk to Logan before the time for the ceremony to start. So I just interrupt. "Hey, Logan. Can I talk to you for a second?"

Logan looks startled at my unexpected interruption, and I start to turn away. I can't do this. What if he says no? What if he thinks I'm rushing things, since we haven't actually dated, and I ruin what we have? What if he decides I'm crazy for doing this here, at someone else's wedding?

"Fee, wait," Logan says.

When I see the concern in his green eyes as I turn back to him, I know I have to do this, right now, before he leaves for Minnesota. I know it's just for a month, but things might be different between us by the time he gets back. There's a big ball of emotion at the back of my throat that is making it difficult to breathe normally, let alone speak. I fumble in my purse and take out the ring box, while still looking at Logan. The concern in his eyes widens into surprise. He obviously knows where I'm going with this before I crack open the box.

I blurt, "Will you marry me?" And then I can't help but whisper, "Please."

He doesn't say anything right away, and I feel that emotion dipping from my throat down into my stomach as he studies the ring box. Does he think I've been too wishy-washy with my emotions? Is he afraid I don't really mean the promise I'm offering? Finally he says, "I always expected that I'd be the one proposing, if I ever got married."

"So is that a no?" My voice cracks into a squeak on the last word. People are staring at us. I have to stop the tears biting at the back of my eyes from falling.

But then Logan gives me a bemused look. "Obviously, I'm not going to say no. Just give me a minute to keep my dignity." He shakes out his hands, loosens his shoulders, and adjusts his bow tie and the edges of his jacket. "Say it again."

"Will you marry me?" I emphasize each word more clearly this time.

Logan steps closer to me and takes the ring box out of my hand. He says, "Yes. Absolutely. For always."

I know none of us can promise that objectively – I've already lost one person I thought would be my always – but I believe that Logan will be true to his word, for life.

He puts his free hand around my waist and draws me in for a kiss. His kiss is insistent and full of promise, and when our lips part, mine are warm and my breath is quick.

Logan says, "You should come with me to Minnesota." Before I can even process how complicated that would be, he says, "I mean not for the whole month. That would be crazy hard with everything going on at Felicitations right now. Just to meet my family. And I can show you around the place where I grew up. I bet my mom still has embarrassing photos of me as a kid, the whole nine yards."

At that moment, it all becomes real. This new life I've chosen for myself solidifies, with new in-laws and sudden ties to a new place. But for once, I don't second guess myself. Even the thought of Minnesota in February doesn't give me pause. "I'd like that," I say.

There's an unexpected noise coming from the auditorium. Part of the swag of flowers has fallen from the arch behind where Autumn and Drake will be standing. It was obviously too heavy for whatever adhesive had been used to stick it up there. People are looking flustered, but I tell Logan, "Let me get the duct tape and that roll of wire out of my backpack, and you can help me fix it."

He grins back at me. "Our first official project as a couple."

I guess it is.

Once we get it repaired, the ceremony goes perfectly. I don't remember much of the details. I keep sneaking glances at Logan, like we haven't been spending time together before. But the giddy feeling is making it hard to concentrate. I do notice that Autumn is beautiful in her wintery white dress. Drake gets tongue-tied trying to recite his vows. They walk out past weepy-eyed relatives and friends to light, airy music.

But the giddy feeling comes crashing down when we get outside, and I find Detective Beckman waiting to talk to me. Straightaway, she asks me, "Have you attempted to contact Preston Shelton?"

"No," I say. Realizing the word sounded defensive, I add, "I've never even seen a picture of him."

Which feels like it is making it worse.

"Good. Don't. His lawyers are already threatening to sue the police department just for asking questions. We can't get the name of the retreat he's staying at, nor will they agree to contact him."

"Oh, wow. That sounds frustrating." I try to put this information together with everything else. "I'm guessing, then, that Pete's information checked out. That Preston probably did kill his wife."

"That is looking probable. We started looking into his past, even his vague connections. And that pouch Logan turned in – that broken watch matches one in a picture of his ex-gardener – who was later killed in a mugging-gone-wrong, which remains unsolved. It's possible that Preston killed the guy and kept the watch – much as Pete supposed that Preston killed his wife and kept the pendant. We believe that each of the items in the pouch could be a trophy from a different victim."

I try to absorb that. Who could have guessed the contents of that marble pouch could be that creepy? I clear my throat and stammer, "In that case, I'm not sure what stonewalling with the lawyers is supposed to do. Won't you just arrest him when he gets back from the retreat?"

"That's the plan. We just need to have enough evidence to make it stick. Thanks to you, we have a big chunk. It helps make Pete's death less meaningless."

I nod, unable to find an appropriate response. I just hope I can find out what happened to Lydia, and how she fit into all of this. She deserves justice, too. The obvious scenario involves Preston having killed her – only, his alibi is one that will be easy to check, once he returns to his office, and gives up the name of the retreat he's been at. People will remember him, even if they didn't have their phones to record his presence. They would note his absence if it was gone long enough to have flown to Texas and back, and spend several days committing multiple murders.

No one would try to fake an alibi like that. They wouldn't be able to return to their life.

So, Lydia's killer could have been tangentially related to the marble bag. Maybe someone wanted the marble bag to blackmail Preston. Or maybe we have been investigating along the wrong track altogether.

I tell Detective Beckman, "There are still a lot of people who might have had reason to kill Lydia, outside of Pete's suspicions."

Meryl says, "Yes, we know about the fight with Agnes Culpepper, the goat yoga instructor. And while it is true that

Agnes has had some anger management issues in the past, it still doesn't seem likely she killed anyone."

I had completely forgotten about Agnes being a suspect. "I'm not talking about that. I've been trying to share information when I'm certain about it, but so much of what I've been dealing with is speculation."

"Go on. Speculate." Detective Beckman takes out her phone, ready to take notes.

I break down the progress of the case with her as quickly as I can. After all, I'm still expected at the reception venue, for photos. Yet, I have to be careful how I phrase some of this, because we weren't exactly supposed to go into the railroad car B&B, so we shouldn't know about the guitar pick. So I can't talk about either Vic or Seth. I'm not sure what either of their motives would be, and they don't seem suspicious otherwise. But yes, I found out today that Vic also plays guitar.

I say, "There are at least five people I think might have had motive." Then I explain, filling in lots of information from interviewing people and online research. Nathan is probably my strongest suspect, from an evidence angle. He claims Lydia gave him the money to start his business, but it could have been a loan, and when she'd unexpectedly showed up in town, he might have found himself unable to pay it back. He is the one, after all, who sells the peach ring candy belonging to the wrapper found at the scene, and he had admitted to having an uneasy relationship with Lydia.

Connection-wise Ray, Lydia's ex who creepy-stalked her by getting a job at Tiff's office, is obviously a suspect. He also had dealings with Preston, and was at the party where Lydia showed up wearing the necklace he might have seen on Adriana Jennings at a previous event. Either Ray or Lydia – or both might have played a part in Adriana's disappearance.

Flip's motive is a bit more enigmatic. From an investment standpoint, both he and his clients had a lot to lose if something negative came out regarding Molten Entertainment. He could be covering up something about the company, and whatever rift that had led to Adriana's abduction. Maybe he was the one blackmailing Preston. Or maybe he could have blackmailed Lydia into giving him the necklace.

If Lydia's book could count as a motive, both Charlie the bass player and that chocolate-throwing ex-girlfriend who believed Cal was innocent are also both suspects. Charlie had been open in his dislike for Lydia's book and what she stood for. And the ex-girlfriend had stated that she didn't consider Lydia to be a real human being. It is possible she could have been disturbed enough to have killed Lydia, without remorse, because she wasn't "real." Of course, she's probably too short to have been the one who actually stabbed Lydia. But she could have had a taller accomplice. Despite what he said about trying to make things right with Lydia, if the accomplice theory proves true, my money is on Ray and the unnamed ex partnering up to get revenge on multiple people in their lives.

Chapter Twenty-Four
Thursday

Ray's car is parked outside when I pull up to Wobble House. What's Lydia's ex doing at Autumn's reception? He could have a logical reason – or something bad might be about to happen. I grab my pepper spray, tucking it into my dress. I hesitate, then take the stun gun out of the backpack and put it in my purse. I'm not sure that I have it in me to use it, but I have a bad feeling about that car.

When I go inside, I see Ray talking to the woman who is overseeing Wobble House until Mitch's will is out of probate. I can't believe it. Ray crashed Autumn's reception to chat with the overseer about a real estate deal, assuming Mitch's heirs are going to put the place on the market, since he died here.

I give Ray a stern look as I walk past, but I don't call him out on party crashing.

I go down the long hallway, to the ballroom. The whole bridal party is seated at long tables not far from the stage. The band is up there, tuning up and getting ready to play. Most of the guests haven't arrived yet.

There are two guys I don't recognize standing near the door. They both nod at me, then go back to talking to each other. When I reach the table, I ask Autumn, "Who's that?"

She waves at the guys. "That's my private security. They came with the ballroom. Apparently, if you serve alcohol in a public venue, the state requires you have somebody on hand."

"At least they blend in," I tell her. Their suits make them look the part for a wedding.

We spend the better part of an hour taking photographs, both in the ballroom and outside. There's a big garden at the side of the building, with a water feature and a bridge. There's a bicycle-driven champagne and cocktails cart set up on one side of the bridge, and a coffee cart on the other. Nobody is manning either one just yet. They're supposed to be for the after party, once the dinner and dancing wraps up inside.

The garden is separated from the back yard of the historic home by a tall wrought iron fence, faced on one side by some bushes. There's not much in the yard, except a couple of mature oaks. I can see the back of the house from where we are posing at the top of the bridge. There's a door leading into the kitchen, where Enrique and his crew are assembling some of Autumn and Drake's favorite foods – plus a chocolate course that I like to think is for me.

Once we've posed with the bridge and the house and the dry grass, we wind up back inside, taking seated photos at the table where we started. By the time the photographers are done, I feel like there's a smile permanently pasted on my face – which makes sense, since Logan keeps accidentally-on-purpose touching my hand underneath the table.

It's fun to feel like a kid again. I'm sure, once we get used to this new direction in our relationship, we'll go back to being mature adults. But Logan has been waiting so long to feel the emotional freedom to show me simple affection, who can blame him? This is so different than the few kisses we'd shared, which had felt like testing out something, dealing with raw attraction. Now that there's commitment attached to it – I hadn't expected it to feel so different. Though what we had before is still there, too.

Kaylee is sitting on my other side. She keeps glancing at me curiously. Finally, she says, "Don't forget about book club on Tuesday. I promised them cake."

"Okay," I say, "But I may have to make it myself. After all this non-stop baking, Carmen may be tired of cake."

Carmen is currently setting up the wedding cake, attaching all of the wafer-paper butterflies to one side in an elegant swoosh. The cake table is just to the right of the bridal party tables. "Speak for yourself," Carmen says. "Kaylee, I'm looking forward to doing your cake. Felicity said you wanted it to look like a book, but I wanted to do a book stack of related titles."

Kaylee says, "That sounds amazing."

The band starts playing through one of their songs for tonight. Unexpectedly, I hear an electric bass. I look up, and Charlie has set his bass against the wall and switched instruments. Certain pieces of modern jazz have a bass guitar in place of the more traditional upright double bass. I hadn't thought much about it, since Charlie played the double bass exclusively during the concert at my shop. That instrument is usually played with only fingers. But he is using a pick on the bass guitar he has now. The group finishes the snippet, and Charlie sets the bass guitar down beside him. As he does so, the pick slips out from underneath the strings, where he had tucked it, and tumbles across the stage. I stand up and lean over the edge of the stage to pick it up and hand it back to him. A bass pick is wider and more triangular than a standard pick. And it hits me that the one we'd seen at the B&B was this same shape.

Could we have been looking for the wrong type of musician? Not a showy lead guitar player and singer, like Ray, but someone who prefers to stay in the background, keeping time. Someone more like Preston Jennings. He's still the only one that makes sense.

Charlie leans over to take the pick. He says, "Thanks," but there's something in his eyes – anxiety or sadness, it's hard to tell – that's deeper than that simple response.

"Sure." I look away from that intensity, down at the stage, at Charlie's feet. Even here, dressed in a suit, he's wearing sneakers. They're black, but they have an undeniable sneaker tread.

I flash back to that moment by the pool, the marks of someone wearing sneakers walking away from the scene. These could be the shoes. But most people wear sneakers, at least sometimes. That's a flimsy hunch to hang a murder accusation on. Unless – maybe Lydia was in on the kidnappings after all, and Charlie could have blamed her for the disappearance of his wife. Maybe Charlie even knew Preston, and they had pooled their information together. I don't know the whys, or how it all lines up, but there's just this vibe I get that the bad guy HAS to be Charlie. But I've been wrong about these kinds of hunches before. And making an accusation about someone here at Autumn's reception would ruin the night – especially if I turned out to be wrong.

But still, Charlie said he was leaving the country. If he is guilty and he gets on a plane, there would be no way to get him back to prove it.

The guests are coming in. There's a whole table off to one side crowded with famous writers, plus Autumn's editor at her new publisher. Kaylee waves, and one of them gestures her over. After all, Kaylee is a high-profile romance author, though most people don't know it, since she writes under a pseudonym.

Kaylee stands up, saying, "Publishing really is a small world." Then she goes over to chat with the other writers. I think Autumn might go too, but when I look over at her, she's turned towards Drake, like they are the only two people in the room.

Yeah, if I make an accusation here tonight – I'd better have incontrovertible proof.

I text Ash, since he's the only researcher I know who isn't here. *Hey, can you find out what kind of musical instrument was stolen from Preston Jennings' home? And if he might ever have been in a band with this man.*

I surreptitiously snap a pic of Charlie and text it over. Only – I think Charlie sees me take the picture, so I play it off, by taking pics of the rest of the band, of the guests slowly streaming into the room, of the beautiful setting here at Wobble House. The last time I'd attended an event in this ballroom, the host had wound up dead. But even that memory doesn't dull the impressive splendor of this restored historic home, with its secret basement tunnel and hidden passages and crazy forced perspectives.

I get a text back from Ash. *On it. Right now, I'm in the garden at the side of Wobble House. I feel like I'm missing all the action, and I happened to be in the neighborhood. You know there's a coffee cart out here? They're serving primo cortados. I'm on my third one.*

I wonder why he doesn't just come inside, if he's feeling that left out that Autumn didn't think to invite him. But I'm sure he has his pride. I text back, *Where's the goat?*

He texts, *Munching on a pine tree. Don't worry, this garden has high wrought iron fences.*

Why does nothing about this interaction surprise me?

I turn my camera back to the entrance. There's Patsy coming in the door – with Nathan. Oh, dear. Right after I talked Arlo into trying to get her back, it looks like she's making big strides towards getting over him – with the help of the cute barista.

Logan asks, "What's wrong?"

I love that he knows me well enough to read that subtle shift in my body language. I whisper, "I didn't realize Patsy would be here. Or that she'd bring a plus one."

Logan whispers, "Autumn invited her, at the concert. A few people canceled at the last minute, so she had extra chairs."

I tell Logan, "Then she should tell Ash to come inside."

Nathan helps Patsy to a seat and takes her coat. He heads towards the coat room, but he has a funny look on his face. Nathan is one of my other big suspects, and I get an odd vibe, so I get up and follow him. If he doesn't do anything odd, I'll play it off like I'm just looking for the bathroom – even though I know very well where the bathroom is, since I'd already dealt with someone being kidnapped out of it during the previous case. Nathan does bring the coats to the coat room, which is in what used to be a drawing room – but then, instead of going back into the ballroom, he turns the other way and heads down the hallway leading to the previous owner's private gallery. Mitch Eberhard had been an art collector – but also an art forger.

I check out the coats. The room doesn't have a coat check station, and a lot of the garments are just piled on the furniture. I move over to the stack where I see Patsy's distinctive blue wool peacoat. Bu when I touch it, the whole stack falls over. Somewhere in the mess, I spot a colorful piece of fabric. I pull the coats off the top of it, and it's a rolled-up scarf. The same scarf Lydia had been wearing that day she'd come to Tiff's office. It's unlikely that two people would have the same hand-printed piece. Which means that Lydia's killer is not only here – but that he was brazen enough to bring a trophy of his murder here. If the stack of coats hadn't fallen, it would be easy to tell whether the scarf had been in the pocket of Nathan's coat or someone else's. For instance, Ray's. Or Charlie's. But now, I'm not so sure.

I follow Nathan, as clandestinely as I can, given the confines of the hallway, which only has a few corners. From around the last corner, I watch Nathan enter the gallery. He moves to the center of the room and just stands there, looking at a painting of a young woman sitting in a beach chair reading a book. The whole thing has a very 1920's feel, with the woman's flowing white dress and the book's solid pink cover. But now that I know more about Mitch's style, his brushstrokes and use of light – and little details, like the faint butterfly tattoo on the woman's wrist – I realize that this is one of Mitch's originals. It's the one painting in this gallery that I've never seen before.

I've collected a few of Mitch's works myself, and aside from the one hanging at Greetings and Felicitations, I've placed them in some of the rooms at the hotel. I'm not sure what I'm going to do with the paintings once we flip the hotel. But then again, I've never collected art before.

I flash back to this very room, to Mitch gesturing around at all these paintings, forged copies he'd made, asking me who

my favorite artist was. He changed my views on art and life –
even in his death.

I jolt from my reverie as I feel Nathan's intense gaze on
me. I make eye contact, and he looks down at the floor.

Nathan asks, "Are you going to tell them I was in here?"

"That depends," I say, stepping into the room. He's one
of my suspects for Lydia's murder – but somehow I feel safe with
him. It's another of those hunches, where I've been wrong before.
But I still find myself trusting Nathan. "Why are we in Mitch's
gallery?"

"Because it's not open to the public, but I heard they
hung the study he did of Dee. That's a beach in New York, where
Mitch went to paint sometimes, before he moved here. The girl I
liked, back when we worked together at the coffee shop, told me
that he had sketched her, but she never saw the finished painting."

I tilt my head, trying to figure Nathan out. "Then what are
we doing in here, aching for the past, when you came with Patsy,
who is waiting for you in the present, in the other room."

Nathan tosses his head, to move his heavy bangs out of
his eyes. "Patsy and I have a long way to go before I'd break into
a room just to see a painting of her. Since I picked her up tonight,
she's mentioned her ex-boyfriend four times. I get the idea that
he's here. And I'm beginning to think she brought me just so she
wouldn't have to be alone in front of him. Because apparently his
new girlfriend is here too."

I laugh, even as I feel my face going red. "That would be
me. But I broke up with him yesterday, because he still has
feelings for Patsy – and I realized I'm in love with someone else."

Nathan gives me a sharp look, like he's trying to figure
out if I'm joking. When it's clear I'm not he says, "That sounds
like something out of a drama. I'll probably just back off and see
how it sorts out. I like Patsy, but I don't do drama."

"Clearly," I say somewhat sarcastically, as I gesture to the
painting of the girl Nathan clearly still has feelings for.

Nathan says, "It's not like that. She's married now, with a kid on the way. I moved here for a new start. This is just a moment of feeling homesick."

"Not resentful that Lydia messed up the possibility that you'd wind up with Dee?"

"I didn't kill Lydia," Nathan says. "I was worried about her, especially after that marble pouch showed up in place of my Chemex. That day I asked you about it, I was just hoping, somehow, that it hadn't been her – that she really was getting better."

I ask him, "When those two guys from the jazz band came into Global Seoul, did you notice anything odd?"

He blinks at my sudden shift in direction. "Not really. One of them asked about the book signing. I hadn't announced it yet, but I figured Lydia must have said something about it on her social media. She has a ton of followers, even though not all of them are nice to her, since her book came out."

"Which of the two guys asked that?" I ask.

"The bass player, Charlie," Nathan says. "I thought it was a little odd, since he didn't strike me as the type who would be Lydia's fan."

"Tell me about it," I say. Charlie had made it clear that he was in fact not a fan of Lydia, or her tell-all type of media presence. If he had been following her accounts, maybe he had been trying to find out where she was staying. After all, they had both come here from New York, so that would be the easiest way to trace her movements.

I try to pull Lydia's Instagram up on my phone, but I'm not getting a signal inside the gallery. I step back into the hall, and my phone immediately registers multiple texts from Ash. I dismiss them for a moment to check Lydia's Insta feed. Sure enough, there's a video where she talks about how lovely her little cottage is by the beach, and how excited she is to see her friend – and fellow real estate agent – in action the next morning at an open house, and how she was going to show up early and make coffee to surprise us. It's all right there – her giving her killer everything he needed to stage her murder.

Nathan watches the video with me, Lydia being so vivacious and bubbly, and I glance up to see tears in his eyes. He's so sad – I really don't believe he killed her.

I tilt the phone more towards me and start to check the texts from Ash, but before I can, Autumn's mom rushes down the hall towards us, saying, "There you are! It's almost time for your speech, and Autumn is worried you're going to miss it."

"Tell her I'll be right there," I say. "I just need a minute to check on something. Maybe Boone or Charlie can tell stories about the old days until I get there."

Mrs. Ellis laughs. "They may be great when they're playing music, but otherwise, all those guys get terrible stage fright. Especially Preston. He's CEO of a startup, but you get him in a meeting with more than four people, and he has an anxiety attack from being the center of attention."

She turns and heads back towards the party, ushering Nathan back along with her. It takes my brain a second to register what she'd actually said. Charlie is the band member who's CEO, and his startup is about to go overseas. But she hadn't said Charlie.

I open the texts from Ash, and it confirms what I'd just figured out. Preston Jennings isn't at a wellness retreat in rural New York. He's here. His full name is Preston Charles Jennings – and he still goes by Charlie Jay when he performs. No one had questioned his name, or referred to him as anything else, so I'd just assumed.

He had said his wife's name was Misty, which sounds nothing like Adriana. I do a quick search for Misty and Charlie J – and that turns out to be a nickname, too.

I text Ash, *Call the cops and come inside. Consider yourself my plus one. Get with Arlo and tell him you called for backup. I'm going to pull Logan aside.*

Autumn is going to be extremely upset if they arrest her bass player in the middle of her dance with her dad.

As I'm heading back into the ballroom, I stop at the door. The band is playing, though it sounds different from before, and for a moment I just listen to it, steadying myself.

Logan isn't at the table. I scan the crowd for him.

I spot Arlo first. He's sitting next to Patsy. I love Patsy's dress. I know she loves old movies, and something about Patsy's look is channeling Myrna Loy. Patsy really is classy. And timeless. I watch as Arlo puts his hand on hers, and the two have a tentative moment, really looking at each other. Then Arlo withdraws his hand and folds his hands together on the table. Neither one of them looks exactly happy. Can they both get over everything that has happened between them? I'm not sure, but either way, I think they deserve it to each other to at least try.

Nathan is sitting at a different table, next to Drake's grandma. Because he's classy, too.

But where's Logan?

I realize what's different about the band. Charlie isn't on stage anymore. Did he see me text that picture of him? Did he make a run for it? After all, it makes sense that he wasn't worried about anyone checking his alibi, if he was already planning to leave the country. He probably hadn't expected anyone to connect him to Lydia, or suspect him in her death. He obviously didn't know about Pete's notes. He hadn't even really been hiding his identity, or the fact that his wife had disappeared. I was the one who had assumed that he and Preston were different people. But the point is, he didn't expect to be a suspect, so he wouldn't have thought his alibi would be needed.

If he realizes we're on to him, not just for the murders committed here in Galveston, but for the wife, and his ex-gardener and whoever had owned that lipstick tube and that padlock, once he gets on that plane, he's not coming back.

Logan steps back into view, and the band goes quiet. All the groomsmen are going to give little words of encouragement to

Drake. It was supposed to be after my speech, but they must have flipped the order around. Should I interrupt?

Tiff, who is headed back from the bathroom, stops next to me in the hallway. As the band's final note fades away, Tiff twirls, enjoying the drape and float of her dress. She says, "It's a shame I have absolutely nowhere else to wear this."

As the fabric settles, I spot something sparkly pinned in the folds of her skirt. I ask, "What's that?"

"Did I spill something on me?" Tiff asks in dismay. She starts pulling at the folds of the fabric, looking for a stain. "You know I'm a klutz."

But she gasps in surprise when she reveals the violet pendant that we've been looking for this whole time, attached to her skirt with a giant safety pin. It's small enough, I can see how it would weigh so little that she would have missed it. This has to be the original.

I help Tiff detach the pendant from her dress. I ask, "How on Earth did Lydia get that on there without you noticing?"

Tiff's eyes glitter with emotion when she says, "She was just that good."

She goes back into the ballroom, while I stand in the doorway, holding up the pendant and trying to get Logan's attention, while one of Drake's friends is speaking.

An arm comes around my shoulder, and a cold weight presses into my side. Charlie says, "Put your arms down."

I comply, though I try giving significant looks at the security guys, who are still standing by the wall. Only, at that moment, Autumn's niece and a couple of other little kids run screaming across the ballroom, trailing wrapping paper and holding up a toaster like it's an airplane. There's no competing with that, for either the security guys' attention – or for Logan's.

After a smug chuckle, Charlie guides me towards the room with the basement steps, where there's a hidden tunnel, leading all the way to the bay. It is a holdover from prohibition days, and it had made the news when we had discovered an entire speakeasy – complete with an old bowling alley – underneath this old house. I get the feeling that if I wind up in that tunnel, I'm going to disappear down there for good.

Charlie says, "Hand over that pendant."

"You don't have to do this," I protest. "The police already know about the pendant. They have enough other stuff to use as evidence that if it disappears, it won't matter. They have the watch, and the rest of it. You probably don't know this, but Pete was keeping notes about you."

"That's not the point," Charlie says. "You've seen too much. I can't let you live, knowing this many of my secrets. Holding my wife's pendant, and taunting me, just like she did. Like Lydia did. She had the audacity to wear that pendant in public, when it was mine. She made a mockery out of what I had done, when I had taken such care." He gestures vaguely around the room with his free hand. "So where's the hidden door?"

He doesn't know? That gives me hope. This house is riddled with hidden passage ways. There's one a room over from here that leads outside. There's at least one other entrance that the police found in this room. It can be accessed by swinging open a bookcase. I'm not sure where that passage goes, since I only saw pictures. But it has to be better than the tunnel.

I move over to the bookcase and slide the panel that opens it, while Charlie keeps a gun on me the whole time. I say, "Be careful. There's booby traps."

"Really?" he scoffs.

"One of the cops broke a foot when a rigged-up bowling ball fell on it." I step into the passage, trying to act like I know where I'm going – and like I'm not nervous about activating any more booby traps myself. It's dark, so we navigate the space by the light of my phone.

It's dusty, and there's obviously mold. I feel a tickle at the back of my throat and in my lungs, precursors to an asthma attack. Which can still happen to me, in spaces like this.

Unfortunately, I realize I left my emergency inhaler in the jeans I had changed out of at the ceremony venue.

As I make my way through the tunnel, I feel like we're moving towards the back of the house. I'm hoping to find a spot where it will be difficult for him to follow, and then I can try to pepper spray him in the face and run away before he shoots me. It's a chancy plan, but it's all I've got.

I tell Charlie, "For what it's worth, I don't think Lydia was trying to taunt you."

Charlie is livid. He says, "I was kind to Lydia. She was beautiful, young, innocent. I even tried to set her up on a date with a friend of mine. Lydia had no business going into my office when I wasn't there. And that she would have the nerve to take the pouch with the most precious things to me in the world – how could she not deserve to die?"

I shudder. His mementos of people he's killed are his favorite things? What exactly is wrong with this guy? "Did you ever actually read Lydia's book? She suffered from kleptomania. She probably had no idea of the significance of what she was taking." I see a 90-degree turn coming up ahead. I pause, trying to sound dramatic. "Though I believe she was trying to send a call for help by leaving me that copy of *The Thin Man*. She figured it out, didn't she? She saw right through you. That your wife made you feel so weak, you killed her."

My dramatic moment is spoiled by a cough. The mold in here is really getting to me.

Charlie still confesses, with relish, like he's been wanting to explain this to someone. "There was nothing weak about it. I really did have a home invasion, and they really did take my guitar. It was signed by Jimmy Hendrix, worth millions. It was never recovered. But it gave me the idea to stage a second robbery, during which Adriana would be 'abducted.' And it would have worked perfectly too, except that Adriana got suspicious. She called that insurance investigator instead of the cops, so a few months after Adriana disappeared, Pete showed up on my doorstep. I told him it wasn't any of his business, since his company wasn't responsible for the life insurance policy."

"But why did Adriana have to die?" I ask. "Why not just divorce her?"

"Prenup," Charlie says simply. "In a divorce settlement, she'd get the entire company."

In his mind, that was the logical solution? I say, "So this all happened because she was planning to axe your land deal."

He actually growls, low in his throat. "Can you believe Misty used to call me her muse? Then she hamstrung every creative idea I ever had."

I don't want to keep making him angrier. He's talking, finally getting a chance to show how clever he'd been, so it's probably best to keep it that way. "So somehow Pete and Lydia found out about each other. I guess that's when you decided to duplicate the pendant, to discredit her. Is that why the jeweler had to die too? So he couldn't tell anybody he'd made the second necklace?"

"It wasn't exactly discrediting anybody. And it was all Pete's fault. Pete 'accidentally' ran into Lydia when we had a meeting about the property, at my office. Pete followed Lydia to Galveston, and I followed him. Pete had already stirred up suspicion, so I needed to get the copy of the pendant from the jeweler quietly, so that I could make sure it was discovered with Adriana's body. All, 'look officers, I don't know whose pendant Lydia stole, my wife still had hers.'"

I try to see his expression clearly in this dim light. It looks like he's sneering. I say, "So you coming to Galveston with your band was just a coincidence."

"A happy coincidence," Charlie says. "I had already hired someone to attend the wellness retreat under my name, so I could travel without any of the board members knowing I'm still involved in music. They tend to think it makes me not look serious enough about the company. I'd kill to keep my company.

I already have, in fact. It's a shame, I'm going to have to leave it all behind when I fake my own death – at your hands."

"You hire a lot of people," I point out, ignoring what he's implying about my impending death, which will be necessary to fake his own. But my pounding heartbeat can't be so nonchalant. "Like the guy who impersonated Pete in Mexico."

Charlie says, "I just told Sam that the guy who was supposed to go down and look at properties for the new manufacturing plant couldn't make it and we didn't want to spook buyers by changing people on them. He had no idea what he was helping me cover up." He sighs, dramatically. "Again, it's a shame to lose my group of such loyal employees." Charlie gestures with his gun for me to start moving. "But it can't be helped."

I grab the pepper spray out from under my bra strap and get it up, pointed at Charlie's face, but before I can spray it, he knocks it out of my hand, and it goes rolling away into the darkness. Pointing the gun at my face, he says, "Try that again, and I'll find my own way out of this tunnel."

"Okay," I say meekly. "It's this way." I'm shaking, but I try to hide it. Just because I had managed to pepper spray Creed, I had gotten overconfident. But I had to try, right? Now, I can only hope for a real chance to change the situation. I keep going, around the corners tracing the uneven outline of the wall, until finally I see a tiny strip of light, where this space leads – hopefully – outside. Moving more quickly, in a dash to escape once we reach whatever is on the other side of this door, I step on a floorboard that bows in. There's a mechanical click above my head. Instinctively, I duck as a dart flies across the space where my head was just moments before. Two other darts fly, and Charlie cries out as one of them hits him in the shoulder. I take the opportunity of his distraction to run for the door, despite a coughing fit that slows me down. It doesn't stop me, and I find the groove that opens the door before Charlie manages to get off his first shot at me.

I slide through the opening door and run face-first into Logan, who is standing outside, trying to figure out a way in. He must have seen Charlie pull me away from the doorway to the ballroom and followed, then gone outside to cut us off since there was no way to easily confront Charlie in the hidden hallway. Logan pushes me out of the way as Charlie fires again. Logan cries out. He doesn't look badly hurt, but there's a streak of blood on his cheek as he stumbles backward, over a stray terra cotta pot and lands sitting down, dropping his gun to brace himself. The gun goes skittering out of reach.

Charlie has his gun trained on Logan now. There's no way Logan can get to his own weapon faster than Charlie could shoot. Charlie tells me, "Go stand next to your fiancé."

I move over to Logan. It hurts that Charlie is the first person to use that word for Logan out loud. I glace into the garden. Ash had said there was someone at the coffee cart. Maybe there's someone at the champagne cart.

Sadly, the booze cart is still closed. Which means that there won't be any witnesses if Charlie shoots us. And the coffee cart is on the far side of the bridge, which means that anyone standing near it won't be able to see into the back yard. So calling for help is pointless.

We're far down the wall from the kitchen door, and they've started serving dinner, so I doubt anyone inside would hear us either. There's a hollowness in the pit of my stomach. I've run out of options for escape. And I just got engaged. I'm not ready to die.

Charlie tells me, "Put the pendant on the ground in front of you. And put your phone down beside it."

I look at my phone. It isn't anything special. I ask, "Is that what you think is iconic about me?"

He shrugs. "You're always taking pictures and posting on social media." He gestures at Logan. "I want the keychain. The one with your plane company's logo. The sea turtles suit you."

Logan takes his time digging in his pocket and removing the keychain from his other keys. I can see him gauging the distance to the gun, or the distance to Charlie, trying to find us a way out of this. He gives me a look, and I know he's about to do something risky to give me time to get away. My heart breaks at the thought of losing him, right after I finally admitted I love him.

I shake my head in a muted movement, begging him to wait, then I try to play for time. Not that I see that working. Ash called the police, but they're probably still too far away. I have the stun gun, but it is in my purse – getting it out would be too awkward. I tell Charlie, "Someone is bound to hear this. We're what, twenty feet over from the kitchen?"

"So what if they do? I have to disappear anyway – right back through that passage in the wall. Look, I know this is bad timing for both of you. And I'm sorry you won't get to have your wedding."

Logan tenses, about to go for the gun. Only, Princess Buttercup notices us and trots over. Sensing the tension, she lets out an uneasy noise. She moves over to Logan, climbing up on him. Then she sees the glittering pendant and – still balanced on Logan's legs – picks it up with her mouth. Most likely she's just exploring it, but when Charlie shouts, "Drop that!" and makes a lunge towards her, she swallows it and runs away. Charlie instinctively turns to look where the goat is going.

I take advantage of his moment of gaped-mouth credulity to grab the Taser out of my purse. I aim it in the vague direction of Charlie and close my eyes as I press the button. Charlie's gun goes off again. Fear is making my body cold and my hands shaky.

I open my eyes. Neither Logan or I got hit, and the goat is trying to climb a tree to get away from all the commotion.

Logan actually laughs, despite the blood on his face, and the near-death experience we just had. He says, "You Tazed him in the butt."

From the ground, Charlie says, "That's not funny. It really hurts."

Logan picks up Charlie's gun. He says, "It's at least a little funny." He takes one of the zip ties from his pocket and restrains Charlie.

Detective Beckman soon arrives and arrests Charlie outside, willing to wait to take our statements until after the rest of Autumn's reception. She gives Logan a bandage for his face. He also agrees to go by the hospital afterward the reception, to get checked out.

Beckman says, "If you don't get it stitched right, that's going to leave a scar."

Logan complains, "That's not the first time I've been shot. You think that's the only place I have scars?"

I arch an eyebrow at him, suddenly curious. After all, I have just proposed marriage to him, so that's something I'm going to find out. But that's a conversation for another day.

From the other side of the wrought iron fence, Ash calls, "I don't suppose I can post that?" He's standing on the champagne cart, which he may have used to help Princess Buttercup over the fence.

"Wait," I say. "Did you seriously take video of Charlie threatening to kill us?"

"What else was I going to do?" Ash says. "He was confessing."

"You could have distracted him," I point out.

He says, "I pointed the goat in your direction. Best I could do."

Logan tells me, "You have to admit, that video is going to make excellent evidence." Then he tells Ash, "Which means no, you can't post it." Logan picks up a piece of paper off of the ground. "What's this?"

"It's Ash's list of the perfect qualities in a guy for me."

There's now a red smear across, *Willing to take a bullet for you*. Logan certainly proved that one. I'm just glad he wasn't badly injured doing it.

Ash says, "I'm still claiming dibs on Logan's new name for the podcast being Damsel in Distress. That's twice you've saved his life, Felicity."

We go back into Wobble House, all three of us looking worse for wear, Ash leading the goat that just helped save our lives. He's going to be in charge of that goat for a while – until we can retrieve the pendant. After all, it is still evidence.

Logan slowly puts his sea turtle keychain back onto the rest of his keys.

I tell him, "Charlie was right about one thing. That really does suit you."

"Breathing suits me," Logan says. "I'm just glad we're both alive."

He moves in to kiss me, but I start coughing again. Logan pulls an inhaler out of his jacket pocket. "Here. I carry this just in case."

I take a puff from the inhaler, and feel the tickle in my lungs subside. "Thanks." It's sweet how prepared he is.

We make our way into the ballroom. Darke and Autumn pause, about to cut their cake. I tell Autumn, "Go ahead. We'll explain what happened after." I look over at the band. "Give me a minute too, before you play. I still want to give my speech."

When Autumn finds out that Charlie got arrested, she looks ashen. She forces a smile and says, "We'll look back on our wedding day and have so many stories to tell." But when she looks over at the band, she looks like she is about to cry. She says, "I guess they can still play, without a bass. It didn't sound great – but this party is about bringing people together, not demanding everything be perfect. I'm the bride. I can choose not to be overwhelmed."

Patsy says something, but the words are too soft for her voice to carry all the way over here.

"What was that?" Autumn calls.

Patsy says, much louder, "I play double bass. I used to be in a community orchestra."

Boone says into the mic, "It's a different kind of music, but I'm sure you'll be able to feel the beat."

Arlo helps Patsy up onto the stage, then he comes over to us. He says, "I didn't get Ash's messages, and I was too caught up reminiscing with Patsy to notice Logan leave. I'm sorry, Lis. I missed the whole thing."

Logan gestures at Arlo's ankle brace. "It's probably for the best. This time. We had a narrow escape."

Arlo looks at Logan, taking in the bandage on Logan's face. It's as close as Logan is going to come to admitting to his friend how scared he was. Arlo asks, "You okay if I ask Felicity for a dance, for old time's sake?"

Logan gestures at Arlo's ankle again. "You can ask. Whether she wants to – and whether you'll actually be able to dance like that – I have no idea."

So Arlo takes me out on the dance floor, while Patsy plays and Logan gets some Tylenol from Drake's grandma, who seems to have everything someone could possibly need in her purse.

Arlo is a surprisingly good dancer for somebody wearing an ankle brace. As we turn, he says, "I haven't said it officially, but congrats to you and Logan. And thanks for solving this one. It's what I needed."

"Hey!" Tiff shouts.

We turn to where Princess Buttercup, having slipped her leash again, is happily eating the paper butterflies off the wedding cake.

Logan is still in Minnesota when we have the next concert at Greetings and Felicitations. I can't decide if the mood is more somber because he's not here – or because Seth is playing acoustic classical guitar. The audience seems to be into it, though, and he's actually really good. Some of the songs are, as he promised, Flamenco style, which requires really fast playing. A friend of Ami's is a Flamenco dancer, and she showed up in costume to dance in accompaniment to those songs. Seth had put together a small wooden platform to serve as a stage. He said we can keep it here, as long as he can take it to use if he needs it.

Ash still hasn't lived down the whole, *I pointed a goat at you, what else am I going to do?* moment, so he's here helping make coffee. Honestly, he's more taking video of me showing him how to make coffee, while Carmen, for once, gets to enjoy the concert with Paul and his son. The kid keeps clapping loudly in time to the Flamenco beats, but nobody is complaining, so I just let them have their fun.

Ash says, "You should see some of the comments on the podcast episode where I mentioned you finally chose a love interest."

I wince. His podcast isn't really up to this point in time – as he's going chronologically through the cases I've been a part of – so I was hoping it would be a while before he talked about it. I say, "I'm sure people are upset for Arlo, and think I'm horrible."

"A few do," he says. "But for the most part, they're really happy for you. I'll print out the best congratulations ones and get them to you. That way you don't have to read the crazies."

"Thanks?" I say. I mean, it sounds like a nice gesture.

He says, "I posted that video from the reception of you doing the "Cha Cha Slide" with Autumn's niece. And the one of me fake dancing with Princess Buttercup. Imogen is totally jealous that she didn't get invited to the wedding."

"You're going to be having a wedding of your own soon," I remind him. "Did Autumn's give you any ideas?"

"Yeah," Ash says. "Don't invite any murderers."

"I'll tell you what I think," Tiff says, bringing two empty plates back to the counter. She and her husband have been enjoying the music and eating chocolate conchas in the annex. "I think I should start a wedding planning business for all these people getting married. Seth just proposed to Ami – from the stage. She started crying and hugging him, so now the music is taking a break."

Ash asks me, "Have you and Logan set a date yet?"

I say, "No, but neither of us want to wait too long. We've decided to take things slow until the actual I-do's."

"I like your scarf," Tiff says.

"Thanks! It's cashmere. Logan got me a goat-hair scarf in honor of Princess Buttercup. I'm trying for an iconic look, since Charlie pointed out I don't really have one. I mean, what really is Felicity? I have to be more than my phone."

Tiff says, "I like that you enjoy photography. And that you go for a variety of fashion styles."

Ash says, "My favorite part of the whole wedding was when the carriage horse showed up to take the happy couple home from the reception. The horse was named Asta. Just like the dog in *The Thin Man*. You could not make this stuff up."

We all look over at the glass case, where the books that have been tied to all these murders are laid out on display. There's *The Thin Man*, at the end of the row. There's an unsettling amount of space still left in the case for more books, should the need arise. Somehow, while my relationship to both Logan and Arlo has changed significantly, I can still see us all investigating things together in the future. I've come to terms that that may well be part of my life now that I have a reputation as an investigator, and people have started seeking me out. I'd been worried about each case cracking open my grief over my late husband. But maybe remembering him is a good motivation for helping other people move forward, too.

Almost as though he's reading my mind, Ash hands me an opened envelope. He says, "This came in your fan mail this morning."

"I get fan mail?" I ask, skeptically.

"The podcast does," Ash says. "I'm technically your fan club president. Most if it is gushy cards and requests for free chocolate. But this one is different. Someone is asking for your help."

"I'll look at it later," I say, taking the envelope and putting it into my pocket. After all, if it's snail-mail, it can't be that urgent. I sigh. "I keep thinking about Lydia. She dressed like she had her life together. But she was a mess inside, which gave her the need to write a tell-all book to rip off the psychological band-aids and finally heal. I can't decide if that's good or bad."

Ash says, "Like, is too public too much?"

I roll my eyes. "With you around, like there's a choice?"

"I have my limits," Ash says.

I hand Ash one of my newest limited edition chocolate bars. It's my own tribute to Princess Buttercup – a milk chocolate bar made with goat's milk and infused with rosemary. It's not something Paul's son is going to like – but I enjoy the complex flavors. I ask Ash, "Do your limits include chopping this and handing out samples while people are waiting for the music to start again."

"I think I can handle that." Ash takes the bar and goes into the kitchen.

My phone buzzes with a text. It's Chloe, of the Mr. Tunaface fame. She's asking, *Why are you not live streaming the concert? Hello!!!! Have I taught you nothing?*

I text back, *You haven't taught me how to live stream. I don't have a dedicated camera, and I'm working.*

She texts, *Whhhhhhugh! I'm on it for next time. Don't make me drive out there. I will you know.*

I text back, *Please do*

Autumn and Drake get back from their honeymoon soon, and it won't be long until Logan comes home. But right now, things feel a little empty. It would be great if whirlwind Chloe showed up, with all her energy. Still, I've never been happier, or more at peace.

Nathan comes in, just as Ash comes out of the kitchen with the chocolate samples. He offers one to Nathan, who says, "I don't mind if I do." Then he turns to me and says, "I knew there was a reason I wanted to collaborate with you guys. This is fantastic."

I tell Ash, "You should talk to Nathan for your next small business spotlight. I'm sure he'd love to show you his roastery."

Nathan says, "That would be great. I'm finding that getting the word out is the hardest part of having a small business."

Ash says, "Anything for a friend of Felicity's. I'll try to think of a few ways we can spotlight your roastery."

Patsy comes in, and there's an awkward moment between her and Nathan, until Nathan says, "I heard you and Arlo have been spending some time together. You should come in for a coffee date sometime. First latte is on the house."

Patsy says, "Arlo's more of an Americano guy, if he can't get Cuban coffee. He makes a good cortadito."

Nathan considers this. "I don't have a Cuban blend. I'll have to look into it."

The band starts playing again. I say, "Since I'm known for taking pictures, you know what's coming next."

I usher everyone into the doorway of the annex, where you can see the people enjoying the concert at the tables behind us. Tracie is sitting at the same table with Carmen and Paul. She really isn't going anywhere. I manage to get Seth into the picture, with his guitar and the skirts of the Flamenco dancer, along with the rest of us. That one's going to go up on Instagram. Then I take a selfie where it's just me, smiling with the chocolate shop behind me. That one I text to Logan.

AUTHOR NOTES

While the railroad car B&B I have in this book doesn't exist, if you want to stay in a rail car while visiting the island, they have accommodations for groups of up to ten at the Rail Hotel at the Galveston Railroad Museum. (These cars are much fancier than my fictional B&B – and even include 24 hour porter service.)

ACKNOWLEDGEMENTS

Special thanks to Jael Rattigan of French Broad Chocolates in South Carolina, who has consulted extensively on this series. And to Sander Wolf of DallasChocolate.org, who put me in touch with so many experts in the chocolate field.

I'd like to thank the Honomu Goat Dairy in Hawaii for the chance to interact with their goats, and Paul Allen at Lost Ruby Ranch in Bonham, Texas for the behind-the-scenes tour, and answering all my pigmy-goat related questions. Princess Buttercup wouldn't have felt real without you! I would also like to thank the Galveston Railroad Museum for the excellent tour, which gave insight to the railroad-related history touched on here.

I'd also like to thank TexaKona Coffee for taking us behind the scenes on how coffee is roasted and espresso shots are pulled, and Maasa at Makua Meadows (Dotour's coffee farm on Big Island Hawaii) for the extensive behind the scenes tour, and answering all my coffee questions.

I have to thank Jake, as usual, for reading the manuscript umpteen times, being my biggest fan and cheerleader, and doing all the formatting things to make this thing happen. He always keeps me going, even when things are stressful.

And thanks to my agent, Jennie, for her input on this series, and her encouragement to keep moving forward.

And for this series especially, I'd like to thank my family for giving me a love of the ocean and a curiosity about history. The Cajun side of both mine and Jake's families comes through in Felicity's family in the books. This has given me an excuse to reach out to family members for recipes and inspiration, many of which you can find on the Bean to Bar Bonuses section of my website. Thanks y'all!

Thanks to James and Rachel Knowles for continuing to sharing their knowledge of bunny behavior, despite the loss of the ever-adorable Yuki.

I'd also like to thank Cassie, Monica and Tessa, who are my support network in general. I don't know how I would have gotten through these years of social isolation without you three.

Thank you all, dear readers, for spending time in Felicity's world. I hope you enjoyed getting to know her. Her seventh adventure will be available for you soon.

Did Felicity's story make you hungry?

Visit the Bean to Bar Mysteries Bonus Recipes page on Amber's website to find out how to make some of the food mentioned in the book.

AMBER ROYER writes the CHOCOVERSE comic telenovela-style foodie-inspired space opera series (available from Angry Robot Books and Golden Tip Press). She is also co-author of the cookbook There are Herbs in My Chocolate, which combines culinary herbs and chocolate in over 60 sweet and savory recipes, and had a long-running column for Dave's Garden, where she covered gardening and crafting. She blogs about creative writing technique and all things chocolate related over at www.amberroyer.com. She also teaches creative writing in person in North Texas for both UT Arlington Continuing Education and Writing Workshops Dallas. If you are very nice to her, she might make you cupcakes.

www.amberroyer.com Instagram: amberroyerauthor